CAGED

LITTLE YŌKAI URBAN FANTASY SERIES BOOK 1

SCOTT WALKER

FIREFLY TALES, LLC

Caged

Published by Firefly Tales, LLC

Cover Designed by MiblArt

ISBN: 978-1-7337396-5-8

BOOKS BY SCOTT WALKER

THE LITTLE YŌKAI SERIES

(A complete 6-book Urban Fantasy Procedural)

In a world where the Japanese supernatural spirits known as Yōkai wander the physical plane, Bureau of Souls Agent Keiko Miller has an oath to protect the innocent and bring justice to the guilty. She also has a secret of her own: she's part Yōkai. She'll have to protect that secret like her job and her life depend on it, because they do.

CLOAK & DAGGER

(Urban Fantasy Dual Assassins)

Val's a human necromancer who talks with the dead.

Timmeron's an elf who communes with nature.

Can these opposites save the world?

After a secret organization recruits a death-dealing necromancer and a life-loving wood elf to become dualcasting assassins, the pair will have to work together to stop a deadly fae from zombifying the planet.

THE MANHATTAN MAGIC SERIES

(Cozy Urban Fantasy Series)

Melina Morgan has the *sight*: the ability to see through any fae illusion. But if the fae find Melina, they'll kill her, which would, you know, totally ruin her plans for a quiet holiday at home. And that's exactly what happens when a drunk dwarf lands in Melina's backyard one night.

In order to protect herself and her town, Melina will travel to the fae-filled city of Manhattan. Armed with a sliver of iron and her sourdough starter, Melina's about to step into a world of magic, mystery, and mischief!

RUNED

(Urban Fantasy Amazon Vella novel)

This year, Ivy Hunter got a lump of coal in her stocking the size of Cincinnati: her father died mysteriously on Christmas Day. Equally mysterious? The message he left Ivy, one which will send her down a path of magic, secret organizations, and monsters from beyond the mortal plane. Ivy's determined to find her father's killer - if she can live long enough.

FOLKLORE TALES OF OLD JAPAN

(Anthology)

This collection contains seven short stories, all based on classic folklore tales from Japan.

DAILY STORY SEEDS

(Anthology)

Thirty bite-sized stories ranging from dark to funny to whimsical, and every mini-narrative in this collection has a seed of truth firmly rooted in our current world.

EXCLUSIVE ACCESS TO "SHADOWED"

Sign up for the Scott Is Writing Readers Group and get your exclusive copy of *Shadowed*, the Little Yōkai prequel novella:

As a freshly minted Bureau of Souls agent, Keiko Miller figured her first week wouldn't be too stressful. A drug dealing oni, a powerful gokudō crime boss, and a mortalization client seeking protection soon prove her wrong.

https://scottiswriting.com/little-yokai-shadowed

GLOSSARY OF JAPANESE TERMS

Caged includes several Japanese words and phrases, as well as references to specific gods and Yōkai spirits. A glossary of terms is provided at the end of this book as a reference.

To all the unseen spirits in the world.

ONE

NO GOOD DEED GOES UNPUNISHED.

That went double in Little Yōkai — the area of downtown Los Angeles formerly known as Little Tokyo — which was where I met a spirit named Yuri. Our paths crossed just once, but that single encounter was enough to intertwine our lives. And it happened in Little Yōkai.

Well, to be more specific, I met her at Hana, a Yōkai-friendly speakeasy.

A single text message from a trusted friend had summoned me to the bar. My kitsune nose picked up the telltale aroma of chalk incense as soon as I opened the door. An unmistakable mixture of citrus, pine and campfire smoke, seeping into the place from censers artfully hidden from view. You eventually got used to the smell. Or not.

The Yōkai who frequented the bar said it made them feel relaxed. Most mortals said it smelled pleasant enough at first but caused headaches and dizziness after a while. I was somewhere in between, able to enjoy the incense for a couple of hours before wanting some fresh air.

My kitsune ears picked up the low murmur of conversation, almost entirely in Japanese.

Rikishi "Riki" Sato, owner and operator of Hana, waved at me from an elevated corner booth. She sat next to a man in a suit. His hair was slicked back, and his eyeglasses and the cut of his jacket reminded me of Western Europe.

A lot of the staff and regulars gave me a nod or a bow as I walked through the early Thursday night crowd. There were a few mortals — rich Euro trash slackers in bright designer shirts, a few Yōkai groupies, a handful of humans well connected with the spirit community — but most of the patrons were Yōkai.

Yōkai.

Thirty years ago, most Americans hadn't even heard the word. Months after we dodged the Y2K bullet, all that changed. Now most Americans knew Yōkai was a term for all manner of Japanese supernatural beings: ghosts, demons, spirits, and a lot of entities we didn't have an equivalent for in the U.S.

Madara, my aka bekko koi and constant companion, darted around me. A beautiful, burgundy-colored fish with black spots, she was no ordinary koi. I alone could see her, and she had some very special abilities, like identifying Yōkai by outlining them in a soft blue light. That gave me a definite edge in my line of work, since a Yōkai presenting as mortal would appear, well, mortal. Most importantly, she hid my Yōkai signature.

And yes, Madara was a Yōkai herself.

Riki's companion slipped out of the booth as I approached, said something to her I didn't quite catch. Not English, not Japanese. A clipped accent. Maybe German? I sat across from Riki, eyed the extravagantly wrapped gift box on the table. Colorful wrapping paper with a wildly chaotic design, a forest of ribbons, and a massive bow. Too ostentatious for my Japanese taste.

"Evening, Sato-san. Another admirer?"

A smile, a wave of her hand. "Some western European syndicate."

"What's the offer?"

"Two-million-euro penthouse with a matching annual salary,

plus ten percent of net profit increases. All the things they think are valuable."

"Sounds like a two-million-euro birdcage and some golden handcuffs," I said.

"Exactly."

I looked around the bar. "Good night?"

"They all are," she replied with a grin. Tonight certainly was. Very few empty seats. "Thank you for coming."

"Of course."

Located in the heart of Little Yōkai — formerly Little Tokyo — Hana's "manifestations allowed" policy had cemented the bar's enduring popularity with Yōkai and mortals alike. A lot of the spirits were taking advantage of the policy and manifesting in their Yōkai form that night, something I wished I could do. My kitsune half was a secret, and I needed to keep it that way.

The bar's eclectic fusion of Western design touches against a traditional Japanese aesthetic felt right at home in Los Angeles, too. The dim lighting came almost entirely from candles, and retro swing music provided a bouncy background to the hushed conversations at the small tables and sofas scattered about the room. An unused piano, an antique typewriter, black and white photos, a white stone bust of some unknown woman — the decor somehow blended perfectly with the exposed wood, earth tones, and furniture a lot lower than Americans were used to.

Riki was presenting in her mortal form, a tousle of chestnut hair loosely cut into a French Bob, a frilly collared blouse sprinkled with sea foam florals. Typical look for her. I was presenting as well: half Japanese, half White.

"Going mortal tonight, I see," I said.

Riki glanced at her body, back at me. She rippled, turned translucent for a moment. The mid-thirties Japanese-looking woman disappeared, replaced by a floating girl in a kimono whose skin and clothes were white light. That was Riki's Yōkai form. As a chōpirako Yōkai, her special ability was to make the places where she lived profitable. So, when she said all the nights at Hana were good, she wasn't exaggerating.

Her special talent had made it easy to get her stamp and leave Japan. The biggest corporations around the world headhunted chōpirako. Recruiting the spirits wasn't just profitable, it was also a bragging right. Riki continued turning down the offers, preferring to run her own bar instead.

Some other Yōkai had similar traits that helped them immigrate, but most of us weren't so lucky.

"Better?" Riki asked.

I smiled. "It's your place. Go with what you like."

The glowing girl morphed back into a Japanese woman in a style of clothes I could never pull off: a Harajuku fashion known as Mori Kei. Riki had tried describing it to me once at a party at her place.

"It's about layers. Natural colors. Your own idea of whimsical."

My fingers had flipped across the hangers in her closet. Scarves. Floral prints. Earth tones. A lot of lace, linen, and leggings. Nothing like the dyed hair and vibrant colors of fairy kei or the more traditional style of kimono kei.

I envied her. I wanted to be comfortable in those kinds of clothes, but the mix-and-match options were too much. Whatever I pulled out of her closet garnered a "well, that *could* work..." reaction.

Riki? She totally rocked that style. I mean, she made Mori Kei look amazing, and the guys definitely noticed. It was a waste of their time, but you couldn't argue with the results.

Compared to her, my usual style of dress was downright boring. Pretty standard fare for a plainclothes female in law enforcement: dark pant suit, blouse, and low-heeled black ankle boots. The SoCal heat of Los Angeles meant I sometimes ditched my jacket, though I preferred concealing my service weapon, Bureau of Souls badge, and the kusari tattoo marks around my wrists. Not that it made much of a difference in Hana. Anyone in there who knew me also knew what I did for a living.

4

Riki handed me a napkin with kanji written on it: "*Corner table. Young woman. Alone.*"

"You want your usual?"

"Please," I said. I spotted the woman across the room, noted the various spirits manifesting in their Yōkai forms. Kitsune foxes. Kappa turtles. Tanuki badger. Yamamba mountain hags. A host of different onna women: taka, hone, and nure. Even saw an oni, the ogre's horns tipping back as he laughed.

In the corner I found a Yōkai presenting as mortal. Generic t-shirt under an olive bomber jacket, loose jeans, over-sized sneakers, and a bright bleach-job of short, spiky hair. Chipped fingernail polish. Female, mid-twenties, Japanese, sitting alone at a table for two. At her feet was a small backpack. An elongated oval-shaped piece of flat gold metal twinkled from one of the straps. I couldn't tell which deity the omamori charm was for.

The pack was nondescript, and if it held anything, it wasn't much. No obvious threat near her, though there was a handsome guy leaning over, talking to her. I caught her expression, and it wasn't hard to decipher: *definitely not into handsome guy.*

I felt for her. Been there too many times myself to count.

Madara didn't seem interested in the guy, not a hint of blue. But the woman? Madara painted her in a rapidly strobing aura. She was new enough to the U.S. that her Yōkai signature was still oscillating.

I came in on the tail end of what had to be an awful pickup line from handsome guy, and I decided handsome guy was now just douchebag guy.

The Yōkai looked down at the table where an empty highball sat next to another, nearly empty one. She seemed to only have eyes for the cocktail in front of her, despite of — or more likely because of — the guy hitting on her. He either didn't notice or wasn't cluing in, rolled right into another pitch for his awesomeness.

"Hey, I'm a nice guy, not some creep. I'm just being friendly. Listen, you like sushi?"

I tapped douchebag guy on the shoulder, gave him my biggest anime eyes and a dazzling smile. Didn't recognize him, which meant he was new to Hana. And that meant he probably didn't know who I was.

"Excuse me, that's my seat." I used my hand to indicate the chair opposite Sad Girl.

"What? Oh, yeah, sure." He moved back, gave me room to sit down, turned his smile on me.

"You don't have a drink. Let me fix that."

I stepped in front of the chair, turned back to face douchebag guy. Put my hand on my hip and cocked my head, looked up at him.

"Got one coming, thanks."

Out of the corner of my eye I caught Mitch, one of Hana's bouncers, lock on to me, start moving in my direction. *He* knew me, and he knew how this might go, even if douchebag guy didn't.

"Well, at least let me buy you ladies some appetizers."

"Thanks, but we're good."

"Okay, cool, cool. Hey, you like sushi? I bet you like sushi. I know a guy, he owns a great place nearby. Maybe afterwards we can hit a karaoke place."

What went through my head was: *You racist piece of shit, you don't know the first thing about me, much less what I do and don't like.*

What came out of my mouth was, "I just want to have a drink with my friend."

The guy's smile widened, and he dipped his head, leaned in so he could talk with his mouth close to my ear. Touching me? No. Invading my space? Absolutely.

"Look, I'm not some asshole. I'm a nice guy. Just give me a chance."

He never got that chance.

"Come on, man, time to go."

Douchebag guy turned around, looked Mitch up and down —

a rather long process, given Mitch's height — and held up his hands like he was being robbed.

"It's cool, dude. Just talking with the ladies here."

"And now you're just walking away from the ladies." Mitch gave him a head nod. I winked at Mitch, blew him a kiss before the bouncer turned to escort douchebag guy to the exit. I didn't need Mitch to look out for me, but it was nice having a guy watching your back instead of your ass for a change.

The woman at the table had a hint of a smile on her face.

"Thank you."

English but with a heavy accent. I replied in Japanese.

"My pleasure. May I sit down?"

The woman blinked a few times, her smile growing wider. She gestured at the empty chair. I took it as an invitation.

"My name is Yuri. It's a pleasure to meet you," she said, switching to Japanese herself. She gave me a half-bow, half-nod deep enough to let me know just how little she thought of herself. It also reinforced how new she was to the states.

I matched her bow and nod. "My name is Keiko Miller. Pleased to meet you as well, Yuri-san." I nodded at Riki's table. "Riki says you could use some help."

"I'm sorry. Riki?"

I should have known. Riki probably never even said a word to Yuri, just sensed she needed help and texted me. Riki was amazing at reading mortals, even better at reading Yōkai.

"Riki owns this place. She asked me to talk with you. May I do that?"

"Um. Yes. Yes."

I smiled, nodded. "Good."

I carried two sets of business cards. The first was for work. The second had my personal info. I pulled one of the latter out of my pocket, used both hands to hold it out to her, careful to make sure the writing faced her. She took the card with both hands, read it carefully.

"It's beautiful. I love the calligraphy," she said.

"Designed that myself, but I'm not very good."

"On the contrary, your skills are impressive."

She studied my card a bit more, placed it on the table after making sure the surface was dry and clean. She went back to studying her drink, avoided making eye contact.

"With apologies, I do not have a card to offer." Embarrassment. A touch of humiliation.

No surprise. If Riki's instincts were right, Yuri probably didn't have much more than the clothes she was wearing and whatever was inside the well-worn pack. My gut said she was a low-level Yōkai back in Japan who had snuck her way into the states. Without an entry stamp, she fell into the category of hakushi Yōkai, entities who had illegally entered another country.

Riki sometimes helped Yōkai who were down on their luck, including hakushi. Sometimes that meant reaching out to me, and if I felt I could help them without losing my job, I would.

I ignored Yuri's comment about her lack of a personal card, changed topics. "So, how may I help you?"

The Yōkai glanced around before replying.

"I need a stamp."

"Ah." The Holy Grail for a hakushi Yōkai. A fresh start. A new beginning. Legitimacy. Legal status. Also, hard to come by and, in any case, not something I was authorized to issue. More than a bit above my pay grade at the Bureau. Yuri cupped her drink with both hands, looked up. Bags under bloodstained eyes under-scored her desperation.

"Will you please help me?" she asked.

I pursed my lips. "Get you a stamp? That would be extremely difficult for me to do."

Yuri caught the gist of my reply: *no way can I get you a stamp.* Her head dipped, then her eyes met mine again.

"I understand, Miller-san."

"Look, I want to help, but I'd like to know a little more about you."

I saw relief on Yuri's face, even a spark of hope, despite my refusal to simply roll out the red carpet. Good. I wanted to find out what had happened to her, how she got here, but mostly, I just wanted to help her. Of all the Yōkai Riki had directed my way over the years, I'd never regretted helping a single one of them.

My employer, however? Well, let's just say the Bureau frowned upon its agents actively assisting hakushi, and that's putting it mildly. If I was caught helping hakushi, not only would I be fired from the Bureau and charged by American law enforcement, the political blowback and social fallout would have massive repercussions.

That was just for starters. If the Bureau found out I was part Yōkai, the likely endgame would be a deport back to Japan followed by a banishment across the veil. I may never set foot on the physical plane again.

Despite the risks, I'd been quietly breaking the rules for years.

"Yes, of course," Yuri said. "I will tell you whatever you ask. Please, I would very much like to show my thanks. May I pay for your drink?"

Like a scene from a movie, a Hana server placed my usual order on the table: a gin martini with four plump olives. Up, dry, and filthy dirty.

I lifted my glass to Yuri.

"To new beginnings."

TWO

I ASKED the server to bring our drinks to the private rooms sections of Hana. He expertly placed the drinks on a tray, led us to a doorway separating the main room of the bar from what Riki called the Pillow Talk rooms. A jorōgumo spider woman Yōkai presenting as a Japanese female in her early thirties stood next to the doorway. She bowed as we approached.

"Good evening, Miller-san."

"Good evening, Yoshiko-san."

"Would you like a room?"

"Yes."

"Please follow me."

Yoshiko gave me a nod as she unclipped the velvet-covered rope, allowing us to pass. The doorway separating the main room from the VIP section didn't have an actual door. Instead, Riki had hung a noren, a special kind of sectioned curtain popular in Japan. Originally a large piece of fabric with the bar's name written in kanji, it had been cut into thirds, each strip hanging from the doorway mantel and stopping short about three feet from the floor.

I pushed through the noren, followed Yoshiko to room eleven. Unlike the main room of the bar, this area was traditionally

Japanese in every respect. The door to room eleven was classic shōji style, a wooden lattice framework covered on one side with a thick opaque paper. The design allowed light to pass through the paper while still providing privacy.

The raised floors of the rooms provided a recessed space below the entrance for shoes. We tucked our footwear out of the way, stepped up and into the room. The server placed our drinks on the small table in the center of the room, backed out, slid the door closed.

The room was about ten feet by ten feet, with an eight-mat tatami floor layout, and a handful of zabuton were scattered around.

I placed one of the thin square pillows at the far end of the room, folded my legs and sat seiza style, with my bottom resting on the soles of my feet. An uncomfortable position for long periods of time, but the zabuton provided a bit of relief. After decades of practice, I could sit through a brief meal without stretching my legs. Yuri adopted a similar position, though she seated herself so she could watch me and the door at the same time.

Madara came to rest on my right shoulder, nestled into my neck. I pretended to play with my hair while giving Madara a few scratches under her chin. Her skin felt dry and smooth, like velvet. Nothing like a real fish.

Yuri looked around. Wasn't hard to see the nervousness in her body language.

"If you want to manifest, it's okay," I said, still in Japanese. "This is a safe place."

Yuri hesitated for a few seconds before changing into an azuki arai Yōkai.

Cool.

Azuki arai translated as *bean washer*, a reference to a sweet red bean called azuki. This kind of Yōkai preferred living in mountainous areas, especially around rivers, streams and lakes. Compared to much of Japan, L.A. was practically a desert in terms of geography. Yuri must have been desperate if she'd decided to come here.

Azuki arai loved washing azuki over and over. They'd rinse the same batch of red beans until it disintegrated, add more beans, and start again. Azuki arai stood two to three feet tall and manifested as little male Buddhist priests. Two features made them unmistakably Yōkai, though. First were their eyes, which were at least twice the expected size of a mortal's. The second difference was their hands, each of which had a thumb and two fingers.

A Hana server knocked on the door before sliding it open. She recognized me.

"May I get you something, Agent Miller?"

"Yes," I replied. "A large bowl half filled with water, a cup of dried azuki beans, a large bottle of warm sake and two orders of hiyayakko."

The server bowed, closed the door. Yuri sat upright.

"How did you-"

"I know a lot about Yōkai," I said. "It's why Riki sent you my way. Are you comfortable talking about how you got here, Yuri-san? It might make it easier for me to help you."

Yuri's eyes shifted downward. She pulled at her kimono collar.

"I do not know where to begin." Her voice had changed, gotten lower as it adjusted to the vocal cords of her new form.

"Well, how did you get into the States?"

"I met someone who said she could smuggle me out. Smuggle many of us out. She put us in a large container for many weeks at sea. She said we'd have jobs and homes once we got here."

"But it didn't turn out that way."

Yuri shook her head.

I sighed, wished her story differed from the hundreds — thousands — I'd heard over the years since the Parting of the Veil in mid-2000. The Parting...well, it was still a complete mystery to pretty much everyone on the planet. The scientists had lots of theories but no real understanding of why it happened. The religious communities took the opportunity to reframe it through their own marketing optics, though they, too, had little more than empty rhetoric when it came to explaining the phenomenon.

I had a personal theory the event had more to do with the hyakki yagyō, or Night Parade of One Hundred Demons. Until the Parting, the parade was a mythological tale of the Lord of Yōkai, Nurarihyon, leading a host of spirits around the physical plane from dusk to dawn. Turned out it wasn't a myth, and in July 2000, the spirits didn't disappear when the sun rose.

Here's what wasn't in dispute: The Parting temporarily rent the veil between the physical plane and the spirit world. At least the Japanese spirit world. No other country had an equivalent experience.

And the veil wasn't just pierced. The Parting ripped it in two. With the barrier between the physical plane and the spiritual plane compromised, Japanese Yōkai made their presence known, concretely answering once and for all the question of whether the subjects of centuries of folklore were, in fact, real.

Japan's Prime Minister responded by creating the Bureau of Souls, an organization devoted to helping the mortal world navigate this uncharted territory. Other countries spun up divisions in their own governments, following Japan's lead. The U.S. created Vigilance, which sat shoulder to shoulder with the FBI, CIA, CBP, and NSA, reporting up through Homeland Security. The Bureau worked with all of them as needed. Only Vigilance regularly gave us any kind of turf-war hassle. The rest were grateful for our help.

Yuri used one of her fingers to invisibly draw on the tabletop.

"They moved the container off the ship once we arrived, but they didn't let us out. We waited. One night they put us into large trucks, drove us away in the dark."

"Hang on, back up. Who brought you to the ship in the first place back in Japan?"

"I do not know names. At least, not real ones. They all used silly, fake names. They were not Yōkai."

Not surprising. A lot of the Yōkai criminals had mortals

working with them. J-pop bands didn't have a monopoly on groupies.

"Okay. So, they put you in trucks."

"Yes. Told us we would get our stamps. Get new homes. Start our jobs in the morning."

"Let me guess. No stamps, no homes, no legitimate jobs."

Yuri nodded.

I took a large sip from my martini, grimace at the bite of the gin. I knew how this story ended.

No passport meant no stamp, and no stamp meant no decent job or safe place to live. And Yuri would think twice about going to the Bureau for help. Without a proper stamp, she'd be treated as a hakushi, which translated as *blank*. Blank meant you never got stamped, never got permission to leave Japan, never got authorization to enter another country. Blank meant you were off the grid, not worthy, non-existent. Blank meant every day was a gamble as to whether you'd be caught and sent back home. Or worse.

Yuri was straight-up hakushi, as blank as they came.

My guess was someone had smuggled the Yōkai into the Port of L.A. or the Port of Long Beach. Nestled next to each other in Long Beach, the ports moved millions of huge shipping containers each year.

"Where did the trucks take you?"

Yuri shuddered, closed her eyes briefly. "A soul shop run by gokudō."

If the Yakuza, the Triad, and the Mob had a three-way and gave birth to a global criminal organization, you'd have the gokudō: Yōkai mafia. And more than happy to lend a helping hand to any unstamped Yōkai who had no other options.

"The top part was a different kind of store," Yuri continued. "A...swap shop? Is that correct?"

"I know about soul swapping. Is that what you mean?"

She nodded. "They did that, too. But that was underground. The place above was a swap store."

I chewed on that for a bit before guessing what she meant. "Like a pawn shop? A place where people sell and buy things?"

Yuri nodded again.

A pawn shop cover located over an illegal soul swap shop? Bit on the nose, even for the gokudō.

"Where did you work?"

"Underground. They trained me to help with rituals for handling the souls."

"Where did the others from the container go?"

Yuri shrugged. "I didn't see them again. But some Yōkai at the shop had worked in other gokudō places. A few had been sent there from other cities. Two of us were taken from the shop before I escaped."

"Do you know where the shop is?"

Shake of her head. "It was not a long drive from the port. Maybe thirty minutes."

That narrowed it down some. Not much, though. Easily over forty square miles of land to scour, and that's if Yuri's sense of time was accurate. I'd need more info to have even a slim chance of locating the shop.

"Do you remember anything about the area of the shop? Any stores, any landmarks, street names?"

Another shake of her head. "I escaped at night. I just remember running, running until I found a place to hide."

"How did you wind up in DTLA?"

"Where?"

"Sorry. Downtown Los Angeles. DTLA." I gestured around me. "Here. How did you get from Long Beach all the way up here?"

She blinked a few times, a shrift of confusion on her face.

"I walked."

Holy shit.

THREE

MY ROUGH ESTIMATES had Yuri walking at least ten miles from wherever the mysterious shop was to DTLA. And she'd done it without being caught by the Bureau, Vigilance, or the gokudō.

"Why did you leave Japan?"

"Living under Nurarihyon was difficult. He became...cruel after the Parting. His power weakens with every Yōkai who leaves Japan." He was not so bad right after the Parting. Now he is more like a," she searched for the correct word, "tyrant."

She delivered the word with the inflection of a question. I nodded. Nurarihyon, Lord of the Yōkai, had a reputation for being oppressive towards Yōkai in Japan. Fleeing Japan to escape Nurarihyon's reach wasn't hard to understand. His control weakened considerably outside of Japan, but inside the country he could still hold any Yōkai in his thrall.

No one was shocked when his grip on the Yōkai had tightened since the Parting, though that policy wound up having the unintended yet unsurprising consequence of accelerating the Yōkai exodus.

Despite back-office hardliners in the Japanese Prime Minister's cabinet calling for Nurarihyon's head, the Bureau had stepped lightly. Peace and stability between the Yōkai leadership and mortal governments had, happily, been the norm for a while. If Nurarihyon or a group of mortals started to escalate things, no one at the Bureau was sure exactly how it would end. One thing I knew for certain, though, was there would be a lot of destruction and death before the dust settled.

So, the current state of affairs was a lot of public posturing, promises that *things were being done* and *promising exchanges were happening.*

For now, Yōkai in Japan faced multiple challenges: falling under Nurarihyon's thrall, dealing with discrimination from mortals, and being unable to present as mortal. Unless a Yōkai could shapeshift, they were limited to their Yōkai form while in Japan. No way to hide and nowhere to run unless you got a stamp or took the chance of illegally immigrating somewhere else.

"I've heard things were bad over there," I said.

Yuri nodded. "But Nurarihyon is not the only danger. Some mortals want to force us into becoming servants, and some want us destroyed." Yuri's eyes slid back down to the table, her finger tracing more invisible symbols. "There are few places that would welcome me in Japan, even if Nurarihyon was gone."

The demand of Yōkai wanting out of Japan far outstripped the supply of secure borders. It was simple economics. A lot of countries balked at the idea of supernatural creatures crossing their borders.

Most Americans called us "tourists" when they were being kind and "hoppers" when they weren't. The U.S. still saw protests against Yōkai, often under nativism slogans ranging from "Send Them Home" to "No Soul, No Citizenship." The latter was hysterical because Yōkai had souls, just like mortals. In fact, some of us used to be mortal. Facts didn't stop the spiritist conspiracy theorists from spinning their own version of reality, though.

Despite the cultural pushback in the U.S., many Yōkai still viewed it as their best chance for a new life. Other countries were more receptive to all Yōkai, not just ones with attractive skill sets.

Tons of Yōkai communities gravitated to places like Canada, Mexico, Australia, and the Nordic countries.

"The gokudō are pretty good at keeping hakushi under wraps. How did you escape?"

"Luck and the will of Ebisu. I snuck out one night." Yuri shifted, her gaze wandering from the table to the walls. My gut told me she was holding something back. "It was dark. I just ran. I do not remember much. There was a strip mall. A coffee shop. Then houses. Many houses. I hid when the sun came out, and I walked at night."

Two clues, both possibly unhelpful. Dozens of coffee shops and strip malls littered the area north of Long Beach. But maybe I could spend tomorrow driving Yuri around the area, see if she recognized anything.

"So how did you know to come to Hana?"

"I met Yōkai on the street. They told me to come here. One of them told me about this bar. They said I could find help."

She looked at me, and the question in her head was obvious.

I had a lot of sympathy and respect for Yuri. Few Yōkai got away from the gokudō, much less stayed alive for a week afterwards. And dodging the Bureau, Vigilance, and local PD? Pretty resourceful.

And I believed her story. My kitsune nose could literally sniff out lies from mortals. Zero help with Yōkai presenting as mortal, unfortunately. But I didn't think she was lying.

"Listen, Yuri-san, I can't get you stamped, and I'm not even sure I could get you back to Japan."

The Yōkai shook her head firmly. "I do not want to go back to Japan. I will not go back."

"I get it, but you need to know staying here won't be fun. If you go to the Bureau or Vigilance for help, they'll deport you. Vigilance might even order you banished back across the veil. If you went up to Canada or down to Mexico, you could get a new identity, perhaps find a decent life."

I put a folded stack of six fifty-dollar bills on the table, slid them over to her. I took three napkins from the table. On the first, I wrote the address of a local motel a few blocks away, plus a simple map. It was run by a friend of mine, Evie, a former Yōkai who had chosen to become fully mortal. I'd known her for years and trusted her. More to the point, she absolutely despised gokudō.

On the second napkin, I wrote the address of a convenience store in Little Yōkai, plus the words "Whisper XR," a special phone with high-grade security software. The Whisper XR used a mix of next-gen cryptography, proprietary banks of telco systems, and VOIP black boxes to make communications to and from the device not only untraceable but automatically able to self-delete any digital footprints of calls and texts.

On the third napkin, I wrote down a virtual number I used with the Whisper app on my cell phone.

"Go to this store. Buy this phone and a fifty-dollar starter plan. Then get a room at this motel. They won't bother with IDs if you pay cash. When you're checked in, text me at this number. I'll call you tomorrow, and we'll figure out the next step, okay?"

Yuri started to say something, paused, then continued. "The gokudō will not stop looking for me."

"Lie low for a week or two, they'll forget all about you. They probably already replaced you with another hakushi Yōkai."

"No, they will not stop. I...I took something. Something they want back very much."

Ah.

If she had something on the gokudō, perhaps I could convince the Bureau to help her out after all.

"What did you take?"

"I am sorry, and please do not be offended, but I do not know you."

She was a criminal on the run from criminals — seeking my help, no less — and she didn't trust me with her secret. Fine. I'd heard enough to feel comfortable sharing my own secret.

"Here." I pulled out my work business card and handed it to her, using both hands as before. "Now you know me."

Yuri's hands shook as she read it. Horror and tears in her eyes.

"You work for the Bureau?"

"Well, I'm an agent, but," I tapped my watch, "I'm off the clock right now."

"You will send me back?"

I frowned, waggled my hand.

"No. I'm not personally interested in deporting you. I really do want to help you. But if you have something the Bureau believes is valuable, I may be able to convince them to give you protection, which would be a lot better for you than anything I can offer. Most importantly, Vigilance wouldn't be able to touch you."

Yuri took that in, seemed to reach some kind of decision. "Will they trade the...will they trade what I have for a stamp?"

"No promises, Yuri. It's not up to me. But I will go to bat for you. If-" Here I held up my index finger to ensure I had her attention, "what you have is valuable enough."

"It is something very valuable. It is something the Bureau would very much like to have."

"Okay. In that, case, you'll need to come to our office and file a statement so I can start working on your protection."

"No. I cannot do that."

"Look, I get it, I do." If the gokudō were after her, she was infinitely safer at the Bureau than wandering the streets alone. I was hoping to parley whatever she had into a deal where the Bureau would willingly provide protection and maybe even a stamp. Adopting a transactional element to our conversation irritated me, but for all its faults, the Bureau could potentially aid her far more than I could.

I worked the system from within when and as often as I could. The Bureau's hands were tied when it came to *Yuri the unstamped Yōkai*. Now, the *Yuri who has something the Bureau wants*? Protection for starters, no question, and possibly even a stamp.

But she was still afraid, and understandably so. Getting her to come with me right now was not an option, and I wasn't going to push it.

Yuri jumped as the door slid open. The server delivered our food and drinks, scents of sake and hiyayakko filling the room. Yuri eyed the large bowl of water and a smaller one of dried azuki beans. I drained my martini, motioned at the bowl and beans, smiled. "Knock yourself out."

Yuri was beyond excited. The lure of the beans pulled a small smile out of Yuri, and she dumped them into the bowl, used a finger to gently stir the water. For the first time since I'd met her, Yuri looked genuinely at ease. She made a sighing sound of happiness.

I placed my hands together, quietly said, "Itadakimasu." I sipped the cold sake and poured a few drops of soy sauce over the hiyayakko. Chilled and cubed tofu didn't sound like much to a lot of people, but when you topped it off with green onions and a few flakes of grated ginger, well, I loved it. Most people preferred it in the summer. I ate it year-round. Besides, Los Angeles was always in a perpetual form of summer compared to the rest of the country.

I pinched one of the tofu pieces with my hashi, carefully lifted it to my mouth.

Oishī desu.

Delicious!

I ate and drank slowly, savoring the tastes. Yuri lost herself in the bowl of beans. She strained them, poured the water back into the bowl, apparently unconcerned the water was dirty. More stirring, and the process repeated itself. I was polishing off the last hiyayakko when the Yōkai sighed, put the bowl on the table.

"Thank you, Agent Miller. It has been too long."

"That's just the beginning if what you have really is important."

"It is."

"Any chance you have it on you now?"

"No, but I can get it tomorrow morning."

"And you don't want to tell me what it is?" Another shake of her head. Still too scared to trust me. Whatever she had, it was her only bargaining chip. She hadn't survived this long without being smart. "Okay. You'll take me to it tomorrow morning?"

"Yes."

On paper, she seemed to be stringing me along, saying anything she needed to in order to stay out of the Bureau office without walking away from a potential deal. My Bureau oath dictated I take her in, but I'd broken that plenty of times. Yes, by not hauling her in immediately, I was aiding and abetting a known criminal, a fireable offense and a prosecutable crime.

Still.

My heart insisted I help her. Something about Yuri had me sold. Plus, she seemed hooked on the idea of getting some help from the Bureau. I was comfortable giving her some extra line for now. I could always reel her in later if I needed to.

I smiled. "Fine. Text me when you're checked in to the motel."

"I will. And I'll text you tomorrow when I am ready to meet. Thank you."

"Would you like something to eat? Are you hungry or thirsty?"

Yuri held up the bowl of beans. "This is all I need."

I texted my friend, Evie, gave her a heads-up about Yuri checking in later tonight. Normally wouldn't have risked it, even over the Whisper system, but something was bothering me. Evie replied with <*nandeimo nai wa!*>

No problem.

We sat there for another fifteen minutes in silence. I dipped into my kitsune power just enough to generate some Yōkai energy, channeled it into my palm. Madara siphoned it off in seconds, the soft tapping of her mouth tickling my skin. Her body glowed a soft baby blue, her tail twitched madly with excitement.

I thought of it as feeding her, which was true to a point. She "ate" my Yōkai signature energy, which is how I've been able to pass as mortal my whole life. The reality was the magical creature could live without it, but, thankfully, she never grew tired of consuming my signature.

Across from me, Yuri slowly stirred the beans around in the bowl, an enormous smile on her face.

———

I still kicked myself for not walking Yuri to the Omagatoki Motel. It was just a few blocks away. Unlikely anyone I worried about would have seen us. But that kind of thinking inevitably tripped you up. You started believing the odds were better than they really were. Or to be more accurate, you started believing you could accurately calculate the odds.

Hana was a wildly popular place for Yōkai, and while I wasn't aware of any active Bureau or Vigilance investigations of the bar, that didn't mean one wasn't underway. L.A. had seen a significant uptick in gokudō activity in the past week. I knew we had every available agent working the streets.

Of course, someone else might have been watching the bar. Another possibility? Yuri was a gokudō plant. I'd experienced some close calls over the years. Trust me, a certain amount of paranoia did wonders for your lifespan.

That's why I took the precaution of retrieving my two cards from Yuri. She gave me an odd look. It would have been an odd request in the states, even odder in Japan. I explained my reasons. She nodded in understanding.

With that taken care of, I mentally weighed the situation. She claimed to have something the Bureau would want, something the gokudō were desperate to retrieve.

Now, if it was intel, why did she have to wait until tomorrow? Was she meeting someone? Expecting an email or text? What could she possibly have that would be worth a stamp? And if it wasn't intel, what might it be? Perhaps an artifact or a powerful magic item? The Bureau would indeed be very interested in that.

I ordered another bowl of water and azuki beans for Yuri, paid the bill. I stepped back into the bar's main room, eager to get up and move around, work off some excess energy.

"Have you seen that Yōkai here before?" I asked Riki, "the one you directed my way?"

"Not before tonight." Riki nodded at her glass. "Care to join me?"

"Normally, yeah, but I've got a lot of shit on my mind. I'd be awful company."

"Oh? Perhaps a distraction is in order."

"How's that?" I asked.

"You're working too hard. You aren't taking care of yourself." A mask of maternity surfaced on Riki's face, though I honestly had no idea if she had a kid. And yes, Yōkai can have kids. I should know.

"What are you talking about?"

"You're caring for your father, Keiko, you're helping hakushi-"

"Hey! Riki, come on." I looked around to see if anyone was paying attention.

"Sorry. My point is, you're always taking care of everyone else in your life. Who's taking care of you?"

I did not need this right now. I pasted on a smile. "Give Audra my best."

Riki lifted her glass at me. "Of course. But I'm telling you, a distraction is just what you need."

Riki doing her usual Riki stuff. I didn't quite catch her drift, but I gave her a wave and stepped off the platform. I checked my watch. Not quite late enough to call it quits, not quite early enough to make staying out a no-brainer.

Maybe chatting with Riki was a good idea after all. I turned around, queued up at the bar behind a couple of young males in dark suits and white shirts with one too many buttons undone. Madara ignored them.

They gave me a once-over and wolfish smiles as they walked away, Grey Goose and Red Bull drinks firmly in hand. I knew the bartender working that night. He nodded once at me — *I see you, I got you covered* — and I turned around to find myself looking directly into the face of a good-looking guy in his mid-twenties. Button-down shirt and indigo jeans. Dark hair with a slight curl, light brown eyes.

"Um. Hey." He put out his hand. "Hey. I'm Benicio." English, and definitely a mortal if Madara had anything to say about it.

I shook his hand. "Keiko."

"Nice to meet you, Keiko."

"You, too. You, ah, you getting a drink?"

"Yep. That is what most people tend to do in bars." Not a trace of sarcasm in his voice.

"Indeed, they do."

And just like that, I found a distraction.

FOUR

GOOD-LOOKING, hunky guys in their twenties have their uses. Sometimes limited but still useful in very specific ways.

The distraction — Beni, short for Benicio, as in Benicio Canales — had been extremely useful. Even better, he hadn't bothered trying to impress me at the bar. If anything, he seemed surprised at me taking the lead. Beni turned out to be an endearingly sweet guy. And he had, to my surprise, quickly shifted from a distraction to more of an attraction.

While we drank and chatted, I learned he was a marketing consultant who drew and painted in his spare time, a fact I soon confirmed when he opened the door to his fourth-floor apartment. The reality of his hobby punched me in the nose. The place smelled of turpentine and oil, and the chemicals hammered my sinuses.

"Sorry," he said. "Guess I'm used to it." He stepped around the easel, cranked open a large window. He disappeared into the bedroom, and I heard him do the same in there. The fresh air helped.

"No pets?" I asked.

He shrugged, grinned. "Never got around to it."

Good. No dogs, then.

I was not a dog person.

Beni put on some music, a forgettable stream of songs halfway between pop and rock, nothing I recognized, and poured two glasses of red wine. We sat down on his sofa.

"Did those hurt?" he asked, pointing to the kusari around my wrists.

"Hurt like hell."

I'd never gotten a regular tattoo, so maybe they weren't as painful as the kusari looping my wrists. I didn't know, and I didn't care, because I had zero interest in getting more tattoos of any kind. A lot of Japanese, especially back in Japan, still frowned on the markings because of their connection to the Yakuza.

The first waves of Bureau agents needed a lot of persuading to accept the kusari, especially since the marks were permanent. Ex-agents had tried everything to remove the tattoos, and short of amputation, nothing worked. Some agents used makeup to cover the kusari just to avoid the unwanted public attention.

I'd witnessed firsthand the reactions to kusari after visiting an L.A. sento. Sento were Japanese bathhouses, and their patrons enjoyed long soaks in large communal baths. Each sex had their own area, and in those areas, everyone walked around totally naked.

I showed the staff my badge and explained how I got the kusari. They politely let me in, but the patrons themselves couldn't stop looking. I didn't want to keep making them uncomfortable, and I didn't want to have to explain myself to every new guest.

I left after ten minutes of whispers and sidelong glances.

Beni started sketching on a small drawing pad. Glanced up at me, sketch, sketch, sketch. Glanced up at me, sketch, sketch, sketch.

"Seriously?" I asked.

"What?"

"You're drawing me right now? Is that your thing?" I didn't find it flattering, but I could imagine some women might.

"My thing is art. I love drawing and painting." Matter of fact, no hint of humor. He looked at me, brows coming together in concern. "I'll stop if you don't like it."

I packaged up my paranoia. Why was I making a big deal out of it?

"It's okay. Go ahead. Might make for a good gargoyle model someday."

He laughed, shook his head.

My phone buzzed. A text from Yuri to my virtual number: <i am safe!>, followed by a half-dozen emojis.

I gave it a thumbs-up, deleted the text.

"You need to leave?" Beni asked. Still sketching.

"No. Would you like me to?"

He closed the drawing pad, put it on the coffee table. "Not even a little."

———

BENI HAD BARELY REGISTERED my badge and gun as we fumbled out of our clothes and performed a striptease dance from the sofa to his bed.

I moaned, rode the wave of orgasms until my senses returned, rolled off him. He gave a post-coital sigh of his own, put his arm across his forehead.

"My God, that was amazing," he said.

Yes, it was.

I smiled as I grabbed my clothes, padded through the semi-darkness, slipped into the bathroom and closed the door. I heard his muffled voice.

"I don't think I can walk."

A standard line, though one usually uttered by a woman. And funnily enough, I was thinking the same thing. Beni had a rare gift for someone his age: equal helpings of passion and patience. I'd taken forever to come, and when I did, the release had been eyes-to-the-back-of-the-head good.

I cleaned up, got dressed, stepped out of the bathroom. Beni watched me from his bed, propped up on an elbow with a silly grin on his face. I pulled my phone from my jacket, checked my messages, found a text from my best friend, Renee: *<just missed u at Hana, here with katia, fumi, and indira>*

Renee and I had been friends since high school and best friends since our college days. She was the pretty one; I was the sort-of-attractive, bit-of-a-nerd tag-along. She enjoyed art and literature; I preferred video games and movies. But we had a common thread in our background that had cemented our relationship. I'd been born in Japan and moved to the states not long after. Renee had been born in France but moved here when she was two.

I replied *<Sorry. Tomorrow?>*

<promises, promises>

"So, I never got your number," Beni said.

"Nope." Had more than my share of dick pics and eggplant emojis. He didn't strike me as that kind of guy, but I'd gotten burned enough times. I was strict about using my virtual number only when helping Yōkai, and I didn't want to pay for a third number. Easier just to say no.

"Um. Well. I mean, can I?" I locked eyes with him, made an *I'm sorry* face. He adopted an apologetic look. "No, yeah, I meant how about your online handle?"

"Not on social media. Kind of a policy thing with work." That wasn't technically true. The Bureau didn't prohibit agents from being online, though it made clear the consequences for being guilty of Posting While Stupid. It was easier to blame work for my non-existent digital footprint.

Less easy was ignoring my desire to see him again. A second date meant sharing more of myself, letting him get inside my carefully constructed defenses. I had lots of reasons for keeping my personal life personal. So, I kicked my own feelings into the corner.

"And this isn't that kind of hookup."

Beni looked genuinely disappointed. He sat up, leaned back against the headboard. "I didn't think this was a hookup."

I laughed. "Hang on. You meet me at a bar two hours ago, we come back to your place for 'just one drink,' and now we're banging in your apartment? What did you think this was?"

Stuff washed across his face, and I realized he truly thought this was more than a one-night stand. He gestured helplessly.

"I don't know, I guess I thought we really connected, you know."

We did.

"Listen, Beni, I just wanted a little distraction, that's all. Nothing serious."

What the hell? Most guys would have killed for no-strings-attached sex. Leave it to me to find the one nice guy in the bar when all I wanted was a quick spin. Also, leave it to me to be attracted to said quick spin. Beni smiled, tried to play it off.

"No, that's cool. Law enforcement Lone Ranger. Half-night stand. I get it. It's cool."

He clearly didn't, and it clearly wasn't. Before I responded, Madara appeared, flicked her tail, pointed straight at the bedroom window. Might have been my imagination, but I swore I caught the hint of a blue shadow disappearing from view outside the bedroom window. Beni's fourth-floor bedroom window. His fourth-floor bedroom window that didn't have a balcony or a fire escape.

Taka onna.

These Yōkai were mischievous but harmless, literally Peeping Toms whose only interest was voyeurism. Being able to stretch their necks up to four stories gave the taka onna plenty of opportunities to catch a couple in the act. Normally I'd have at least drawn the curtains on Beni's window, but tonight I'd been, well, distracted. Apparently, my little bedroom rumba with Beni had attracted some attention.

"Hey," I said, "This was a hundred, all the way. You're amazing." I'd found compliments about sexual prowess were catnip to twenty-something guys, and I landed the earnestness of mine with a perfect score. I didn't need to lie; Beni knew his way around the female body.

He made a point of taking in my figure.

"Girl, you are hands-down the finest thing I've seen. This was cool."

It was an awful response, an awkward mix of bravado and nervousness. I leaned over, kissed him on the forehead. Put my left hand on his cheek. I leaned forward, whispered in his ear.

"Good. Glad you're okay with cool. Now, I need you to stay very still and very quiet. I think someone's hanging outside your window."

He started to get out of bed. I put a hand on his chest. "Stay still."

He nodded.

Between the dim lighting and the carpeting in Beni's bedroom, I tiptoed to the window. Thanks to Madara, I clearly saw the blue silhouette of a person clinging to the building with one hand, the other holding something. I reached out, grabbed the wrist, jerked the Yōkai through the window. A yelp of surprise, followed by the loud fumbling of the Yōkai hitting the floor in a tangled pile. I held on, twisted their arm, cranked the leverage. Whatever it was holding thudded to the floor. I caught a whiff of cinnamon.

"Let me go! I'm not going to hurt you!"

I recognized the voice, peered closer, tried to pick out the face in the dark. Beni switched on the lamp by his bed. A Yōkai, presenting in their mortal form. Japanese male, early forties. A familiar face.

"Gerrald-san? Is that you?"

A pause. "Hai."

"What the fuck, man? Have you lost your mind?"

Not a taka onna, then.

Kevin Gerrald was a stamped hitotsume-kozo. These Yōkai manifested as one-eyed boys who enjoyed pranks. Legend had it they loved tofu, but I can tell you for a fact they loved Manhattan-style clam chowder nearly as much, if not more.

Gerrald had presented as a middle-aged male when he left Japan. He'd helped me plenty of times, but his fascination with breaking into the gokudō network meant we kept crossing paths. I knew he was committing petty crimes. More than once I'd cut him loose instead of hauling him in. But stalking me? This was new, and I couldn't figure out why he'd do it.

"For fuck's sake, you're breaking a half dozen laws, any one of which is grounds for deport."

"It's not what you think. I was, uh, trying to warn you."

"About what?"

"A taka. A taka onna. I tried to catch them, but they took off when I got close. That's when you grabbed me."

His story made no sense. If Gerrald had startled a taka onna, the Yōkai would have simply moved on. Also, taka onna don't have to climb walls. And Madara would have warned me, just like she did Gerrald.

The thing I'd heard fall to the floor was Gerrald's cell phone. I picked it up, saw it was still unlocked. The screen's back light was set to super dim, and a video recording app was still running. I released Gerrald's wrist, let him stand up.

How he'd scaled the building was a feat of agility though far from impossible. I peeked down, saw there were plenty of hand-holds. It was an older building with lots of architectural character, not like the simpler, cleaner designs of modern apartment buildings.

Beni was partway out of bed, the sheet bunched together around his waist. "Keiko-"

I cut him off. He seemed to struggle between wanting to get out of bed and not wanting to flash us.

"It's fine. Sit tight."

"Can I have my phone back, please?" Gerrald asked.

I stopped the video, rewound it, watched me and Beni talking before I turned off the lights. Looked like Gerrald had begun recording not long after Madara had pinged him.

"Gerrald-san, I'm going to ask you a question, and I'm only going to ask it once, so take your time before you answer."

Gerrald scratched at his neck. I caught another whiff of cinnamon, my heart breaking a little with the realization.

"Yeah, um, okay."

"Why were you spying on me?"

The Yōkai looked offended. "I wasn't. I just told you-"

I pulled my sidearm, a modified Sig Sauer P320, aimed it at the floor. Gerrald astutely took the hint and shut the fuck up. I tossed him my shimenawa handcuffs.

"Put those on."

"Hey, Agent Miller, come on. We go back a long way. I'll do whatever you want, okay?"

"Right now, I want you to put those on."

"After all the info I've given you, after all I've done, this is how it goes down, huh?"

"Gerrald-san, I can smell the Crimson Candy on you, and I'm willing to bet you're hopped up on it right now. You were recording me, plus you used your powers to carry out a crime. You really think I can ignore all of that?"

"Look, I wasn't going to post the video online or anything. What do you want me to say here?"

"I want you to tell me why you were following me." He scratched at his neck again, and it was like I'd buried my nose in a bowl of those heart-shaped red-hot candies. The thought of how Crimson Candy was made sparked a fury I couldn't fully stamp out, and I knew I had some paperwork in my future.

Under different circumstances, I'd have let Gerrald go, just like I had in the past. But he'd stacked the deck so far against himself, I couldn't wave it all away. The video, the drugs, the lying. And he was holding something back, more afraid of telling me whatever it was than being arrested.

I needed to know what could possibly be that threatening.

FIVE

ARRESTING Gerrald made me angry and left me more than a little depressed.

I'd saved his ass more times than I could count, stuck my neck out much farther than I should have. It hurt to catch him following me, spying on me, lying to me. Hurt even more finding three vials of Crimson Candy in his pocket. At a grand a pop, Gerrald must have come into a small fortune.

More concerning was the nature of the drug, whose chief ingredient was blood taken from a living mortal. Outlawed in nearly every country, possession of the substance in the U.S. got you an automatic deport. Distribution? Automatic banishment.

I checked the cuffs, made sure they were secure. A specially crafted version of shimenawa lined the insides of the cuffs. In Japan, people used shimenawa rope to mark physical places or objects believed to be spiritual in some way, such as an unusual tree or a boulder. The Bureau had found a way to adapt shimenawa for its own purposes. A thin shimenawa cord lined the interior of its handcuffs and forced Yōkai into their mortal forms.

Plain shimenawa would work, too, though the cuffs prevented anyone from easily removing the cord. Also made it safer to transport a suspect. I carried a short loop of shimenawa to use when a Yōkai was manifesting, and cuffs wouldn't fit. Once the Yōkai was in their mortal form, the cuffs went on and the cord came off.

Beni used the bedsheet as cover to get dressed while I read Gerrald his rights. I gave Beni an embarrassed look.

"Helluva way to end things, huh?"

Beni grinned. "Definitely the most exciting date I've had."

The idea of navigating the rest of this conversation with Gerrald standing two feet away was, shall we say, unappealing.

"Look, I'll call you," I said. I wasn't sure I would, wasn't sure I could. Part of me wanted to, no doubt.

"You have my number?" Beni asked.

"Actually, no, I don't." Guess the don't-let-him-over-the-wall part of me was beginning to crack.

Beni got his drawing pad, wrote down his cell number, folded up the paper, handed it to me. "So. Yeah."

I put the paper in my jacket pocket. "Yeah."

We stood there in an awkward silence. I flashed on the end of my very first official date when I was in middle school. This was worse.

Gerrald groaned. "For fuck's sake, kiss already."

———

I DROVE Gerrald to the Bureau office in DTLA. He spent the time pleading for his freedom. Outwardly, I ignored it. Inside, I was floored he'd done what he did. Floored he was using Crimson Candy.

We almost made it to the office when Gerrald groaned.

"Gerrald-san, you good?"

Another groan, and he leaned forward, his head hung low.

"I don't...I don't feel-"

Sound of vomiting from the backseat. I hit the window buttons as I eased my Crown off the road. The good news was almost all of it had gone straight to the floorboards. The bad news was my car's back floorboards were completely covered in vomit. Gerrald sighed, slumped sideways. He looked like he was sleeping.

"Gerrald-san?" I tapped his cheeks. "Hey, Gerrald-san, wake up."

His pulse and breathing were steady, but I hit him with a light healing han just in case. His eyes blinked open. A second later, his nose wrinkled.

"What's that smell?" he asked.

"That's the smell of a Crimson Candy overdose."

He sat up, closed his eyes. "I don't know what you're talking about."

I pointed at the vial on the backseat. "You don't know how a vial of Crimson Candy fell out of your pocket?"

"Never seen that before in my life."

I checked his pupils. The healing han seemed to have taken the edge off the drug's effect. I took the vial, shook my head.

"I'm sorry, Gerrald-san. You haven't left me any other choices."

I took him to Sub-level 3, the uppermost floor for processing and holding suspects. SL3 was known as Containment, a polite euphemism for holding cell area. It was also one of the domains of the Jewels in our office.

Bureau agents fell into one of three categories, each a reference to one of the pieces of Imperial Regalia, also known as the Three Sacred Treasures of Japan. Japanese coronation ceremonies were private, as in no photos or videos. Very few people witnessed the ceremony in person. During the coronation, a priest presented the new emperor with a sword, a mirror, and a jewel. Much like a crown and scepter, the Imperial Regalia denoted the rightful ruler of the land.

The sword represented valor, the mirror represented wisdom, and the jewel represented benevolence. Field agents were called Swords. Mirror agents focused on intel, Yōkai research, magic, and oversaw our Archives Department. All other agents were called Jewels, and they handled the rest: back-office ops, logistics, equipment, local liaison, and more.

One of the Jewel agents raised his eyebrows when I ran down the charges. The Jewel shook his head, looked at Gerrald.

"Boy, did you pick the wrong window."

SIX

THE BUREAU DIDN'T ISSUE uniforms. Back in Japan, most agents were more formal in their dress, but Assistant Chief Mei Okada, head of the Los Angeles Bureau office, gave in to a more casual dress code. Upside? I got to dress as casually as I liked, which usually meant a pantsuit and blouse. I carried a Bureau badge and a concealed sidearm, pretty much like any plains-clothes LEO in the states. That's about where the similarities ended, though.

In addition to arming its agents with an encyclopedic knowledge of Yōkai, the Bureau issued us a handful of weapons and tools only we could wield.

The Bureau called our wrist and ankle tattoos "agent capability augmentation and enhancements," but most agents just called them kusari. The inch-wide strip of blue kanji and ancient symbols allowed us to deliver han-powered punches and kicks. To date, the only mortals who could successfully use kusari had been born in Japan. Current thinking was it had something to do with the Parting having occurred in Japan. Intel suggested Vigilance was desperately trying to backwards-engineer the process with U.S.-born citizens, but they hadn't publicly commented either way.

If the kusari weren't sufficient, we could turn to the omamori placed inside the back cover of our badges. A Shinto priest on staff at our office created the paper-based talismans, which were sealed in a thin bag before being placed inside our badges. In the first week or so of January, the priest would collect the old ones and issue new ones.

The talismans served as both a lucky charm and a connection to the o-kami Hachiman, god of war and protector of Japan. In answer to a plea for help, the god might grant us temporary powers like extra strength or a bit of immunity to physical damage, but honestly, I'd found him to be a fickle deity.

Next up was the official Bureau of Souls firearm: a han-forged Sig Sauer P320. Modified under the most secretive of conditions back in Kyoto, our versions had han-powered kanji stamped into their barrels. The magically powered automatic handguns turned ordinary bullets into rounds lethal enough to kill supernatural beings.

I personally also used a katashiro, though not all agents did. My katashiro was a hand-sized doll-shaped piece of sheet metal, but many agents used paper. For me, metal made sense, as I was constantly tweaking the wards on it.

A drop of blood on the metal would bind the object to me, and the katashiro would offer protection from whatever curse, threat, or harm I wrote on it. The more general the protection, the weaker it worked. And no extra buffing points for stacking wards — every extra copy of a ward diluted the katashiro's overall effectiveness. In the wrong hands, it could be used against me, so I kept my katashiro locked up in a safe at home.

If all of those failed me? Well, I still had a few cards up my sleeve that were not Bureau-issued. Being part kitsune, I had access to some Yōkai abilities like casting minor illusions and an enhanced sense of smell. I kept those cards incredibly close to my chest, though there was one person besides me who knew all about them: my father, David Miller. I called him Pop.

"Long night, Petal?"

Pop gave me a look I'd seen more than once, though not in many years. It was the *you played too late, and now you're paying the price* look, a standard load out in the parenting arsenal. I was absolutely exhausted, as one gets after staying up until four a.m. cleaning someone else's vomit out of one's car.

I was paying a price all right, but it had nothing to do with any kind of playing on my part.

"Yeah, Pop, you could say that. Had a suspect barf all over the backseat of my Crown."

I took a bite of my rolled omelet. Oishī desu, big time.

Sumiye, Pop's night shift caregiver and one of my aunties, clucked her tongue. She was a yosuzume Yōkai. Rough translation: night sparrow. Sumiye rarely manifested while working.

Yosuzume would accost travelers at night, swarming around their targets. Depending on what sources you believed, the spirits were either harbingers of ill fortune or warnings about dangerous Yōkai nearby.

So far, all Sumiye had brought to our home was love, laughter, and the best natto I've ever tasted. A lot of people didn't like natto, said the fermented soybeans had an unappealing smell or they didn't like the sticky texture. They hadn't tasted Sumiye's version.

"You should get a job in an office," she said. "Work regular hours for once. Find a nice boy, get married, and give your father lots of grand babies."

"I'm at the point where I'd settle for regular hours," Pop said. Sumiye laughed, and I swatted Pop's arm with my napkin.

I'd lucked out and found a handful of Yōkai and mortals to look after Pop twenty-four-seven, mostly for when I couldn't be home. They were all super sweet to him.

"So, which client redecorated the interior of your car?" Pop asked, then he caught himself. "Sorry, sorry. I know you can't talk about your work."

"Not much to talk about. And they weren't a client, they were a suspect." I shrugged. "What are you going to do, right?"

"Well, for starters, you could always get a different job. What? Don't look at me like that. The FBI or CIA would love to get their hands on a Bureau of Souls agent, and Vigilance would offer you the moon to get you on their payroll. How bad would that be? Working for a place where you actually have some leverage. Where they appreciate you."

"It's not like that, and you know it."

"What I know," he said, over a cup of steaming black coffee, "is you're a damn fine agent, a fact the Bureau of Souls doesn't seem to have noticed. How many promotions have you been passed over for?"

"I wasn't passed over, I turned them down. There's a difference."

Pop was looking at his plate, his cup in his hand, just staring at his eggs.

Crap. Pretty early in the day for an episode.

After several seconds, he looked back up at me, returning from whatever mental vacation he'd been on.

"So, which client threw up in your car?"

Sumiye turned around, gave me a sympathetic look that nearly brought me to tears.

"I can't give names, Pop."

"Right. Sorry. You know, I'm really struggling to find a reason not to swing by the office and have a word or three with Mei."

I placed my hashi on the porcelain holder. "Whoa. Stop right there. Even if you and Mei go way back as friends, we agreed you'd stay out of my career. Personal is personal, work is work. Please."

"Okay, okay. I promise." He held up three fingers, which I think was a scout thing.

I checked the time. "Gotta run."

I kissed Pop on top of his head, ruffled his silver-speckled hair. He'd aged very little compared to the photos of him around the condo. Same gunmetal grey eyes and Roman nose. Same amiable smile. He was one of those guys who looked more distinguished the older he got. I'd inherited his smile and a hint of his eyes — at a certain angle my eyes sparkled with flecks of grey — but thankfully not his nose.

"See you at dinner, Pop."

"Love you, Petal."

"Love you, too."

Sumiye gave me a hug and a look she held just long enough for me to catch her silent message: *It's going to be okay.*

Before leaving, I presented our daily offerings to the Shinto kamidana shrine we had installed in our dining room. I placed fresh water, salt, sake, and rice into separate, small, and specially shaped containers. The containers rested on a tray in front of our kamidana, a small, three-sectioned wooden structure sitting on the shelf of the shrine.

The kamidana housed multiple ofuda, tall wooden talismans that represented each of the kami we worshipped. Displayed in an upright manner, the thin talismans were wrapped in protective paper. I checked the sakaki sprigs on either side of the kamidana. The evergreen tree clippings looked fine. I'd replace them in the middle of the month.

I offered a brief prayer to the kami in the shrine, especially Inari, the fox god I felt closest to.

Next to the kamidana shrine was our butsudan, a Buddhist altar dedicated to the Buddha and my family ancestors. The intricate and beautiful wooden cabinet had two small doors on the front, and inside was a statue of the Buddha, incense, candlesticks, a bell, and memorial tablets for various family members.

I lit a candle and a stick of incense, quietly rang the bell, and placed a small bowl of rice and an orange in front of the altar. I offered a series of well wishes and pleas for guidance and protection from my ancestors.

Before the Parting, the practice of maintaining kamidana and butsudan at home had been in a steady decline. Interest skyrocketed post-Parting, and Pop had made sure I grew up with them in our house. The daily offerings and prayers were part of my morning routine.

If I'd known just how badly my morning would go, I'd have prayed a helluva lot harder.

SEVEN

I STEPPED through the Bureau's insanely warded street entrance and the even more heavily warded inner doors. Madara did her job. I waltzed through without a peep from the Yōkai sensors. Good thing, too, as the Bureau had a policy strictly forbidding Yōkai from serving as agents.

I took a sip of my mocha as I weaved through the Pen, the large room holding three dozen desks where most of the Swords worked. Assistant Chief Okada's private office was in a back corner of the Pen. She waved me over before I even got close to my desk.

I bowed low, took a seat. Mei flicked her hand over a device on her desk. The windows looking out at the Pen smoked.

Not the kind of thing you'd expect if they were giving you a medal, so...

Mei had me sit for a few more minutes in silence as she read, scribbled a note, read some more, scribbled again. She capped her fountain pen, took off her glasses, tucked a stray loop of grey hair behind her ear.

"Why do you insist on needling Agent Martinez?" she asked in Japanese.

Valeria Martinez, one of the few non-Japanese agents in the

L.A. office. Her parents hailed from Mexico, but, like me and every other agent, Martinez had been born in Japan. Her parents had moved to L.A. when she was ten, and she spent the rest of her life here. Old money, as far as I knew, and her haute couture wardrobe and BMW 7 Series seemed to back that up.

I thought our unusual connections to Japan might have given us some common ground, but Martinez had shredded every olive branch I extended. After several months, I gave up and avoided her as much as possible.

Answering Mei's question presented a bit of a quandary. I bit back my first response — *because she made it so easy* — jettisoned my second response — *Look, I tried being nice, she's the one with the attitude problem* — and instead opted for something less likely to move me to the pole position on the Chief's shit list.

"We just have different styles when it comes to law enforcement, I guess."

"Styles."

Slapped down like an unbeatable winning poker hand and packed with a ton of unspoken baggage. She knew Martinez and I hadn't gotten along for, well, ever. I'd been intentionally steering clear of Martinez lately, barely interacted with her. I wasn't sure what Mei was driving at.

"Chief, did you call me in to discuss how poorly I play with Martinez?"

Mei leaned back in her chair, folded her hands in her lap. "No, I didn't. Miller-san, I supported your application to the Bureau under circumstances that raised several eyebrows."

Mei had spent most of her life in Japan, and she retained a reticence for explicitly calling people out. According to the office gossip and Pop's comments over the years, she'd been on her way up the ladder, the likely candidate for eventually snagging the Section Chief's desk in Kyoto. Possibly even the Director's seat, as in head of the entire organization.

Six years ago, she'd requested a transfer to head up the L.A. office. Hard not to view it as a self-imposed demotion, and it definitely derailed her shot at getting tapped for the Kyoto office. Mei never spoke about her reasons for coming to the states.

Mei's reference to her role in my application's approval got my attention. She expected me to connect the dots. A triple dose of guilt flushed through me — one for realizing I was making things unnecessarily hard for Mei, one for not realizing it sooner, and one for not just sucking it up better — and I bowed my head.

"Please forgive my lack of discipline and poor judgment."

"Words. Words I have heard many times, yet your actions stubbornly remain the same." There was no exasperation in her voice, just a resigned stating of facts. I left my eyes on the floor, kept silent. There was a pause, and somehow I knew the next thing out of Mei's mouth was not going to be good. Sometimes you got that feeling of dread. Most of the time it turned out to be nothing, a false positive. Not today.

"IA has opened an investigation on you."

Son of a bitch.

If the Bureau of Vigilance had learned about my extracurricular activities or if one of the hakushi I'd helped in the past had slipped up or sold me out, I was screwed. And so were Mom and Pop.

"What's the charge?"

"Extortion and planting evidence on a suspect."

I laughed. I'd never done either of those things and couldn't imagine a scenario where I would.

"Chief, I can promise you that is a lie."

"I believe you."

I mentally exhaled a sigh of relief. "Who's the accuser?"

"Kevin Gerrald. He claims you planted the Crimson Candy on him when he refused to pay you protection money."

Huh. Didn't see that coming.

Gerrald never struck me as the type of person who'd try a stunt like this. Maybe my arrest had forced him across a line. Or maybe someone put the idea in his head.

Mei leaned forward. "Keiko-chan, I always honor my

promises. But if things with the IA do not end pleasantly, I may be greatly restricted in my ability to protect you."

Mei's switch to my first name and the more personal honorific of -*chan* twisted like a knife. Mei wasn't threatening me. She was warning me. And making a plea for my own good, if I was mature enough and smart enough to hear it.

"I understand, Chief. But I clear almost twice as many cases as anyone else in the office. Figured that would carry some weight."

A smile tugged at Mei's mouth, and I admit to taking some satisfaction at her acknowledgement of my statement.

"In many ways, you're the best agent in this district. That is likely what has kept you in the Bureau for so long. But your other traits are the ones that open you up to uncomfortable lines of questioning."

"I understand. I really do, Chief."

"Good, because if you do, I'm sure you won't mind me exercising my judgement and making a decision that's clearly called for."

"Of course." Whatever she had in mind, I could handle it. Would gladly handle it.

"Effective immediately, I'm assigning Martinez to shadow you, 24x7."

Except that.

I opened my mouth to spout off eighteen reasons why that was such a crappy idea.

"Chief, we're dealing with a huge increase in gokudō activity. We need every agent working as many leads as possible. Doubling us up is a waste of-"

Mei held up her hand.

"You will do no official work without involving Martinez. Given the special circumstances surrounding your father, she will sleep at your apartment. I'm reassigning your current cases."

I didn't think things could get any worse. I was wrong, of course.

Mei handed me a red manila file with a black X across the front. "That will be your one and only focus for now."

I scanned the first page, skimming the details. A Jane Doe Yōkai death, almost certainly a murder, no identification, etc. I'd seen dozens of them.

But none of them had a victim's photo of Yuri's face.

EIGHT

I WALKED out of Mei's office, Yuri's jacket heavy in my hand. I dropped the jacket on my desk, took a swig of my lukewarm mocha. Across the Pen, Martinez was making a beeline for me.

Nope. I soooo cannot deal with this right now.

I pretended not to see her, walked towards the elevators. Martinez broke into a jog. When I pivoted towards the staircase, she actually sprinted. In heels, no less, I begrudgingly noted.

"Miller-san, I need you to file your report from last night's booking. I can't finish yesterday's daily summary report until you do."

She put her arm across the door to the stairwell, blocking my way.

"Have it to you within the hour, Martinez-san. Gotta check on a suspect."

"Now, Miller-san."

Title-wise, Martinez was my peer and had only a few months of seniority on me. Not nearly enough to be ordering me around like this. She could whine to our mutual boss about me holding up her report, but even that was a stretch in my opinion. Most agents assigned to the daily summary reports didn't even start on them before eleven, which gave their fellow co-workers plenty of time to finish any late-night case paperwork. I looked down at her arm.

"You want to move that, or shall I?"

"I need your report."

"I heard you."

I sipped my mocha. Took my time. Watched her over the lid of the coffee cup. Part of me wanted to upend the drink over Martinez's head, watch it pour down her perfectly coiffed black hair, genetic lottery-winning face, and designer clothes.

Okay, not really. And I didn't hate her so much as I wished she wouldn't always act like the rich, popular girls from my high school. But learning of Yuri's death and my new tethered assignment to Martinez left all of my de-escalation Bureau training in a smoking heap. My patience was rice-noodle thin.

"I can do this all day," she said.

"I'm sure you can. But I'll make this easy for you. Give you an excuse to back down."

This was not how Martinez thought it would go. She shifted her weight, and I saw her run the calculations: just how high could Keiko crank the crazy? I already had a rep in the office for being unpredictable. May as well lean into it.

I used my right hand to pull back my jacket, rested my palm on the grip of my holstered Sig.

"You can either walk your Johnny Choo heels away from this door, or I can shoot them off." I gave her the most deadpan look I could muster. "Your choice, but it'd be a shame to have to spend your lunch break shopping for a new pair."

Martinez's mouth fell open.

"That's a criminal threat. And intentionally discharging a weapon in the office is a fireable offense." A sour smile split her face, and she shook her head. "HR and IA are going to fight over who gets to string you up first."

I unsnapped the leather safety strap on the holster, making sure the only person who could see it was Martinez. Anyone else in the Pen would just see two fellow agents talking. A lot of the agents in the DTLA office spent most of their lives in Japan. They brought with them the tendency to avoid outright conflict. Raising your voice, directly criticizing someone to their face, even politely but explicitly rejecting a co-worker's request — those were unusual in Japan.

Assistant Chief Okada's approach to office culture was, in my humble opinion, to her credit. Example: all U.S. agents were fluent in English and Japanese, and while Japanese was the language of choice, several agents regularly used English in the office. On the other hand, Mei preferred we keep our Japanese sensibilities when it came to intra-office interactions.

Point was, me threatening to discharge a firearm in the office and in the direction of a fellow agent, no less, was the very opposite of Mei's preferences. It was a total bluff, of course, and I was being childish and wildly unprofessional. But I couldn't stop myself. Martinez just got under my skin like nothing else.

"One."

Martinez's lips went tight. She wasn't backing down as quickly as I would have guessed, I gave her that.

"Two."

Martinez's arm dropped. She stepped aside just enough to let me through the stairwell door. Guess my reputation for being a loose cannon was still intact. I'd certainly goosed it with this stunt.

I gave a curt nod of my head, opened the door, and headed down to the Archives. From behind, Martinez hurled a final retort.

"And they're *Jimmy* Choo's, you tasteless piece of shit!"

Bingo.

Not only had I gotten her to blow her cool and yell in front of everyone, she'd also cursed. Pretty sure Mei would have heard it, too.

On a scale of one to ten, my happiness meter popped to a solid eight.

———

LOCATED in the top two underground levels of our office, the Archives Department was a bit of a misnomer insofar as a lot of our data was digital. But some things couldn't be digitized or needed to be kept locked up safely behind a ton of wards and spells. Sub-level 1, or SL1, was where most of the Mirrors worked. It contained their offices and a heavily warded safe room. SL2 was a mix of filing cabinets, computer servers and terminals, and vaults.

As a Sword, I was a rare sight in the Archives Department. Most of what we needed we could access via the office network. But I didn't want Mei or Martinez or anyone else seeing what I was pulling up on my cubicle desktop.

In fact, the only reason I was working at the Bureau in the first place was because of my desire to reunite my parents. According to Pop, the Bureau had banished my mom, Narumi, from the physical plane when I was less than a month old. She was currently staring down a hundred-year sentence for not registering herself with the Bureau in the early months following the Parting.

Agents had caught Mom when I was three weeks old, but not before she and Pop had found a way to bond Madara to me. With some help from Mom's friends on the physical plane, Pop and I managed to sneak out of Japan. He wasn't fond of the idea of me working for the Bureau, and I can't say I blamed him. He didn't know about my plans to bring Mom back early — and I didn't want him to know — which meant stoically accepting his silent condemnation of my career choice.

Point was, my relationship with the Bureau was *conflicted*.

I found Koji Oshiro, the senior Mirror agent in Archives, at a large table, hunched over a washi scroll. He peered at the thick paper through a massive magnifying glass mounted on a moveable arm. Despite its age, the scroll was in excellent condition. Japanese washi paper was known for its durability.

"Hey, gorgeous," I said. "What you got there?"

Oshiro didn't look up, muttered quietly to himself. "Intact, too. And if I had to guess, it's-"

A puff of green gas appeared above the scroll. Madara flipped out. I scrambled back away from the small cloud.

"-still active," Oshiro finished saying.

"Why aren't you working on that in the safe room?"

Oshiro tapped a small box on the table next to the parchment. "Portable ward."

I shook my head. The Mirrors in Archives had a reputation for being odd. Personally, I found them inquisitive, intelligent, and focused. I'd slowly befriended Oshiro over time, my frequent trips downstairs finally cracking the ice.

I stepped back up to the table, examined the box.

"Nice work."

"A trivial matter," he replied, deflecting the compliment.

"You have any luck on that signature modulation detection ritual?"

"I'm making progress."

"Please let me know when you have it ready for a test, will you?"

A single nod was the only reaction I got.

NINE

BY NOW, I'd calmed down enough to face Martinez again.

I walked upstairs to my desk, my earlier anger pushed aside by an oil slick of remorse. Yuri wasn't going to get stamped. She wasn't going to enjoy any kind of protection from the Bureau. And it might be a very long time before she touched another azuki bean on the physical plane.

Unlike mortals, when a Yōkai's physical presence was destroyed, their soul crossed into an ethereal world the Yōkai called home. We referred to it as Furusato; literally "home" or "hometown." Furusato existed in a kind of overlapping, intersectional way with our physical world.

Yuri's soul was already across the veil and back in Furusato by now, and theoretically, she could return to the physical plane in the future if she wanted. Emphasis on theoretical.

The Parting had only lasted a night, but when the curtain closed again, it was like the slamming of a door. Travel in either direction was extremely dangerous, though for different reasons.

Crossing the veil from Furusato to the physical plane used to be relatively easy for Yōkai. Several first-hand accounts of them doing so post-Parting confirmed the transition was near impossible. Those who succeeded said they'd think twice before trying it again.

Going in the opposite direction was no picnic, either. Yōkai returning to Furusato had to shed their physical bodies by dying. As Yōkai were essentially immortal, that meant suicide or allowing their physical bodies to be destroyed. Once in Furusato, they had to reconstruct their physical forms, which was a slow and painful process.

Yuri had needlessly suffered because I hadn't done enough to protect her. And now, instead of being able to track down her killers on my own, I was going to have Martinez riding shotgun, which meant riding my ass.

Mei called Martinez into her office. Out of the corner of my eye, I caught James Balingford walking towards me.

Inari's nine tails, can I not catch a break today?

"Morning!" He perched himself on the corner of my desk, his right leg swinging slowly back and forth. Rumor had it Martinez and James had been an item at one point. He'd hit on the good-looking female agents in the office, and when he'd gotten around to me, I should have been flattered, I guess.

His assets, if you could call them that, included his looks and a decent sense of style.

But did I mention he hit on all the female agents? Balingford had put me in his sights my first week as a full agent. I politely told him I wasn't interested. Didn't mix personal and professional worlds, it's not him, it's me, I was just coming off a bad break-up, etc. It all sluiced off him like liquid Teflon.

Finally, I couldn't take it anymore, and I "accidentally" nailed him in the balls with a full cup of piping hot coffee. Made it look like I had turned around without noticing him, so I had to apologize profusely for being such a klutz. We both knew it wasn't an accident. He got the message.

His reaction shouldn't have been surprising. What's that old saying? "Hell hath no fury like a woman scorned." They forgot to add, "but rebuff the undesired advances of a young white male with privilege syndrome, and it's probably a tie." Balingford had been making my life as unpleasant as possible ever since.

I ignored him, my head cranking on Yuri. I chided myself for not following up with her. Berated my failure for not paying better attention. Second-guessed my decision to let her back on the streets on her own. If I had brought her in — if I'd done my job — she'd still be alive. While I was spiraling down the drain of self-criticism, Balingford launched into the reason for his visit.

"Word is you just got a babysitter." His voice was low enough that only we could hear it.

I blinked, looked up at Balingford. "What?"

"I just got handed two of your mortalization cases, and it looks like one of them's a schizo hopper. Thanks for the extra workload, Miller."

Hopper.

The insulting slang reference turned my stomach. Bad enough to face that level of prejudice from a spiritist, but to hear that kind of sewage come out of an agent's mouth made me embarrassed to be associated with the Bureau.

"Any time," I said, punctuating my reply with a swing of my mug. The cold coffee rose dangerously close to the cup's edge. Balingford jumped back, nearly tripping over himself.

"Hey!" The polished facade fractured, anger briefly peeking through. Balingford caught himself, smiled, plastered over the cracks. "Guess you finally fucked up a little too much this time, and the Chief jerked your chain. Long overdue if you ask me."

I got a text from Evie: <*Please come. Important.*>

Guess she'd found out Yuri was gone.

"I gotta answer this."

"Sure, sure." He walked away, satisfied with how the conversation had gone. I put the coffee cup down instead of hurling it at Balingford's head.

My morning had started with a guy vomiting in my car, followed by the joy of cleaning up that mess, and just a few hours of sleep. From there, it descended into discovering I was the focus of a bogus IA investigation. The topper on this layer cake of shit? Learning Yuri was dead.

I checked my watch.

Huh.

I'd managed to squeeze all of that in before ten o'clock.

"Agent Miller?" I looked up at someone I recognized but didn't personally know. "I'm Agent Mitsui. Internal Affairs."

It was going to be a long day. A very, very long day.

TEN

MULTIPLE CHOICE QUESTION: Mr. Gokudō needed an easy way to dispose of a corpse in Los Angeles. He should:

A) toss the body in the Pacific

B) give the victim a prolonged soak in a bath of acid

C) roll the corpse in a blanket and dump it up somewhere in the winding hills of Griffith Park.

The answer was C. While only a handful of murders actually occurred in the municipal park each year, the LEO community widely acknowledged a lot more corpses got dropped off there. The park had over 4,200 acres of hills, ravines, and caves, and only a dozen or so park rangers assigned to patrol the entire area. It was safe to say we'd never find all the skeletons in that particular closet.

Unless, of course, Mr. Gokudō figured no one's going to care too much about the body when it was found. Unless he'd counted on the corpse of yet another unstamped Yōkai barely warranting a mention on the six o'clock news. Unless he felt that even if someone identified the body, they wouldn't be able to track it back to him.

In which case Mr. Gokudō probably just tossed it out of a

moving van along one of the roads in the park, not even bothering to roll it into a deep chasm, much less bury the body.

According to the case jacket, a jogger had discovered Yuri's body just after six in the morning. Yuri's body lay sprawled between one of the major roads and a trail running through the park. No indication anyone had even tried to hide her body.

The jogger had called 911, who notified local PD, the Griffith Park Rangers, the Bureau, and Vigilance. Vigilance rode oversight on Yōkai crimes, but they were no more equipped to deal with the supernatural beings than LPD. To date, the Bureau had held a zero-sharing policy when it came to han magic.

That, of course, drove Vigilance out of their mind. They were desperate for the ability to bring Yōkai policing under their control or even hire an agent. Vigilance had covertly approached me multiple times over the years, ostensibly as a "consultant." I'd rather shave my legs with bleach and broken glass than help them.

My interactions with Vigilance reinforced their reputation for covertly supporting all efforts to permanently deport and ban Yōkai, and they took every opportunity to undermine the Bureau's authority, take credit for its collars, and all but demand the Bureau share their secrets.

Since none of that had happened yet, the Bureau handled most aspects of Yōkai cases. A Jewels sweeps team had likely already transported Yuri's body to the Bureau for processing, where a Jewel coroner was probably just now starting the autopsy. At some point, Vigilance would task one of its officers to oversee until the case was closed. The good news was Vigilance rarely liked messing with John and Jane Doe cases. Nothing flashy about those. I'd probably only have to deal with a couple of calls with the Vigilance case officer.

Before I could start solving Yuri's murder, though, I'd lost an hour with Internal Affairs. Mitsui laid out the claims. Gerrald said he was performing a citizen's arrest against a taka onna when I stumbled onto him. He said I'd demanded protection money from him or else I'd arrest him. When I declined, he said I'd planted the Crimson Candy on him and hauled him in. I disputed the claims, gave my side of the events. IA would now methodically evaluate the accusation, which could take weeks.

For the time being, I turned my attention back to Yuri.

The assigned Vigilance officer was a guy named Darnell Durante. I'd worked with him a year back. Surprisingly not a complete ass, though with the Vigs, that didn't carry as much weight as it should have. I texted Durante with a peremptory check-in to hopefully keep him off my back and buy me some time.

Time I desperately needed if I was going to check out the motel for clues without Martinez looking over my shoulder. The daily summary report would have to wait a little longer.

Quick sweep of the Pen showed everyone was busy with their own work, and even Mei was nose-deep in paperwork. Martinez was nowhere to be found. I stood, walked casually to the stair-case, which would get me to the underground parking deck and a side-street exit. Like the front entrance, this exit had wards and a round-the-clock video camera. I didn't need to sneak out, per se — just leave without Martinez noticing.

To her credit, Martinez was waiting for me in the stairwell.

"Where we off to?"

Well, shit.

"Work the Jane Doe case like the Chief asked."

"Still waiting on that report."

Much as I wanted to tell her what to do with the report, having a showdown with her right now would only make things worse. And a small voice in the dark corner of my mind scolded me for being so immature about the whole thing. I was holding her up because...why? I enjoyed having the upper hand in some petty power play? Not super professional of me.

"Right, right. Okay, I'll polish that off, then we can head out."

She followed me back to the Pen without a word, hovered over my shoulder. If it was any consolation, and it was a minor one at that, she didn't seem as thrilled as I would have guessed. I finished entering the report in our case management system, creatively named the CMS. Martinez went to her desk to finalize her summary report for Mei, eyes lifting every so often to make sure I hadn't bolted. I focused on the mountain of reports waiting for my attention, and half an hour later, we headed back to the parking garage. When I turned for the street exit, Martinez stopped me.

"Wait, where's your car?"

"At home. It's just a fifteen-minute walk."

"You left your Crown at home?"

"I felt like walking today." Which was true. Some days, I left my Bureau-issued car at home.

"Don't bother, we'll take mine." Martinez pointed at her dark blue BMW. She consistently drove her Bimmer to work and in the field, only getting behind the wheel of her Crown if she had to. She'd worked out some deal with Mei and the Jewels, got an exception to use her personal vehicle on the job. My guess was she paid the Bureau for whatever customizations were necessary to her personal car, agreed not to request reimbursement for gas and miles.

And I won't lie. Part of me tweaked at the thought of slipping into the Bimmer. A huge step up from my personal Camry or my Bureau Crown. And having Martinez chauffeur me around town? Normally, I'd be all over it. Not today.

"That's awfully sweet of you, but I'll grab my Crown and swing back here to pick you up." She cut me a *don't even* look. I crossed my heart. "Promise."

"Miller-san, that's worth about as much as last week's losing lottery ticket. We'll take my car."

"The Chief said you were shadowing me, and she said I was the case officer for the Jane Doe, so..." I left the implication hanging, watched her weigh the decision of whether to run crying to Mei about something as inane as which car we'd take or just let the whole thing go. She put on a sour look, opted for the latter.

"Fine. Let's go."

I eyed her shoes. "Okay, but you're going to wish I'd shot those heels off before this is over."

ELEVEN

MARTINEZ KEPT up with me without breaking a sweat or her stride. We spent the walk without saying a word, and it wasn't until we were in my Crown that she broke the silence. She sniffed, made a face.

"Is that vomit?"

I bit my tongue to keep from smiling, offered her a mournful look.

"Yeah. Had a suspect puke his guts out last night. Tried to roll down his window in time, didn't make it. Projectile crap everywhere."

The look on Martinez's face was abject horror. She gagged, scrambled out of the car even as she tried to avoid touching anything. Seeing her brush at her dry-clean-only designer duds almost made up for the morning. The smell wasn't that bad, and truth be told, I'd thoroughly scrubbed the small amount of vomit that had wound up in the front seat. I felt she was over-doing it.

"Didn't you clean it up?"

A flash of anger. What did she think I was, a moron?

"Yeah, I cleaned it. I got home at two a.m. this morning, spent an hour hosing down my car, got a few hours of sleep, and dragged my ass into work. As soon as I have a spare half-hour, I'll get it to the car wash for a deep clean. In the meantime…" I gestured for her to get in. "Unless, of course, you'd prefer the trunk."

"I'd have preferred you mentioned this before we walked all the way to your house. We could have taken my car."

"Slipped my mind. Got a lot going on. Sorry." I turned over the engine. "In or out?"

Another few seconds of hesitation before she delicately climbed into the seat.

"At least tell me the windows work." I made a face, shook my head. Was I deliberately poking the bear? A little. Okay, maybe a lot, but I couldn't help myself. I thought she was going to have an aneurism. "How do you live like-"

I mashed the passenger window button on my door armrest, watched her face go from full-on shock to full-on rage as the glass slid down. I grinned over my small and admittedly petty victory. That small voice in my head crossed its arms, tsk-tsk'd me.

"It's a wonder for the ages you're still single, Miller-san."

"Who says I am?" Actually, I'd been single for a while. Riki wasn't totally off base in her assessment of my level of self-care. I had plenty of reasons to skip the dating scene — living with my father, my job, the fact that I was half Yōkai and no one knew.

Martinez frowned, sighed, closed her eyes. She breathed in and out slowly, looked back at me. Her voice had ratcheted down to something approximating a normal tone.

"Listen, I don't like this anymore than you do. Mei insisted, against my objections."

I didn't believe that for a second. Having her riding along, watching everything I did, just waiting for a chance to report the slightest error to Mei? This assignment had to be a dream come true for her, especially if she knew about the IA investigation. On the other hand, given what I was about to do, I decided not to argue with her.

"Okay, Martinez-san."

She sat on that for a bit. "I'm serious. I've got far better things to do than babysit a fellow agent who doesn't respect herself or the Bureau."

That was unexpected. Much as I hated to say it, I'd never considered Martinez's animosity to be anything other than simple jealousy. Maybe a competitive streak. It was irritating to think she was always looking for a way to undercut me in Mei's eyes, but I could handle that. Barely gave it a second thought.

But the idea she considered me a poor excuse for an agent?

That arrow found its target, lodged its head deep into the meaty slab of my pride.

"Hang on," I said. "I bend the rules once in a while, but that doesn't make me a shitty agent. You can hate me, but you can't accuse me of slacking my way through the Bureau."

"Your words, not mine. Besides, IA will reach its own conclusion. Let's go, Miller-san. Case won't solve itself."

Martinez wasn't stupid, and she already didn't trust me. My hopes of solving this case without her learning about my connection with Yuri took a solid punch to the kidney. A couple, actually.

Her accusation was still rattling around my head as I put the car in gear. I pulled out of the parking space, braked. I checked the small storage space in the center armrest, opened the glove compartment.

"Shit," I muttered.

"What?"

"My sunglasses. I think they're behind you. In the back pocket of your seat." I gave her an apologetic look. "Would you be a doll?"

Her face was a mix of distrust and disgust. She scowled, opened her door. As soon as she was clear, I pulled away. Momentum swung her door closed before it clipped a parked car, and I gunned it. In the rearview mirror, I saw her typing away on her phone.

Okay, maybe Martinez was a *little* stupid.

TWELVE

THE OMAGATOKI MOTEL was one of the last old school holdouts in DTLA. Hell, Little Yōkai itself was the embodiment of holdout. After the Japanese spirits started turning up in Los Angeles, it didn't take long for Little Tokyo to get renamed Little Yōkai. The section of northern DTLA became a haven for all manner of spirits. The existing mortal residents and business owners had a few things to say about their new neighbors, some good, some bad. After a decade, though, it was no longer a question of whether Yōkai were going to congregate in Little Tokyo, it was just a matter of how many would.

And so Little Yōkai was born.

The area became a magnet for Yōkai, stamped or not. It also drew a fair share of mortals who were sympathetic to the spirits' plight. I grew up in DTLA, and Pop made sure I regularly spent time in Little Yōkai. Pop warned me about not revealing my Yōkai side, which meant no matter how much I enjoyed being around a community of fellow Yōkai, I was always a little on guard, a little reserved, a little walled off.

Despite that, fewer places gave me more joy than Little Yōkai. Soak up some gossip, enjoy some dumplings, listen to musician tease tunes from a traditional Japanese guitar called a samisen... I'm talking paradise.

Today, Little Yōkai was a vibrant community that had somehow struck the perfect balance between welcoming Yōkai and mortals alike. And it had dodged the gentrification bullet by not just keeping but expanding on property owned by Yōkai. The result was not perfect — no neighborhood ever was — but the resulting blend of a Yōkai community that included a mortal-oriented tourist area was my happy place.

Perched on the south-eastern edge of Little Yōkai, the Omaga-toki Motel was a two-story, old-school motel that stubbornly refused to update its 1930s exterior. It looked increasingly out of place, especially considering the towering buildings flanking the motel, each at least three times taller and sporting a modern archi-tecture.

But I knew the owner, Evie, and I knew that was kind of the point. She was smart enough to give a Wall Street broker a run for his money. Despite the dated outward appearance, the rooms were modern. Evie counted on the appearance to scare off most of the riffraff, and she'd encourage the rest of the dregs to kindly fuck off if they caused any trouble, and she didn't truck with the gokudō no matter how many times they tried shaking her down. Evie could protect her motel just fine, thank you very much, *now get your asses out of here; I've got a shotgun and a broom, and I know how to use both of them.*

Bold words for a mortalized Yōkai who no longer had the powers she once possessed. But there's the kind of power you had and the kind of power others had that you could access. Evie was solidly in the latter category, at least according to some of the gossip I'd heard on the street. Drunken, two-in-the-morning gossip, so I took it with a shaker of salt.

"Evie's a former member of the Ryū Kiri, Miller-san. Watch your step with her."

Ryū Kiri translated as *Dragon Mist*. A supposedly all-powerful, mysterious group of Yōkai secretly pulling the strings of Los

Angeles and doing so under the unsuspecting noses of the mortals. Modern-day folklore, if you asked me.

Regardless, it carried weight in the Yōkai community, and Evie enjoyed no small degree of respect as a result. She rarely had issues with the gokudō, and that's why I pointed hakushi in need of some help to the Omagatoki Motel. I knew they'd be safe.

Guess I'd have to reevaluate that belief.

I pulled into the underground public parking lot of the motel, drove to the third and bottom-most level. Took the stairs to the tiny lobby, which sat perpendicular to the rest of the motel. The lobby was empty. I tapped the bell on the front desk counter. From behind a half-closed door, I heard Evie call out.

"Coming!"

Evie's now-permanent mortal appearance was a grey-haired Japanese female. She'd learned English and a smattering of Spanish. Preferred a type of kimono called a tsukesage, which was on the more casual end of the kimono fashion scale. She kept a pair of eyeglasses on a chain around her neck, though I'd never seen her wear them. Her eyes, neither yellowed nor dulled by age, told you everything and missed nothing.

"Keiko-chan! Oh, sweetie, I'm so sorry about what happened." She shook her head. "I'm so, so sorry. I should have-"

"Not your fault, Evie-san."

"Do you have any idea where she is?"

I told her what I knew. Evie took the news hard.

"Can I see her room?" I asked.

Evie nodded. I could see the guilt still clinging to her. Probably never forgive herself, though it truly wasn't her fault. She unlocked a cabinet behind her, pulled out a dark green diamond-shaped keychain, locked the cabinet again.

Evie led the way out and up to the second floor, opened the door to room four. I grimaced — an unlucky number in Japanese culture. Evie didn't buy into all the superstitious stuff some Japanese did, and frankly, neither did I, to a certain extent. Never occurred to me to tell Yuri about avoiding room four. Another wave of my own remorse rolled through me.

"I didn't go in once I realized she was gone. You come find me when you're done."

I nodded, thanked her. I pulled on a pair of plastic gloves, flicked on the lights, and closed the door.

Madara didn't make herself visible, meaning there wasn't a whisper of anything Yōkai currently in the room. A quick visual sweep generated a handful of observations, but none were overtly sinister. The bed cover looked tousled, like someone had sat on top of it. A TV remote was on the floor. The initial Jane Doe report mentioned nothing about a backpack being found near her body, but it wasn't here, either. No other personal effects, either.

I cast a han of seeing, and the spell turned up the afterimage of a Yōkai signature. But it was far too strong of a burst for it to be just Yuri. Make that signatures, plural. She was definitely not the only Yōkai to have used the room in the last day or two.

Based on how strong the afterimage presence was, I guessed two powerful or maybe up to four low-level Yōkai had been in the room. More powerful Yōkai had a stronger signature. The doorknob and lock had looked fine. No signs of forced entry.

I began methodically sweeping the room, took my time. Thirty minutes later, I had absolutely nothing. A large towel hung on the hook on the back of the bathroom door. A soap wrapper was in the trash can, and a used bar was in the shower.

Okay, how had this gone down? Yuri had come in, taken a shower, lain on the bed while watching some TV? Someone got inside the room or convinced her to come outside? Did the absence of a struggle mean she knew them and went willingly, or had she given up right off the bat? Either way, what did that tell me about who the intruders were? For that matter, had Yuri voluntarily left the room, gotten spotted, and then killed somewhere else? Or were the Yōkai signatures from friends of Yuri's, other Yōkai she'd invited to her room?

Too many questions, not nearly enough answers.

I cast another han of seeing, this time with a slight twist. Instead of looking for indications of Yōkai, this version detected the use of magic.

Bingo.

I got a faint read off the lock. Someone *had* spell-picked it. Also got residual traces of both offensive and defensive Yōkai powers. So Yuri had not gone willingly. Still didn't tell me who had taken her.

Time to check in with Evie.

———

"PLEASE SIT HERE, KEIKO-CHAN."

Evie put me in front of the computer, told me how to pull up the motel surveillance footage from the night before. She'd installed two cameras, one at each end of the building, so she had two angles on all room doors.

"That's the north camera feed?" I asked.

"Yes." Evie sat next to me while I went through the video. Not much activity, and the few bodies crossing the camera's view were easily identified by Evie. At 12:24 a.m., the feed went dead. "Skip to 12:51."

I did, and the feed resumed. "Same on the south camera?"

"Yes."

I continued scrubbing the video right up to the moment I saw myself entering the motel office. Nothing unusual. I pulled up the south feed, went through it with identical results.

"Spiked or a glitch?"

"Both cameras are less than a year old and have separate hard-line feeds to the computer, which hasn't given me a problem in years. I'm thinking spike."

"So we've got nothing." I leaned back in the chair, rubbed my eyes. Not a good idea. Felt like I was raking them with a cheese grater. I had counted on finding something here to get me on the trail of Yuri's killer. If I'd ditched Martinez only to come up empty-handed…

"Where's the feed for that?" I gestured above us at a camera pointing at the lobby door. Evie leaned over, tapped at the keyboard. A view of the lobby appeared on the monitor. Evie and I watched the feed. At 12:38 a.m. the camera captured two large males heading to the southern staircase. The guys were built like pro wrestlers. Both wore their dark hair pulled back in a short ponytail and sported suits worn over dark t-shirts. Madara was no help, as she could only identify Yōkai physically near her.

Evie and I watched the pair descend, each with a hand gripping one of Yuri's arms. Impossible to identify their ethnicity, given how far they were from the camera. The timestamp was 12:49 a.m.

I pushed the puzzle pieces around, trying to fit what I'd learned into some kind of picture.

Two dudes, probably gokudō, used magic to knock the outside cameras offline. Smart. But they weren't smart enough to knock out the lobby camera, so maybe they were the B-team? Or just a touch arrogant?

And Yuri may or may not have known the two goons, but she hadn't gone willingly based on the residual magic in the room. For some reason, my head went to the guys being oni. The handiest reference for oni was a cross between an ogre and a troll. Intelligent and hard to stop if they got angry. I'd learned to respect their abilities.

But that was purely a guess. The rules for how Yōkai presented as mortal only allowed for a few general presumptions. First, Yōkai only gained the ability to present when they left Japan, and that ability ended as soon as they returned. In fact, the Bureau had learned early on crossing Japan's airspace would eliminate a Yōkai's ability to present.

Second, unless a Yōkai could shape shift, they only had one mortal form available to them when they left Japan. Could be a kid or an adult, male or female. The youngest on record was a five-year-old girl, but most Yōkai presentations fell between fifteen and sixty.

Finally, Yōkai had no control over how they presented. We were always Japanese in appearance, and however we presented the first time we left Japan was how we presented every time. Our mortal form never aged.

There were two exceptions to these rules.

Exception the first: shapeshifting Yōkai got a default mortal form, but they could present any way they wished, change any aspect of their appearance.

Exception the second: for part-Yōkai people like me, our presentation form appeared to age like mortals.

Kitsune were known for being innately gifted shapeshifters. Unfortunately, my powers did not include this ability. Not yet, anyway. My best guess was I needed to obtain at least one more kitsune tail before I could unlock that power.

I had little more than a hunch about whether Yuri's kidnappers were Yōkai. And if they were shapeshifters, the video wouldn't have been much help, anyway.

The facts I could confidently rely on were few. The pair of intruders had taken Yuri from the motel, and a few hours later, someone had murdered her and dumped her body in Griffith Park.

"Any chance you recognize these guys?" I asked, pointing at the screen. Evie shook her head. "When was the last time you rented out room four?"

"At least a week. Most guests avoid room number four. But with the craziness on the streets right now, I've been full up for days. It was the only available room I had left last night. I think I need to change the number."

"Yeah. Couldn't hurt. Say, you still using any hakushi on your cleaning crew?"

"Wish I did. But my last one got pinched a couple of days ago. Haven't had time to hire a new one, been doing most of the work myself."

No chance the signatures I'd picked up were from house-keeping or a previous guest.

"Anything else I should see?" I asked.

"I got a visit from a couple of gokudō yesterday around noon."

"Yeah?"

"Wanted me to let them know if any *hoppers* checked in matching Yuri's description." Her mouth curled at the word. "Like they had stamps themselves."

"Think it's the same pair from last night?"

Shake of Evie's head. "One was female, the other male. Both thinner and shorter than those two. I mean, they could have been shape shifters, but I don't think so. I'd bet my soul the male was nikusui. The other I couldn't say."

Nikusui? I didn't like the sound of that. A couple of oni was one thing, but if a nikusui was asking about Yuri, that was a whole different level of danger. Nikusui were vampiric in nature — fast, lithe, dangerous. Plus, they could charm you if you let them talk to you for too long. I'd rather take on a handful of oni than a single nikusui.

My gut told me the A-team had tried to squeeze Evie, and they'd sent the B-team when Yuri showed up. But that meant finding Yuri in the first place. An unpleasant thought surfaced in my head: if a gokudō tailing Yuri had followed her into Hana, they would have seen me with her. Seen the two of us head into the Pillow Room.

"The nikusui. You said he was gokudō. Any idea which gang?"

A shrug. "He didn't say he was with a gang, but the woman was Crazy Nate, through and through. Moved like an itachi weasel, anyway. The nikusui left me a number to call if I saw anyone fitting Yuri's description. Said it would be the most prof-itable call I ever made."

Evie held out a piece of paper with a 909-area code on it. Inland Empire territory, east of Los Angeles, well inside the Crazy Nate turf. The Nate was an all-itachi gokudō gang led by Mikasa, AKA Miki, AKA Mia. Weasels in appearance, they had razor-sharp claws and were rumored to be able to start huge fires if they got together in a big enough number. A few of the California wildfires had been blamed on the itachi gokudō.

More problematic for the Bureau was the fact that they could also shapeshift into other forms, including animals, mortals, and Yōkai. Legend said they could hypnotize mortals, but so far, the Bureau hadn't been able to confirm that.

I ran the numbers, which refused to totally add up. The Crazy Nate wasn't the most powerful gang in the area, though they were easily in the top ten. Up and comers, too, always looking to throw an elbow at the competition. Far as the Bureau knew, they didn't go much into soul shops, preferring to stick with more traditional crime: protection rackets, extortion, drugs. And Long Beach was Shiny Kites territory.

Little doubt the Nate were looking for Yuri, however. I filed away the discrepancy for now.

Yuri might have been on the run, but she wasn't far ahead of whoever wanted her. In fact, if they were canvassing Evie, I was willing to bet they were sweeping the entire town. And if they were checking the usual list of Yōkai sympathizers, they wanted Yuri back. Badly.

Or they wanted back something she had taken.

THIRTEEN

I CALLED THE 909 NUMBER. It rang five times before someone answered in Japanese.

"Hello?"

I spoke in Japanese. "I'm trying to reach Mikasa."

The person on the other end hung up. I tried again. Straight to a default voicemail. Same thing on the third attempt.

I'd been at the motel for an hour. Not a single call from Martinez or Mei.

Hmmm.

Since no one seemed to be demanding my attention for the moment, I called an old acquaintance, Ninagawa Miyako, a stamped daitengu. She'd immigrated here a decade ago, gotten her psychiatric license, and focused on the narrow but lucrative niche of providing therapy to other Yōkai. Miyako once told me she didn't want to become mortal because it would make her less effective as a therapist. I didn't know about that, but I did know she was a bleeding heart with a borderline Nightingale complex. I'd referred more than a few Yōkai her way over the years, and I'd asked her for help with a couple of mortalization cases.

Hey, Yōkai need shrinks, just like everyone else.

———

"Miller-san. Been a while."

"Yeah, it has. How are things?"

I detected the smallest pause in Miyako's reply.

"Is this a personal call or a professional one?"

"Professional."

Her voice shifted slightly to a more formal tone. "How may I be of help?"

"I'm looking for a way into the Crazy Nate gang. Got anything you can give me? A name? Address? Maybe a rumor from a friend of a neighbor of a cousin's barber who once said they saw a bunch of weasels committing arson one night?"

"This is an official inquiry, correct?"

Shit.

I'd hoped to quietly bypass that formality. Miyako was a professional, and she'd remained on the right side of the Bureau by being very good at following the rules. Something I, on the other hand, sometimes found challenging.

"I'm waiting on the sanction. Should have it shortly. Listen, this is time sensitive. And important."

"I'm sure it is. Please call me back as soon as you have the sanction."

I grimaced, decided not to push it. "Will do."

We hung up, and I rifled through my mental Rolodex for another way into the gang. I had contacts on the streets I'd culti- vated, and I could ping some Little Yōkai residents if push came to shove. I started calling one of them when a text from Miyako popped up on my screen.

<Peaks on Robertson. 45 min>

———

Not unsurprisingly, allowing Yōkai to immigrate around the globe wasn't a universally accepted idea. The notion of helping

Yōkai become mortal and more seamlessly integrate into society made more than a few mortals apoplectic. Even some Yōkai, too.

Most mortals who opposed Yōkai immigration and mortalization did so from a place of hate based on fear. I didn't fear the imaginary threats of a spiritual creature. I *did* fear the real dangers, of which there were many, and the victims were, more often than not, Yōkai.

Yes, a tiny percentage of Yōkai joined the gokudō. An even smaller percentage were straight-up bent on spreading chaos and mayhem. The Bureau spent a great deal of time trying to prevent these Yōkai from harming each other and mortals, and when it failed, it spent even more time tracking them down and bringing them to justice.

The Bureau also spent a lot of time protecting Yōkai from threats, both mortal and spiritual. This meant working with LEOs around the world when a Yōkai had committed a crime.

But at the end of the day, the vast majority of Yōkai were simply trying to find their way in a new world, one which presented challenges they were often unprepared to deal with.

I saw it on a regular basis, and I'm not just talking about work.

Even this late in the morning, Peaks was packed. A cross between a hipster coffee shop and a health-food cafe, the local chain had caught on like wildfire. A few dozen locations popped up from the West Side all the way into San Gabriel Valley. I admit to liking the coffee, but I found most of the patrons annoying. I lumped coffee and wine into the same category: liquids to be consumed and enjoyed but not discussed any longer than it took to order them. And ordering them should be a matter of seconds.

Happily, Miyako spared me from stepping inside the shop. She leaned against the building near the front entrance, a couple of to-go cups in her hands. For all her prim and proper manner, she dressed in a kind of shabby-chic style I envied. Funky ankle boots, loose-fitting slacks, a tight-fitting vest over a linen blouse. Long black hair styled in a just-rolled-out-of-bed look. The good kind.

Depending on your point of view, she'd lucked out and

presented as an attractive Japanese woman in her mid-twenties. Great as far as it went, but Miyako had privately shared with me the struggle to be viewed as an extremely talented psychiatrist when she perpetually looked like a recent college grad. Given she was a few hundred years old, I could only imagine how frustrating it must have been for her.

She held out one of the coffees.

"Thank you," I said, accepting the cup with both hands and a bow.

"Don't mention it," she replied.

I sipped the coffee — a mocha. She remembered. We walked down Robertson, dodging the sidewalk lunch crowd. This part of Robertson felt like a time bubble, a version of L.A. from the past that refused to acknowledge the actual year. Decades-old architecture, no consistency in the store signs, one random shop after another. We passed a shoe repair shop, a used bookstore, and a massage parlor in the first block.

"I could have my license pulled for divulging confidential client information."

I adopted a hurt look. "I said thank you."

Miyako smiled. "Luckily for us both, I don't have to break confidentiality to give you what you want."

I raised my mocha. "Here's to small fortunes."

"Why don't you reach out to Ron Espen. He's-"

"I know Espen. Stamped daitengu. Splits his time between here and Japan. He's already on the Bureau contractor list. That's as close as you can get me to the Shiny Kites?"

Miyako shrugged. "You wanted a name, that's the best one I've got."

Espen wasn't all that odd of a contact. He'd somehow slid into the image of a law-abiding Yōkai after getting tripped up in the early gokudō explosion right after the Parting. Publicly, he'd walked the straight and narrow path after his initial straying from the righteous path.

Some at the Bureau suspected him of double-dealing, believed he never truly left his gokudō roots. Couldn't argue with his intel, though, which was consistently valuable and accurate. I'd met him twice, and in my opinion the jury was still out on where his loyalties laid.

As a connection to the Crazy Nate, Espen was farther from the gang than I would have liked. Or maybe not. Maybe Miyako knew something I didn't. She was absolutely committed to protecting her clients' privacy. That didn't mean she hadn't helped me out in the past with some nudges in a general direction.

"He'll be here this afternoon." Miyako handed me a postcard flyer for an art gallery called Beyond the Veil. A new showing for a Yōkai painter named Muko. "He's her patron. I have it on good authority there's a private pre-show viewing at one today."

"Are you keeping tabs on Espen? Is he a client?"

"Sanction first, answers later." Delivered in a sing-song voice.

Wave of my hand. "Fair enough. And thanks again. I owe you one."

"You already owe me lots. I'll add this to your tab."

I went to put the flyer in my jacket pocket, felt another piece of paper already there. I unfolded the paper. Beni's name, his number, and the sketch he'd done of me.

Beni, you sly fox.

Miyako peered at the paper. "What's that?"

"It's a picture. A drawing. Of me."

"It's good. Really good. Who's the artist?"

"A guy I met."

"Oh?" Miyako arched an eyebrow ever so slightly. She knew me well enough to realize the significance of me not providing a name right off the bat. When I simply smiled in reply, she nodded. "Good for you."

FOURTEEN

THE CLASSIFICATION of Yōkai was anything but a science. It also didn't help that their general behavior sometimes morphed over time, as did, to a small degree, their Yōkai form. Such was the case with tengu.

Forget most of what you've read or think you know about these mountain goblins, the reality right now was they broke down into two groups: daitengu and kotengu.

Daitengu generally leaned towards the law when they chose to get involved with mortals. Most of them hung out in seclusion and meditated the days away, but when they decided to interact with the mortal world, they did so in a helpful manner. Their Yōkai form was in line with the old tales and stories passed down over the centuries: mortals with a long, often curving nose.

The other kind of tengu were called kotengu, and they were a lot less inclined to navel-gaze. Quite the opposite, as they often played the part of the prankster and partier, the very epitome of extroverts who liked to gather together as much as possible. The Yōkai form of a kotengu was a bipedal bird around four feet tall.

Unlike most Yōkai, daitengu and kotengu had a close dynamic. Kotengu tended to congregate around daitengu, who often provided guidance and acted as caregivers. Daitengu were the stabilizers, the ground for the charged energy of the kotengu, who were less likely to cause mischief when around the calming presence of their Yōkai cousins.

Given how few daitengu moved openly in the world, the Bureau had gone to great lengths to court them in the hopes of building bridges with the larger tengu community. Espen was one such daitengu, and he'd been on the Bureau payroll as a contractor for years. In fact, he was the first, the poster child for the program.

The Beyond the Veil gallery was mostly a large, open space formed by lots of glass, metal beams, and concrete. My badge got me past the receptionist. I watched Espen addressing a knot of folks. Madara painted almost everyone in the room as Yōkai, and most of them were manifesting.

Espen stood next to a Yōkai who was presenting. Long pink hair completely obscured her face and nearly touched the floor. Pink combat boots, tight jeans, and a t-shirt completed the artist's look. The only exposed skin on her body were her arms and hands. Then I realized she wasn't presenting, she was manifesting.

The clothes pegged Muko as a creative, but her hair pegged her as a kejōrō. These Yōkai looked like beautiful mortal women. Traditional legends said they styled their hair to hide their face and used to live as prostitutes, which made it easy for them to prey on mortals. Kejōrō could control and animate their hair, allowing them to grasp, hold, and manipulate objects. They could also form razor-sharp blades.

My experience? Most kejōrō had no taste for mortal blood and were more than happy to leave their streetwalking history in the past. Some cut their hair short on purpose to avoid being identified or stereotyped. Others had embraced their special powers and applied them to professions like art.

Muko practiced a form of multi-tasking art, which meant she could wield multiple brushes at once. It was a mesmerizing, impressive technique, and countless time-lapse videos of the process filled the Internet. I'd watched more than my share of them.

Espen's voice filled the gallery as his speech came to a close.

"-and visionary artists like Muko create works that explore the intersectional spaces between mortals and Yōkai, helping us understand both ourselves and our shared world in new, insightful ways. Critics often categorize her work as 'depression art,' though I'm sure you'll agree it's anything but depressing. I prefer the term 'emotive art,' which I believe is far more accurate. Distinguished guests, I'm honored and privileged to support such a talented artist, and it's my very great pleasure to share her inspiring visions with you all today."

The crowd politely clapped, many doing so while awkwardly holding champagne glasses. Small talk echoed around the room as the group broke up, began exploring the exhibit. Mostly paintings, though I also saw a handful of elaborately designed sculptures scattered about and perched on stone pedestals.

The art hanging on the walls was a mash-up of sumi-e painting and what I presumed was modern art. I loved sumi-e, but modern art had always been a lost cause for me. Renee had given me a crash course, walked me through some of the more important pieces. It just never landed with me.

I couldn't see myself hanging any of Muko's pieces on my walls at home, but that just proved how bad of an art critic I was. Based on the six-figure prices listed for the pieces, her works were hella popular in the fine art world.

I agreed with Espen about the term depression art. An unfortunate misnomer. This style of Yōkai art had picked up its moniker after someone suggested it triggered suicides in mortals. A more accurate description was "emotional art," as it often evoked powerful reactions across a wide spectrum in mortals. A few countries still had bans on this kind of Yōkai art.

I fed Madara while I waited and tried not to look too closely at any of paintings. Being a mix of Yōkai and mortal, I wasn't likely to react as strongly as a mortal might. I knew from experience, however, that I was anything but immune.

Espen worked the room, bows and smiles all around. He presented as a middle-aged Japanese male with dark brown hair, light brown eyes, and rugged good looks. An elongated nose was the only obvious hint he was manifesting.

He moved easily in a charcoal turtleneck, slate grey slacks, and an all-black traditional haori jacket, a visible nod to his Japanese roots. The loose, open jacket fastened with two thin cords, leaving a gap about two to three inches wide. I found them stylish in an understated way.

I called Espen's number, watched him glance at his phone, excuse himself from a conversation.

"Hello?"

"Espen-san, this is Bureau of Souls Agent Keiko Miller. I'd like to ask you a few questions." I spoke Japanese.

Espen put his hand in his pocket, smiled. He switched to English.

"That sounds rather ominous, Agent Miller. It's been a while. How are things at the Bureau these days?"

"Busy, which means I don't have a lot of time for niceties. How quickly can you meet me at the office?"

"I'm a tad busy myself. May we chat first thing in the morning, agent? Just name the time."

"Yeah, I was thinking less tomorrow morning and more like right now."

"I'm afraid that's not convenient for me, Agent Miller."

"Won't take long. I promise. And I did drive all the way out here to see you."

Espen made a slow circle, spotted me across the room. The smile on his face widened. "It appears my schedule has just opened up." He walked over to me. "I didn't know you were a fan of the arts, Agent Miller. I can get you a ticket for the premiere."

"Some other time, thanks. Espen-san, I need access to the Crazy Nate."

His eyebrows arched, and he guided us towards a corner of the gallery. "Please define 'access.'"

"One or more confirmed locations of their operations. Short of that, I'd settle for the name and current address of any of its members."

The daitengu smiled at me, the way a father might just before he delivered the bad news about not making the cut for the soccer team.

"I have always assisted the Bureau honestly and transparently, and I will continue to do so. I have also been very clear on the limits of my assistance, and what would happen if I ever felt I was being asked to exceed them. Your request is falling outside of my scope of influence."

Espen saying he couldn't help felt more than a little off. I didn't believe he had zero connections to the gang, and even if he had no direct connections, he had plenty of other ways to put me in touch with them. His deep Rolodex, knowledge of the Yōkai community, and willingness to help the Bureau were, after all, the reasons why he'd landed his consulting gig in the first place.

Did he have a connection with the gang he didn't want me to know about? Or was he trying to protect me?

I'd heard multiple rumors Espen had avoided being fired by pretending to work with the Bureau after getting tangled up with the gokudō right after the Parting. And by fired, and I mean killed in a special way that destroyed his body and soul.

No crossing over to Furusato. No reconstruction of his physical body. No returning to the mortal plane.

The Bureau called it being fired because it involved a fire ritual that literally burned the Yōkai's essence into nothingness. Euphemisms aside, it was a true death sentence for Yōkai, with no chance for parole, no chance for reincarnation.

Views were mixed on the practice. I objected to the practice, but I'd learned to keep my thoughts to myself in the Bureau.

"You don't have anything at all?" I asked.

"Agent Miller, I'm sorry to have wasted your time. Do let me know if you change your mind about the premier."

I put my cards on the table. "Someone murdered an unstamped Yōkai last night, dumped her body in Griffith Park. She got caught up in some gokudō syndicate shit."

"Yōkai and mortals are killed every day, Agent Miller, and usually it's a mortal who deals the fatal blow. L.A. is a violent city. Mortals are violent creatures. I'd presumed you already knew that."

Okay, time for a gut-based Hail Mary.

"I'm not saying you're connected to the Crazy Nate, Espen. I'm just asking you for some information. And I gave you the courtesy of tracking you down instead of making you come down to the office. Please. Help me find her killers."

Espen pursed his lips, looked at me for a few seconds, deep in thought. "There's a Yōkai-friendly bar in El Monte off Rush St. It's a magnificently trashy little place called Roku Roku. No signage out front. I'm told several Crazy Nate members are regulars there."

I pulled up the address on my phone. El Monte was in San Gabriel Valley, east of DTLA. "See, that wasn't so hard."

He gave me a serial killer smile. "You like to pretend you're the upstanding Bureau agent, out here protecting mortals and stamped Yōkai from the mean and evil gokudō. The reality is you'd probably fit in just fine as a fixer for any of the gang bosses. I'd certainly love to have access to your talents. Oh, what the two of us could achieve."

I shook my head. "See, this is why I don't like you. I have to beg you to do the decent thing, and when you finally do, you immediately shit all over it."

Espen sucked air through his teeth, grimaced. "Not much traffic in decency these days, and besides, the pay is awful. A word of advice, Agent Miller? Loyalties are fine as far as they go. I appreciate that. Just make sure the people you pledge your loyalty to continue to be worthy of it."

"What the hell does that mean?"

Espen glanced away, took on a reflective look.

"Some people can never be trusted. A few might have been in the past. The line between allies and enemies is getting thinner all the time." He swung his gaze back to me. "There's a war coming to these shores, Agent Miller. Not this week, not this month, but soon. You might want to review your list of confidantes, make sure they're all still reliable."

"Well, that's funny, coming from you."

Espen stiffened his back, assumed a posture of subtle insult.

"I may be many things, but I've never lied about my past or about my intentions. And I've never betrayed someone who placed their trust in me."

"You can't take the high ground now that you're stamped and expect it to wash away your past sins. It doesn't work that like."

"Indeed? Before I rejoin my guests, please educate me."

"You do the hard work. You keep things legal. You follow the rules."

"Like you?"

I couldn't tell if he was trying to be funny or playing it straight. "You're one to talk about allies, considering you used to be a heavy hitter in the gokudō. I'm still not sure how you managed to get stamped."

Espen smiled. "It pays to choose your allies wisely. It pays even more to choose your enemies wisely." He glanced over my shoulder. "Speaking of allies and enemies, which one is she?"

I turned and saw Martinez striding towards us. Angry didn't quite capture the expression on her face.

Inari's nine tails, it certainly took her long enough.

FIFTEEN

"JUST WHEN I think you can't shock me with your obsessive self-destruction bit, you rise to the occasion, Miller. Honestly, I don't even care what you were up to. I'll file a report with the Chief and let her handle it."

We were sitting in Martinez's BMW, the air conditioner keeping us cool while heatwaves snaked across the road. My kitsune nose picked up the distinctive *new car* smell. Faint and probably not something a mortal would detect. I'd read somewhere it was the result of the plastics, adhesives, and fabrics in the vehicle releases gasses as the new components aged. I know most of my friends loved it, but the smell gave me headaches. Based on how weak the odor was, I guessed Martinez's car was just a couple of months old.

To her credit, Martinez had waited until we were alone in the car before laying into me. She was beyond furious, had moved into the silent, slow-burn kind that was far scarier than any screaming, table-flipping version.

Her comment explained why Mei hadn't been melting my phone with job-ending texts. I guessed Martinez didn't want it known how easily I'd given her the slip.

"How'd you find me?"

Martinez held up her phone, showed me some kind of map. "Tracker."

"What? Wait, when did you tag my car?"

"As soon as I got in it. Dropped the tracker between my seat and the door."

I couldn't stop the grin on my face. "Well, look at you, Martinez-san. Gotta say, I'm impressed. I'd be more impressed if it hadn't taken you four hours to find me."

"Yeah, the signal went dead for a while. By the time I picked it up again, I was already back at the office. I chased you all over town after that, but I kept missing you." Right, the underground parking deck at the motel. Must have blocked the tracker signal. "So, did you enjoy your little excursion? Am I going to have to worry about you ghosting me again?"

I crossed my chest. "Nope. Promise. I'll be a good little agent from now on."

Martinez wasn't even looking at me anymore. "Just tell me something, Miller. Off the record. Are you bent?"

Her question shook me. It probably shouldn't have, but it did. Just how much of a fuckup did she think I was?

"No."

"It's fine if you are, I just want to make sure I don't become collateral damage if you self-implode while I'm babysitting you. I'd appreciate an honest answer. Call it a professional courtesy."

I took a long, deep breath, looked her directly in the eyes. "I'm not bent, Martinez. Rough around the edges, maybe, and someone who isn't fond of red tape. That's a far cry from being a crooked agent."

A nod from Martinez. "It's no secret I want Okada's job. It's also no secret you're going to jump to the front of the line, regardless of your less-than-spotless file. That wouldn't bother me so much if you were at another office. But you aren't. You're at my office, and if you get promoted, I'll have to report to you. I don't think I could do that."

I knew about Martinez's aspirations — everyone did. Her

intention to claim Mei's corner office was public knowledge, without apologies. What I didn't know was she had bought in on the office gossip about me. I shook my head.

"Well, here's some good news for you: the last thing I want is the Chief's desk. You can have it. But since we're being all open and honest, I'm not sure I could report to you, either."

"If you aren't going for promotion, why do you spend so much time in Archives? Why all the overtime?"

That was not an answer I was prepared to give. I opted for a truthful response, even if it wasn't the real reason.

"I think a lot of agents overlook the value of Archives. Tons of useful intel in there if you know where to look. Did you know that in the 7th century, villagers would wrap their newborns in water-proof clothing when it rained to keep the ame onna from stealing their babies?"

"No. But so what? That's not how you ward off the Yōkai rain women. You're supposed to leave a cup near the entrance of your home or the window of the nursery so the ame onna will drink the rainwater in it instead of taking your newborn."

"Yeah, but if that's true, why did we stop putting them in water-proof clothing?"

That prompted a roll of Martinez's eyes. "Because it doesn't work."

"How many ame onna cases do we handle out of our office each year? Twenty? Thirty? And of those, how many were abducted even though their parents left a cup of rainwater by the window?"

"I don't know."

"I do. I looked it up. Around twenty percent."

"Well, then, the parents forgot to refill the cup, or it got knocked over."

"Or," I held up my finger to keep her from cutting me off, "the ame onna figured out a way to get us to change our beliefs hundreds of years ago. To change how we acted, so it would be easier for them to prey on us."

"That seems a little far-fetched."

"I'm just saying Yōkai have been around a lot longer than mortals, and their memories are a lot better than ours. Time has a way of erasing the footprints in our past. We've forgotten so much of our own history, it's little wonder we fail to connect the historical dots."

I could see her chewing on that, looking for the holes in my theory. I didn't have any evidence to definitively prove what I said, but if you dug into the Archives deep enough, you started to see the patterns. Old beliefs about Yōkai changed over time. For that matter, the nature of some Yōkai morphed over time.

Just a thousand years ago, iso onna — spirits vaguely reminiscent of mermaids — were rumored to rescue drowning swimmers near the coastlines of Japan. For some reason, that stopped around the end of the 12th century, when they started luring their victims to watery deaths in the surf. None of the Bureau's Mirrors were quite sure why the change had happened.

Like almost all post-Parting Yōkai, iso onna no longer hewed to the legends surrounding them, but this only begged more questions: were they ever violent? And why the change in their reputation if their behavior remained the same?

According to the iso onna, they didn't have a clue, either.

Point was, Yōkai weren't any different from mortals. We changed our attitudes and behavior over time, and while a very small number of us were malevolent, most just wanted to survive, not take over the world. Even the most traditionally evil Yōkai had the random outlier, someone who bucked the numbers.

I'd shared my theory with Oshiro in Archives, and he hadn't dismissed it out of hand. Said he'd dig into it and let me know. That alone gave me confidence it might hold water. Oshiro did nothing he considered a waste of time.

Skip all that, though. The real reason for trotting out a hard-to-disprove theory whenever someone started eyeing my time in the Archives? I didn't want them knowing the truth: I was trying to sneak my mother across the veil before her banishment was up.

She had over sixty years left on her sentence, and even if Pop was still somehow alive when she crossed back over, his dementia-induced decline meant he wouldn't even recognize her. A Bureau agent essentially trying to spring her mother out of jail? Yeah, that type of stuff didn't go over too well during an annual performance review.

So I was thrilled to have everyone think I sported a tinfoil hat if it meant they wouldn't give my time in Archives a second thought.

Martinez appeared to buy my story. I changed topics.

"Hey, we don't have to be friends, but we do have to be partners. No point making this any worse than it is. Let's agree I have zero interest in standing in your way, and you could maybe ease up on me, give me the benefit of the doubt when it comes to my job and my loyalty?"

She gave me a long stare. I sensed the wavering telegraphed by her hesitation.

"Okay. Truce."

"Cool," I said.

"So, where are we on the Jane Doe Yōkai case? I presume that's what you've been working on?"

"Yeah, checked with some local contacts, started putting together a couple of leads for us to run down." I spun a story about getting an anonymous tip that pointed to the Crazy Nate, which prompted me to reach out to Espen. "Super thin, but it's all I've got. Espen pointed me to a bar in El Monte. I was going to shake some more trees in Little Yōkai before checking it out."

"Sounds good."

I decided an olive branch was in order. "Tell you what, I'll leave the tracker in my car. You follow me back to the office, we'll walk over to Temple St. Market together, and you can drive us out to El Monte. What do you say, partner?" I nearly choked on the word, but it had the desired effect.

A nod. "Deal."

SIXTEEN

TEMPLE ST. Market was a portion of Little Yōkai that had started as a handful of sidewalk vendor carts and exploded into three blocks of covered stalls and shops. The forward-looking spirits in Little Yōkai established an open-air market with a decidedly touristy angle. A pair of massive red torī bookended the market at either end, the wooden arched structures symbolizing the threshold to another world.

In many ways, it wasn't just a figurative border. Plenty of manifesting to be seen, spirits walking around in their Yōkai forms. I longed to transform into my kitsune fox, but that just wasn't just an option.

So, I hid that half. The last time I'd fully manifested was over two decades ago. I was seven at the time, and Pop had found me in my room, a kitsune admiring herself in the mirror. The light brown patches on my paws broke up my nearly all-white coat of fur. I looked at my reflection, wondered how much I resembled my mom. Pop said I looked a lot like her as a mortal. As a Yōkai, she had six tails to my one and a lot more brown in her fur. I took his word for it, since we had no pictures of Mom.

"Keiko! You can't do that! It's too dangerous!" Pop's words had come from love and a desire to protect me, but his reaction to my

Yōkai form left a painful mark in my memory. I can count on one hand how many times I've manifested since.

As much as I hated it, I hid my Yōkai side. And that went double for my hoshi-no-tama, or "starball." All kitsune carried this tiny glowing sphere with them. Some of us carried them under our tongues when we manifested, others on a necklace or tied to one of our tails.

The hoshi-no-tama were the source of our kitsune powers, and if separated from them for too long, we could die. The starballs held a bit of our life force in them, and we guarded them accordingly. I've kept my starball in a fox-shaped necklace for years.

The upside was that presenting as a hafu — half Japanese, half White — gave me an insight few would ever experience: the challenges and rewards of being a Yōkai but navigating a Yōkai-centric community LWM or living-while-mortal.

And while I couldn't give you an exact date, I can tell you my time in Little Yōkai as a teenager triggered my interest in the Bureau. Deciding I might be able to help my mom was the tipping point for becoming an agent, but the seeds of desire to help my fellow Japanese spirits, particularly hakushi, were planted in Little Yōkai.

Martinez and I dropped our cars off at the office and walked the two blocks to the Market.

"Let's duck in here for a sec, I need to get something." Martinez followed me into Notoro's, a Japanese confectionary store. Martinez raised her eyebrows at my selection. I bought six boxes of mizu manju, little jelly cakes made from flour or rice powder and filled with a variety of sweet paste. Next up were four large bags of amanatto, which were candied azuki beans.

We stepped into Temple St. Market's mid-afternoon lull. About half of the stalls offered items aimed at mortals and tourists. We passed tables overflowing with a variety of art, Yōkai offering to perform various feats for money, a few musicians with hats or bowls at their feet, and tons of food vendors. My nose picked out several amazing smells that prompted a pang in my stomach, even though I'd just eaten. Lots of stalls sported little trinkets, figurines, and carvings that fell under the *kawaii* umbrella. Kawaii was a catch-all term for "cute." Think *Hello Kitty*, and you're spot on.

Takumi Row was my favorite part of Temple St. Market. Basically, a small collection of artisans who focused most if not all of their lives to mastering a single craft. Woodworking, pottery, washi, cookware, and a lot more.

The rest of the stalls offered goods that skewed slightly more Yōkai, and more often than not, you'd catch a whiff of chalk incense in the air. Or you might hear music that didn't seem to have a source. Or feel cold on a sunny day.

As someone who was part Yōkai, I knew for a fact the stories about us experiencing the physical plane differently from mortals were absolutely correct. My dad would describe something as sweet, but it might have been bland to me. I heard voices when it rained, unintelligible but lyrical, which I'm told no mortal could detect. Pop said I used to fall asleep to a rain machine when I was a baby. I don't think it was a coincidence.

Madara got excited whenever I went to the Market. I had no way to be sure, but I preferred to believe she loved identifying all the different Yōkai. She darted about like a kid at an amusement park.

"Hello, Chemistry-san. How are you?" I asked in Japanese. I rarely used English in the market.

Chemistry was a sunrise spirit, a mortal-turned-Yōkai spirit. In this case, a kowai. Kowai had features vaguely reminiscent of a large fox, large sharp teeth, and a long tongue. At the moment, she was presenting as mortal, a female Japanese teenager. Her stomach growled. She grimaced, placed a hand over her belly. Kowai were eternally hungry spirits with emaciated torsos and legs. Always on the hunt for food, they ventured out at night, when it was less likely for them to be seen.

A few charitable haradashi Yōkai, known for their good-natured and jovial hospitality, coordinated with DTLA restaurants to provide prepared food from their excess inventory. Kowai could usually count on at least one free meal a day, but for a kowai, it was always a frustratingly temporary fix.

"Sorry about that. Good to see you, Agent Miller." The Yōkai looked at Martinez, a bit guarded. She switched to English. "Hello."

"It's okay," I said. "She speaks Japanese. This is my new partner, Agent Valeria Martinez." The word rolled more easily off my tongue, to my surprise. Martinez's body language hinted she had caught Chemistry's cultural dance.

"Hello," Martinez said. "Pleasure to meet you."

"Pleasure to meet you." Chemistry's eyes never left the bag in my hand.

I held out the amanatto. Chemistry shimmered, manifested into her Yōkai form, which was more ghostly in appearance. Her fox features became more prominent, and her mouth grew wide, revealing large canine-like teeth and a long red tongue. She opened the bag, tipped it skyward, and emptied its contents into her mouth. Two loud gulps, and she closed her eyes in relief.

"Thank you."

"Bit early to be out, isn't it?" I asked.

"Well, you know, things have been tough recently. Making a go of things here, even with a stamp, it's not easy. Some days, I wish I had never left Japan." Another growl. Chemistry licked her teeth with her tongue.

"You don't mean that."

"No." Chemistry wrapped her thin arms around her, hugged herself. Another growl. "Listen, the gokudō, they're looking for an azuki arai."

"Which gokudō?"

"All of them. Shiny Kites, Crazy Nate, Deadballs, all of them. It's why they've been tearing the city apart the last couple of weeks. The Yōkai stole something from one of the gangs, perhaps a powerful artifact. With the kind of reward the gokudō are offering, I hope they never find her. She'll be lucky if all they do is fire her soul." I decided not to tell her about Yuri's fate.

"Thanks. You let me know if you hear anything else."

"Of course."

I'd been trying to get Chemistry into the mortalization program for over a year. The waiting list was long. She wanted to be done with her suffering, and I felt lousy for not being able to do more for her.

As for her mention of the artifact, well, that wasn't a shock. Occasionally, a magical artifact turned up in the physical world. Sometimes Yōkai brought them here, sometimes they appeared under unexplained circumstance. And a few had, apparently, already been here before the Parting.

The Bureau collected them when it could, secured the objects in the Kyoto vaults. A loose artifact in L.A. could easily explain why the gokudō were going at each other.

Martinez and I returned to Temple St., resumed our walk.

"What's with the bag of beans?" Martinez asked, switching back to English.

"Chemistry says they take the edge off her hunger better than most food."

"How do you know that?"

I shrugged. "She mentioned it at some point."

"You come down here a lot?"

"Sure. Almost every day. Don't you?"

Martinez seemed to struggle with my reply, a square peg to the round hole of her question. She looked around at the stalls.

"No. I mean, I've been here before. I-"

"Miller-san! Where you been hiding, pretty lady?" Gumdrop, a stamped Yōkai and a long-time regular at the Market. Closest thing Temple St. Market had to an unofficial mayor.

Gumdrop's mortal form was a squat Japanese male, perhaps in his early forties. He moved in for a bear hug, but the squeeze was butterfly gentle. "You ladies need a charge?"

"Always," I said and pulled out my cell phone. The Yōkai

rubbed his hands together, covered my phone with them for a second or two. "There you go! How about you, gorgeous?"

Martinez opened her mouth, looked at me. When she didn't say anything, I filled the silence.

"Gumdrop-san, this is Agent Valeria Martinez. Martinez, he can top off the charge on your phone."

"Pleasure to meet you, Agent Martinez. First-time customers get a complimentary charge."

"Um. Sure. Yeah." She held out her phone. Gumdrop sandwiched it between his hands. Martinez checked the battery level, smiled. "Thanks."

I gave Gumdrop ten dollars. "Got anything for me today?"

"I heard a couple of Shiny Kites came round to Evie's place, hassling her about some hakushi they're looking for."

"Shiny Kites?"

"What I heard."

"Thanks. Be good," I said.

"Now where's the fun in that?"

SEVENTEEN

I WONDERED if Evie might be losing her touch. She had a knack for identifying Yōkai and spotting gokudō. Maybe her eyes were finally going. Or maybe the two oni were somehow connected to the Shiny Kites?

Martinez shook her head. "He hit you up every time you come down here?"

"Yeah."

"Did you really need to charge your phone?"

"Not really."

"So, you're just handing out candy and currency for leads? Did I skip an entire chapter of protocol in the Bureau handbook?"

I waved an arm around me.

"This is Little Yōkai, Martinez, emphasis on 'Yōkai.' It's a whopping two blocks from where you work every day. As a Bureau of Souls agent, you didn't think this would be a good place to spend some time once in a while?"

She turned in a slow circle, came to a stop with her hands on her hips. I waited, watching her try to form a response. I was almost as speechless as she was. How could any decent agent not view Little Yōkai as a goldmine for understanding the lives of the very people we were supposed to be serving? And if you couldn't see how much information flowed through the Market, how it was a data sink for much of the Yōkai and gokudō activity in Los Angeles, maybe the Bureau wasn't the best place for you.

"I come here a few times a year. I've been to a matsuri." She held up her hands. "Look, I don't live close by, and you know our work schedules, Miller."

"I hear you, but the next time you consider having lunch out somewhere, maybe consider making it in Little Yōkai?"

"That's fair." Martinez looked at the boxes of mizu manju. "Another bribe?"

Deep breath. Stay centered.

"A gift."

"Okay. Since you seem to have an entire tour planned, why don't you lead on?"

I bit back a sarcastic comment. "Sure. There's one more person I want to see."

Satsuki's stall was awesome. I had no idea where she sourced her stuff from, but her table was brimming with odd knick knacks from Japan. Lots of obscure pop-culture merchandise, unusual antiques, and some of the rarest anime DVDs I'd seen.

"Is that *Gravity Guns: Super Nova*?"

The zashiki warashi Yōkai looked up from her magazine. She was manifesting, her Yōkai form being a young girl around ten years old. Short bob haircut and a kimono. Satsuki grinned at me from her perch atop a tall stool. Legend had it zashiki warashi Yōkai brought prosperity to the households they inhabit.

Much like Riki, Satsuki had been approached by several wealthy individuals. And like Riki, Satsuki had shrugged them off, preferring to enjoy the freedom of running her own place in Little Yōkai and living where and how she liked. Her abilities paled compared to Riki's, though, and Satsuki had initially struggled after coming to the states.

"Agent Miller! Good to see you!"

"You, too, Satsuki-san."

"You've got good eyes. That's a sub-titled copy."

"Get the fuck out. Seriously?" The Yōkai took the DVD off the shelf, handed it to me. A rare commodity in the anime world, the remastered GG:SN collector's edition included the entire first season of *Gravity Guns*. The show ran from 1977 until 1994 and produced multiple movies and spin-offs.

But that all came later, and it might not have come at all. The network almost cancelled the show right out of the gate. Quality copies of the first few seasons were hard to come by, especially subtitled ones. The dubbed ones were garbage, the translation wonky at best.

"How much?"

"$650."

I whistled. "Bit above my price range as long as I'm on the Bureau's payroll."

"Aw, come on, Agent Miller, I wouldn't charge *you* that much. How's $250 sound?"

I shook my head. "Awfully sweet, but I'd be ripping you off at that price. Plenty of diehard fans would pay you top dollar for it."

"Least I can do. I owe you." Satsuki seemed to notice Martinez for the first time. Her friendly face turned frosty. She adopted a more business-like attitude. "You got a partner now, Agent Miller?"

"Satsuki-san, this is Agent Valeria Martinez."

The Yōkai switched to English. "Pleasure to meet you, Agent Martinez. You like anime?"

Martinez responded in Japanese. "I, uh, I tried watching a couple. Couldn't really get into it."

"No sweat," Satsuki said, switching back to Japanese. She leaned closer, dropped her voice. "I hate 'em myself, but they're good business."

I adopted a look of mock horror.

"Heathen."

Satsuki laughed. "Least I'm not worshiping some fox trollop." My reaction must have been all over my face. Satsuki dropped the smile, and Martinez arched an eyebrow. "I'm sorry, Agent Miller, I didn't mean anything. Inari's a good kami."

I recovered far too late and far too unconvincingly. Wave of my hand, a half grin. Martinez was going to find out soon enough, anyway.

"I know, Satsuki-san, it's fine. Look, I just wanted to drop these off. Dole 'em out however you like, okay?" I put the boxes of candy on the table. Satsuki peeked inside.

"Oh, they're going to love these. Thanks."

"I gotta go. You take care, all right?"

"Will do. Nice meeting you, Agent Martinez."

"You, too."

We walked back to the office, Martinez giving me an odd look. "What?"

"Nothing. I just didn't realize how plugged in you were to the Yōkai. To Little Yōkai. You're really comfortable here."

I fought down the spike of panic in my chest, forced a casual smile I didn't feel. Martinez gave no hint she thought I was anything other than mortal, but I was always on guard, always afraid I'd accidentally give up my secret.

"I grew up here. I've lived in DTLA almost my entire life." An honest answer, and one she appeared to accept. Even so, my heart rate didn't return to anything resembling normal until we were back at the office.

———

MARTINEZ NAVIGATED her BMW along Figueroa, eventually merging onto the Arroyo Seco Parkway, an eight-mile stretch also known as the 110 State Freeway between DTLA to the south and Pasadena to the north. The Arroyo Seco was the first freeway ever built in the U.S.

It was either bumper-to-bumper, with traffic crawling well below its 55mph speed limit, or it was pretty open, with folks hitting 60mph or 70mph along the curvy six-lane freeway. A fun drive when traffic's moving, especially in a 7-series. Martinez slip-streamed around cars, and she topped out at 65mph on the straightaways. Seeing her exceed the speed limit surprised and somehow pleased me.

"All right, break this down for me, Miller-san. What was up with Satsuki?"

Ugh.

"What do you mean?"

"'I owe you?'"

"For fuck's sake, Martinez, I thought you said you were going to trust me. Truce and all that." She glanced at me for a second, said nothing. "It's none of your business, but Satsuki was struggling to make a living after she landed here. Stamped but wildly unprepared for life in the states as a Yōkai. She refused to be a living ATM for some billionaire who wanted to add another zero to the end of their bank account balance. I came across her one day near the Market, baked out of her gourd on warnal stems. I helped her get a part-time job at the Market. That's it, no big deal. Satisfied?"

"Sure." She didn't sound satisfied. "So, why'd you give her the sweets?"

"Oh. That. Well, Satsuki tries to pay it forward. She collects stuff for some of the spirits in Little Yōkai who are struggling, hands them out after work."

Martinez sighed, frowned. "Can I ask you a question?"

"You mean another one? Sure." I expected a barely veiled probe into my dark underground dealings, but she surprised me.

"What's with the unusual names? Chemistry, Gumdrop."

"You really don't know?" Shake of her head.

Hoo boy.

This would not be easy. I tried to frame what I'd learned over the years about how Yōkai reacted to adjusting to the mortal world, distill it into something easy to understand. It wasn't easy, and it got even more complex when you layered in the challenge of leaving Japan's unique culture for America, which was equally cool but obviously different.

"When Yōkai arrive here, whether or not they have a stamp, they often take the path of least resistance, which means fitting in instead of standing out. Some change their name to better suit their new appearance, their mortal presentation. Other times, they adopt names that sound exotic to them but also have a personal connection. It's a bit of acclimation and a bit of reinvention. You follow me?"

A nod. I continued.

"Gumdrop picked his name from an anime show, and Chemistry probably just likes the sound of it. Look, a lot of these Yōkai working the Market are unstamped and completely off the grid or stamped but living on the fringes. Some prefer to stay in their own form as much as possible, and Little Yōkai is the closest thing they have to a safe space. But even there, many adopt a name and an identity they feel they have to in order to survive, even if it's not who they are in real life."

I was getting worked up, and I heard it in my voice. My comments applied equally well to myself. I took a breath, calmed down.

"A lot of mortals in America fear Yōkai. You've seen the bulletins about the spiritists, you know the drill: *kick the Yōkai across the veil, we don't want them here*. Despite that, a lot of Yōkai make it. They find a way to navigate their new home, either by hiding in a niche or carving one out for themselves. But they never do it fully on their own terms. Success for them always comes at a cost."

Martinez nodded. "I think I need to spend more time in Little Yōkai."

"I think that's a fabulous idea."

EIGHTEEN

ESPEN WASN'T KIDDING about Roku Roku. It was a clichéd caricature of wildly incorrect views about what life was like in Furusato. Some American mortals designed the place based on references that strongly evoked Bosch's hellscape painting, a Western eye projecting its values onto an Eastern esthetic.

The decor was baroque. Lots of asymmetry, visually assaulting color schemes, and images unsettling to most mortals. Like the full-size, lime-colored fake bull hanging from the ceiling, innards falling out of its dissected belly. That was bad enough, but the topper was the four-foot-long maggot pushing its way out of the offal, its face a large daisy. The sight evoked a stomach-turning recall to my required 7th grade experiment involving a frog and a scalpel.

To hear the Yōkai describe it, Furusato wasn't a lot different from the mortal realm, but that didn't stop a bunch of mortals from interpreting it their own way. It also didn't stop a bunch of mortal groupies who would do anything to feel like they were part of the Yōkai community from flocking to places like Roku Roku.

My eyes spent the first few seconds adjusting to the light,

which was minimal. The scent of stale beer filled the air, as did a lazy acoustical guitar piece. Heavy curtains concealed the windows in the place, and most of the tables were empty. Madara didn't ping anyone as Yōkai. I noted the exits, mapped out the locations of everyone in the place.

At the bar, I held up two fingers. "Nirasa."

The bored bartender nodded, reached under the counter. Martinez eyed me sideways. Guess she was fine speeding and weaving along a freeway, but a late-afternoon beer was strictly off limits.

Whatever.

The bartender set down two icy bottles of the Japanese beer. "Tab?"

"Yeah."

"Just need a card."

I pulled out one of my Bureau business cards, tapped the bar twice with it, slid it over to him. He looked at the card, back at us. An expression of extreme unfriendliness settled on his face.

"This some kind of joke?"

I sipped my beer. Icy and excellent. "Not at all, good sir. I'd like to ask you a favor. Please pass along a message to the next Crazy Nate member who comes into this fine establishment. Unless, of course," I pointedly looked around the room, "you see one here I can talk to."

"I don't know any Crazy Nate."

I smiled, took another sip. The safe money was on the bartender throwing my card away as soon as I left. I couldn't let that happen. I leaned forward, adopted a conspiratorial tone.

"The next time you see a Crazy Nate, please tell them I'm requesting a sit down with Mikasa. It's in her interest to call me. If I have to come back here, I won't be this pleasant."

The bartender frowned. "Seem pretty pleasant to me."

I threw my beer at the shelves of liquor behind the bar. Two bottles on the bottom shelf exploded, covered the area in a layer of white foam. The bartender's eyes went wide. I heard motion behind me, sensed Martinez already on her feet, stepping between me and the patrons. The bartender pulled a bat from behind the bar.

"God damn it! What the fuck-"

I picked up Martinez's beer, prepared to throw it. The bartender froze in place. I placed two one hundred-dollar bills on the counter.

"Like I said, sir, I need a favor. Please pass along the message. The Nate need to get their boss to call me. And don't forget: if I have to come back-"

"Yeah, yeah, you won't be so damn pleasant."

———

"I'VE SEEN some over-the-top shit before, Miller-san, but that was completely inexcusable. You already have one open IA complaint; what do you think they're going to say about this? Hope you like late night security guard work at the local mall."

"Relax. I more than paid for the liquor and beer. Besides, they're not going to file a complaint."

"And why not?"

"Same reason you backed off yesterday at the stairwell." I recalled our showdown, which already felt like ages ago. "Most people will shut down when faced with an unpredictable opponent."

"This is exactly the kind of crap that gives you a loose cannon reputation around the office."

"It's also why I'm so good at my job."

"That's not the word I'd use."

I chuckled. "Fair, but that place is owned by the gokudō. It's a front for a Yōkai brothel. The last thing they want is the Bureau or any other LEO investigating them."

My phone rang. Renee.

"Hey," I said.

"You busy?"

"I'm being chauffeured in a 7-series BMW at the moment, so no." Martinez gave me the middle finger. "What's up?"

"I just got a shoot. Thailand. Leave in a couple of days. Hoped we could get together before then. I can text Katia, make it a girl's night out."

"Doubtful. Working a case right now, real time sink."

"You sure?"

"Trust me, I could use a girl's night out, but I'm probably going to have to pass. Have fun in Thailand, and text me some pics, okay?"

"I'm going to have to since you're not on social media."

"This is me hanging up."

"Bye, sweetie."

Inari bless Renee. She had no clue my mom was a kitsune. And she certainly had no idea I was half Yōkai.

Keeping that secret from her was a near-constant pricking of my conscience every time I double downed on the lie. And it wasn't just Renee. It was Riki, Mei, and everyone else in my life who thought I was just a regular old mortal whose parents divorced, leaving a single child raised by a father who never remarried and an estranged mother in the wake.

Hard enough being a hafu, but at least that wasn't a lie I had to hide behind. I couldn't, even if I wanted to. Living a hidden life as a Yōkai, while working at a law enforcement agency that forbade Yōkai employees? That was a far harder path to walk.

"I'm going to have to report this to Mei." Martinez white knuckled the wheel, a scowl on her face.

"Okay."

"I'm serious."

"Okay."

Maybe I should have been more worried. Maybe I should have felt guilty about what I did at the bar. Maybe, a small part of me said, I shouldn't have thrown the beer at all.

Later, I'd think about her reaction, realize her anger was more about me putting her in a position of having to choose whether to report me.

Rightly or wrongly, my experience in the Bureau had taught me the fastest way to get information and move a case along. How to get to the point where you knew a criminal was no longer roaming free. That a Yōkai had successfully transitioned to a mortal and was beginning a newer, happier life. That a dead hakushi had gotten justice.

I didn't know any other way, didn't know how else to do my job.

Or sleep well at night.

———

POP HAD MADE an impressive chunk of cash in the finance markets. He didn't love the work, even though he was very good at it. When he figured he had enough to live comfortably and still leave me a sizable inheritance, he pulled the ripcord, sold his company, and took an early retirement. I'd known we were rich by any standards, but Los Angeles could always find a way to make you feel poor.

Martinez drove us out to her place in The Flats, a high-end neighborhood a stone's throw from the L.A. Country Club and the old Playboy Estate. I didn't stay on top of the real estate market, but I was pretty sure the hacienda mansion set Martinez back several million dollars.

"Nice place."

"Thanks. I'll pack a bag, make yourself at home." She disappeared down a hallway, her heels clicking on the tiled floor, leaving me in the middle of a cavernous living room with vaulted ceilings. The design was all about looks, with furniture that felt more like art than functional objects to sit on. The actual art itself was a mix of traditional Mexican and modern.

As far as I knew, Martinez was single. I had a feeling her parents lived somewhere in L.A. I could see a pool in the backyard, and the two-story house must have had at least four bedrooms. What she was doing knocking around alone in a drafty place like this was beyond me. Plus, her commute to work must have been a nightmare. Why didn't she snag a swanky condo penthouse in DTLA if she had this kind of money?

The tapping echo of Martinez's shoes returned.

"Ready?" I asked.

"Yeah. I packed for three days, figured I could come back if I needed to."

I looked around. "Shame we can't stay here." A half-joke, but Martinez took me seriously.

"Well, no reason we couldn't if you're up for it."

"Ah, yeah, no, that's…that won't work for me."

"Right. Your father." Martinez ran a hand through her hair. "Well, I mean, if you want, he could stay in the pool house. That's private. Or he could take the downstairs bedroom."

I honestly didn't know what to say. Every time I thought I had her pegged, Martinez surprised me.

"Super generous of you, thank you, but I've got round-the-clock help for him. Don't feel good asking them to drive out this far. Plus, I don't want to drag him out of his home." I had other reasons for not accepting her offer, like the illegal wards on my apartment.

Martinez sniffed, shrugged. She seemed offended at my rejection.

I smiled, held out my hands. "Hey, I'd love to hang here for a few days. Seriously. Who wouldn't? It's just my father. With his condition-"

She cut me off with a half-smile. "Of course. No problem. We should probably get going. Traffic's going to be hell."

"And unless you're in a rush, I want to hit one more place tonight."

Martinez raised her eyebrows. "Another informant? What do we need this time? Grape-flavored bubble gum?"

"Just a hole in the wall Indian place with amazing food," I said.

"Oh. Okay. I like Indian."

"But afterwards we'll hit Boyle Heights. There's some Yōkai in desperate need of gum."

Her laugh was genuine and a joy to hear.

NINETEEN

WE AWKWARDLY STUMBLED between prolonged silences and stilted small talk over garlic naan, vegetable biryani and chicken tiki masala. I don't consider food to be a meal unless it involves some form of meat, but the biryani was tasty. I was glad Martinez had ordered it.

After making some bridge-building headway earlier in the day, we'd retreated to our separate corners. On the upside, the food was as good as advertised, and Martinez made a point of complimenting it several times. The olive branches were still being exchanged, and it was a pleasant, if not surprising, way to end the day. Certainly a far cry from how it started.

The worst of rush hour traffic had bled off, and we made decent time heading to Boyle Heights, just east of the L.A. River and adjacent to DTLA. I tried to offer Martinez some tips on the best places to look for street parking, but she insisted on dropping off the car at a valet stand. Said she'd rather pay the $15 or $20 than waste fifteen minutes looking for parking.

It was dark by the time I pulled open the single large wooden door to Mad Alice, a large Craftsman-style house someone had repurposed into a bar. My nose picked up a bunch of odors: a mixture of tobacco, weed, and a couple of other, much more illicit substances wafted outside. Mad Alice had started out as a forgettably bland bar but had quickly taken a different path. The heavy chandeliers, skulls, and gargoyles gave it a solid Goth feel, and the hookahs added an exotic feel to place.

That night hookah business was good. Not an empty seat in the place. Small knots of people stood and sipped their drinks, waiting for a table or bar stool to open up. The place was a sea of pork pie hats, colored hair, and extreme mascara. Dim lighting and a low-level dub-bass beat under a trippy instrumental tune gave the joint a mellow feel.

Madara pinged at least a dozen Yōkai in the crowd, a few manifesting. A couple of familiar faces, though the most I got in terms of recognition was a slight lift of their heads.

I walked through the bar, Martinez behind me, waved at Dinks. He nodded, smiled, finished closing out someone's tab. Dinks looked right at home in his bar, fit in perfectly with his customers. Tweed vest over a plaid button-down shirt. Multiple piercings and a shaved head below his own vintage hat. A line of tattooed kanji down the inside of his right forearm.

"K. What can I do you for?"

"Five minutes of your time?"

"Right this way, then, my ladies."

Dinks' office cut off the bulk of the music. Where the bar was a haunted, dim space, the office was still displaying the original architecture of the building. But it needed a facelift. Cracked paint and scratched wood beams.

Dinks took a seat behind a beat-up antique desk, propped his boots on it, and placed his hands behind his head. He'd taken a deep dive into the assimilation pool. Rarely spoke Japanese, acted more American than Japanese. He seemed happy, and I certainly didn't judge.

And I knew about the pressure of fitting in.

Until I acquired shapeshifting abilities, I only had two forms to choose from: kitsune and my given mortal form. I knew I only had two because I'd tried on multiple occasions to change my appearance.

The first time had been in elementary school. One day, a White girl in my class challenged my ethnicity.

"But your eyes have grey in them. You speak perfect English. You're not *really* Japanese, right?" She wasn't being intentionally mean; was, in fact, sort of a friend. She just couldn't reconcile the young woman standing in front of her with her own definition of what it meant to be "really Japanese." When I got home, I tried so hard to look like a blonde, blue-eyed girl that I gave myself a migraine for days.

"Dinks, this is Agent Valeria Martinez. Martinez-san, this is Dinks."

"Hello," she said.

"Pleasure meeting you." Dinks turned to me. "So, what's up?"

"Curious if you've seen this Yōkai before." I tossed a picture of Yuri on the desk. Dinks looked at the photo, shook his head. "You had any unusual visitors recently?"

"Business has been off a little thanks to the gokudō dust up. I mean, I get a few of them in here on a regular basis, nothing unusual about that. What's unusual are the questions they've been asking lately."

"About a Yōkai?"

"Yeah, but also about a tamashi. Promised me a good bit of cash if I could help them find it."

"A soul cage? Whose soul?"

"Didn't say. Could be anything. A gokudō rival, a mortal in debt to the gokudō, some trophy soul."

The agent's voice in my head muttered to herself. So maybe the gokudō weren't after a powerful artifact after all.

Or the tamashi is a cover, my training countered. *Don't rule anything out just yet.*

I could feel pieces of the puzzle moving about, starting to reveal more about Yuri's death, but the bigger picture remained agonizingly obscure.

"Do me a favor, Dinks? Show that photo to your staff. Ask your regulars."

Dinks gave me a two-finger salute. "Anything for you, Agent Miller."

"Thanks."

Dinks snapped his fingers, grinned. "Hey, I just got a fresh shipment of-" Dinks stopped, cut a quick glance at Martinez. "Sweet Jasmine. Brand new strain, straight from the blender. Hasn't even hit the dispensaries yet. Super smooth kick, you don't even see it coming, then it's just a slow ride home. Happy to give you ladies a sample."

Martinez leaned forward, I'm sure to lay down some righteous indignation on the poor guy. I put my hand on her arm.

"Some other time, Dinks. But I wouldn't turn down some of that 20-year van Winkle behind the bar."

"Done!"

When the office door closed, Martinez stood up, shook her head. "This guy's dealing, and you're asking him for a shot of liquor? What the hell?"

"What dealing? Marijuana's legal in California. This bar is a consume-on-site dispensary, or hadn't you noticed?"

Martinez pointed a finger at me. "Don't make the mistake of thinking I'm an idiot, Miller. He wasn't about to offer us weed. You think I don't know the smell of haze or what a bag of warnal stems looks like?" She pointed at the not-quite-hidden sack on Dinks' desk.

I nodded. "You're right, you're right. Dinks is an old client of mine. Mortalized years ago. I was his transition agent. He hit a rough spot, and I helped him out. The van Winkle is just his way of showing his gratitude."

"As opposed to his way of breaking, shit, I don't know how many laws? This. This is the crap I'm talking about, Miller-san. You want to know why no one trusts you at the Bureau? It's because you pull this kind of sketchy crap. Balingford? He's convinced you're on the take."

And another domino toppled.

Martinez unclipped her badge from her belt, started for the office door. I put out a leg, planted a foot on the desk to block her path.

"What are you doing?" I asked.

"What you should have done a long time ago. I'm going to shut this place down."

"No, you're not," I said.

Martinez pulled back her jacket, put her hand on her Sig. "You want to wind me up? Go ahead. I can be unpredictable, too."

"Have a seat and take a breather for two seconds." I gestured at her chair. "Please?"

She crossed her arms instead, stared down at me, waiting.

"You saw the tattoo on his arm, right?" I asked.

"Yeah. 'Mitsuko.'"

"Let me tell you the story behind that. First off, Dinks doesn't just run this place. He spends his nights here, sure, but he spends his days down at the Yōkoso shelter in Little Yōkai. Hell, he's been on the board there for three years. And he makes donations. Sizable donations. Like six figures a year. You think he keeps his office this way because he likes the sight of mold and beat-up, second-hand furniture?"

"How the hell should I know?"

"He donates a lot of his money to the shelter because back in Japan he watched his daughter, Mitsuko, get run over by a car while crossing the street. Never recovered from it. Grief ate him up until he turned into a Yōkai, and then he spent every minute of every hour of every day obsessing over Mitsuko's death. He wandered into Yōkoso one day, and they helped him get his life in order."

I nodded back at the door.

"The kind of money that guy gives Yōkoso doesn't come from weed, it comes from stuff like stems and kelp tea. Non-addictive and less dangerous than alcohol. No Crimson Candy, no Sweet Strings. Besides, his customers are rich, they can afford it."

"It's still illegal. Rich doesn't enter into it."

"Hey, you got me there. No argument. But his customers aren't hurting, Dinks gets to funnel their money into a worthy cause, and maybe I ignore the fact that he flips some stems under the table. Think it through. You put him away, fine, you get another arrest under your belt, and this bar becomes the latest foodie hipster restaurant in Boyle Heights. Dinks' customers move on to the next place willing to deal with them. They don't even miss a night out on the town. But within a few months, Yōkoso will have to let some of its staff go, and the clients they serve will have a much harder time finding the help they need." I dropped my leg. "Do what you want."

Dinks kicked the door open, hands filled with a bottle and three short glasses.

"Ladies, this is some of the finest-" He saw Martinez's badge, looked at me, raised his eyebrows. I shrugged, nodded at Martinez.

"Your call, partner."

She glowered at me, turned her gaze to Dinks, put her badge away. "It's nothing. Never mind."

"All right," Dinks said with a lot less enthusiasm in his voice. He put a double pour in each glass, handed two of them to us. "To a better world."

We clinked glasses, but only Dinks and I took a sip.

"Not a bourbon lover, eh?" Dinks asked Martinez. "No problem. Name your poison."

Martinez put her glass on the table. "I'm going to show this around the bar." She picked up the photo of Yuri, walked out of the office. Dinks let out an enormous sigh.

"Shit. I thought I was a goner there. New partner?"

"She's a bit of a stickler for rules."

"Ah. Should I be worried?"

I weighed the situation before answering. My gut told me Martinez probably wouldn't arrest anyone. She would have booked Dinks already if she'd planned to.

"I think you're fine."

"Guess that'll have to do. And since she won't be needing that…" Dinks waggled his eyebrows at me, poured Martinez's glass into mine. "Here's to not getting arrested."

The van Winkle was a rarity for me. Even if I could have afforded it on a regular basis, I'm not sure I'd spend my money on it. I've got other commitments. Dinks somehow always had a bottle of it floating around, and I didn't turn it down when he offered.

"So, what can I really do you for?"

"Looking for some intel on the Crazy Nate."

The grin threatening Dinks' face completely faded. He eyed me for a long time before holding up his glass, pointing at the drink with his other hand.

"Did you know that over the course of two months in 2013, someone stole 195 bottles of this glorious amber? Most of it disappeared, never to be seen again. The suggested market price for a bottle is $169, but it goes for ten times that. It's funny."

"What?"

Dinks shrugged. "Who's to say how much this bourbon's worth? I mean, we let the market decide, right? Supply and demand. And in the end, it's worth exactly what people are willing to pay for it. From the market's point of view, this bottle is worth over a grand. For someone who hates bourbon, on the other hand," he jabbed a thumb at the office door, "it's worth fuck all. I don't know what it's really worth, but it's for damn sure some fine bourbon."

"And this has to do with the Crazy Nate how?"

Dinks looked over his desk at me. "How much is your life worth, Keiko? Because that gang is all kinds of bad news. If you take them on, make sure your backup has backup. Killing a Bureau agent isn't nearly as distasteful for them as it should be."

"You're saying I should be careful."

"I'm saying you should stay the fuck away from the Nate if

you have anything resembling a desire for self-preservation. Or for the welfare of those you care about."

I didn't like hearing the word "no."

Madara swam into my view, darted furiously to the office door, flicked her tail like she was being chased by a shark. At the same time, someone rapped three times on the door, quickly, then two more times. Dinks put his glass down as he rounded the corner of the desk.

"Shit."

"What?" I asked.

"Stay here, K."

I didn't, of course.

TWENTY

I FOLLOWED Dinks back out into the bar, watched as he lifted the top of one end of the counter, slipped through, moved to the far side. A slim male dressed all in black was leaning on the counter, half-closed eyes panning across the place, lazily taking it all in. Short jet-black hair cut into a messy, spiky kind of style you'd find on a fashion magazine cover. Presenting, for sure. Late thirties Japanese.

That's the Yōkai who had set Madara off, no doubt about it. He had the thousand-yard stare some of the older Yōkai developed, and his signature was steady. He'd been in the states for a while. I looked for Martinez, found her in a corner. Her body language said she was enjoying the scene. She laughed loudly, presumably at something said to her by one of the two guys hitting on her.

My Bureau training told a different story. Martinez was on edge, gearing up for a fight. And she was keeping Goth Guy in her sights.

From my view, Dinks seemed to be talking fast, his hands animated and gesturing wildly. Goth Guy stared impassively, his head cocked to one side, hands resting on the bar. A swivel of Goth Guy's head — barely a noticeable shake — cut short Dinks' chatter. Dinks went completely still.

I caught Martinez's eye, walked around the bar. When I got close to Goth Guy, I pretended to trip and fall into him. Well, almost. Instead of bumping into him, I found myself being half-spun around by the Yōkai. It was like a dance move, a graceful display of dexterity and strength. One second, I was about to body check him, the next I was standing where he was. Goth Guy was now behind me.

Note to self: *this Yōkai was fast.*

"Whoa!" I grabbed the bar, continued with the girl's-had-too-much-to-drink act. "I mean, ta-da!" I broke out into a giggle fit. A sea of white expanded around Dinks' irises. I turned to the Yōkai, who might have been looking at a potted plant for all the expression on his face.

"Nice moves, brother." I gave him an exaggerated thumbs up, grinned widely. "Where'd you learn to dance like that?"

The Yōkai looked past me at Dinks. "We're done."

His voice was honey on hot glass, sweet and smooth, and had an almost musical quality to it. Training kicked in again, my mind scratching for a classification. A hinoenma? Maybe a nikusui? Somewhere in a part of my brain, neurons fired, made a random connection that seemed hard to ignore.

Shit, was this the nikusui who had paid Evie a visit?

I called up what I remembered about them.

Strengths: a lot

Weaknesses: disturbingly few

Physically fast, abnormally strong, could jump extremely high, immune to nearly all mortal weapons, able to put you under their spell if you listened to them for long enough.

I swayed a bit, pretended Goth Guy had been talking to me.

"Done? Hey, don't be a party pooper." I reached out a hand for the Yōkai's arm, grabbed empty air. He'd backed up in a way that made it look like he'd never moved his feet. An eel-like writhe that opened the distance between us.

But Martinez had slipped in behind the Yōkai, boxed him in. I pressed on, starting something that approximated dancing. I hoped it had the impression of dancing. Despite popular opinion, not every girl automatically knew how to dance well.

"Come on," I said, reaching out again, "let's dance the-"

Goth Guy cast a han, a low-level kinetic spell, most likely meant to knock me back into the bar. It rocked me off my toes but not enough to put me off balance. I chalked it up to the omamori behind my badge.

Thank you, Hachiman.

Martinez didn't hesitate, reached for her weapon.

"Bureau of Souls, you're under arrest!"

I went for my shimenawa cuffs, pulled them out just in time to see Martinez drop out of view. Goth Guy swung at me. I dodged backwards, waited for the now claw-tipped fingers to rake past, stepped in close and drove my right fist up into his rib cage. He twisted at the last second, but the blow still knocked some of the wind out of him.

Having missed me, his arm reversed direction, and I threw up a forearm to block the elbow whipping towards my head. It was a sloppy move, but it worked. It did not, however, prevent a punch to my stomach. I responded with a head butt. Goth Guy turned enough, and my nose crusher became a glancing cheek bruiser.

I adjusted my stance, tried to plant my right foot behind his, use his body weight to get him to the ground. Even with my own Yōkai speed, I wouldn't last long in a standing fight with the nikusui. I pushed him backwards, felt him momentarily go with the motion, begin to tip over my right foot. I thought I had him. Instead, he twisted away from me, leaving me off balance, and I caught four claws across my face.

Martinez appeared, wrapped her arms around Goth Guy from behind. I reached for the cuffs on the floor, nearly got my head kicked in by the nikusui.

Fuck this.

I drew my Sig, put it in Goth Guy's face.

"Stop fighting!"

The room went completely dark.

TWENTY-ONE

GOTH GUY MUST HAVE HAD a partner skulking about. Nikusui weren't known to have spell-casting abilities, and in any event, channeling magic was hard while fighting, especially when someone had you in a bear hug. Either way, the darkness wasn't natural, it was magical. And strong. Like, industrial strength. I was totally blind.

Martinez groaned, and I reached for where Goth Guy was. I snatched nothing but air, the nikusui's scent already fading.

The patrons in the bar screamed, scrambled, bumped into each other.

"Martinez-san!"

"Here!" she answered.

A brilliant sphere of light appeared above her head, floated weightlessly. It was much dimmer than it should have been, but it brought the level of panic from *complete* down to just below *near-total*. Goth Guy was gone.

I told Martinez to secure the area and forced my way through the front door. I put Madara on the hunt, followed her trail of glowing bubbles without letting her get too far ahead. She could only hide my Yōkai nature if she was close. Now, I wouldn't involuntarily manifest if we got separated, and unless someone was casting a han of seeing, they wouldn't notice my Yōkai signature. Still, I preferred keeping Madara close at all times.

In less than a block, the nikusui's scent faded out, and Madara came to a stop. Most likely, he'd jumped in a car. I jogged back to the bar. Dinks and Martinez were taking care of the patrons who'd suffered injuries. Martinez and I doled out some minor healing hans, including a hefty one to a guy who appeared to have broken his ankle.

The healing hans had limitations. Wouldn't cure a fatal wound, but they could slow the damage from serious wounds and cure minor ones. While I finished tending to the injured, Martinez called in a sweeps team and worked on fully dispelling the darkness han. Took her a while, which pissed her off.

"Bastard kicked me before I could draw," she said. "He's fast."

"Nikusui fast," I said.

"Yeah, I was thinking the same thing. Here, let me get that." Martinez gave my face a healing han. Despite having already casted a metric crap ton of spells, she cast one more, and Goth Guy's slices closed up.

"Thanks, partner." I touched my face. "And well done."

She smiled, took the compliment without comment.

Within an hour, the guy with the broken ankle was on his way to a local hospital, and the sweeps team of Mirrors had descended on the place. I'd helped Dinks hide his contraband before they arrived, and while Martinez hadn't lifted a finger to help, she hadn't complained, either.

The sweeps took statements from everyone, checked for han magic residuals, confirmed a darkness spell had been fired off. When the Jewels finally vacated the place, Dinks ducked behind the bar, filled a rocks glass with a colorless liquid, took a large gulp. Grimace of satisfaction. He pointed the bottle at me.

"I told you to wait in the office."

"All of my report cards said I don't play well with others. It's kind of been a lifelong problem."

Dinks took another drink, glared at me. "They're going to think

I talked. That I went to the Bureau. Fuck." Dinks sighed, gazed around at the place.

"Hey, bartender," I replied, "hit me with a shot of something expensive. And put it on her tab." I nodded at Martinez. That brought Dinks back to the here and now. He poured me a glass of scotch, which I raised.

"To old friends."

Dinks gently knocked his glass against mine, and we both drank. I heard Martinez walking to the door.

"I'm going to check the area," she said, "see if I can find any witnesses who might have seen the nikusui heading out."

That might have been true, but I suspected she'd read the situation, decided I'd get more out of Dinks if she wasn't in the room. Again, I found myself giving her credit. When Martinez had gone, I leaned forward, got Dinks' attention.

"That Goth Guy, he a regular here?"

"No. Never seen him before."

"You sure you left the gokudō stuff behind?"

The bottle slammed down on the bar. "I did. I have. He was asking me about a tamashi, God knows why. I don't know anything about it." Dinks knocked back another shot, sucked air through his teeth.

"Next time the gokudō come sniffing around, please let me know, okay?"

"Every time you get between me and the gokudō, things don't exactly turn out platinum."

It was a fair point, though the last time had been his fault. I'd been lucky to pull us both from the shit hole he'd dragged us into.

"I can swing you some protection."

"No, that's just going to make it worse."

I eyed the bottle in Dinks' hand. "At least let me follow you home."

Dinks set the bottle on the bar. "No, thanks. I'm good. I just want to lock up and go home to Bonnie and Alex."

I wanted to say something to make him feel better. Anything

to avoid parting on such a negative note. Tell him how proud I was of him. Tell him he'd beaten the odds with his transition, found a lovely wife, had a lovely kid. Was making the world a better place.

Instead, I nodded and left.

TWENTY-TWO

I DON'T REMEMBER EXACTLY when I started calling my father Pop, but he'd been calling me Petal since I was born. I asked him about it once. He said he got the name from one of his favorite cyberpunk novels. Like flashy night clubs and loud bars, cyberpunk wasn't really my thing. I grew up reading mostly fantasy. Dragons, monsters, magic. My fantasy reading slowed down big time after the Parting and stopped altogether when I took the job at the Bureau. I was living in a fantasy world now.

Most days — on Pop's good days — I was Petal. When he had his episodes, I might be my mother, Narumi. Or my Aunt Lisa on Pop's side. Or, and this one hurt the most, just some strange woman. Dementia did that to you.

Chika, Pop's nighttime caregiver, greeted me in the front hall of our condo. A tōfu kozō Yōkai, she appeared as a boy dressed like a Shinto priest, though she presented most of the time while working. I introduced her to Martinez. Chika leaned close, whispered to me.

"He's still up, in the kitchen."

"Good day?"

"Wasn't a bad one. Niko told me your father tried stepping out after lunch, said he needed to go to the office. She stopped him.

Other than that, it's been fine. Sumiye texted me, she's running a few minutes late, but I'll stay till she gets here."

I shook my head. My watch read 11:58pm. Chika's shift ended at midnight.

"Nah, don't worry about it. Head home as soon as you're ready."

She gave me a hug. "There's some sesame anpan buns wrapped up in the kitchen. Might still be warm."

"Thank you!" Chika made the best anpan buns, period. Her signature version was an airy sweet roll filled with a mouth-watering sesame filling.

I walked into our kitchen, found Pop standing in front of the fridge, the door open. He wore a dark blue robe with white trim, softened from years of use.

"I can hear you two talking out there, you know," he said. "You think you're being quiet."

"You hear anything juicy?"

"Just a couple of nosy birds needlessly worrying about an old man."

I kissed him on the cheek. "Hey, Pop."

"Hey, Petal."

He had a jar of pickle spears in one hand, a half-eaten spear in another. One of his favorite snacks, and a taste I'd adopted as well. I tweezed out a spear and held it up.

"Cheers."

"Cheers."

Pop made a *ding* sound like two glasses clinking together as the pickles met. A silly tradition, but one that stretched back as far as I could remember. Pop put the top on the jar, returned it to the fridge.

"Working late?"

"Mmm-hmm," I said. "Running down some leads on a new case."

"Interesting one?"

"It's not boring." I played it off, not wanting to talk about

Yuri. I found the bowl of anpan buns, brought them out to the family room. Chika had gathered her things and said good night.

Please, Inari, don't let Pop remember how much I've complained about Martinez...

"I didn't know you were bringing a friend home, Petal."

"Sorry, Pop. This is Agent Valeria Martinez. She's working the new case with me."

Pop smiled. "You expecting to solve it in our condo?"

Martinez, smiled awkwardly, turned in my direction for help.

"I'll explain later, Pop," I said.

"Fine. I'm David Miller, Agent Martinez. Pleased to meet you."

"Valeria is fine, Mr. Miller."

"So's David." He yawned. "Sorry. I'm sure the case is in good hands, and it's late, so if you ladies will excuse me, I'm getting some shuteye."

I put the bowl down, told Martinez to help herself, followed Pop to his room. He looked at his bed. Chika had turned down the sheets, something she did any night she was working for us.

"What does she think I am, three years old? That woman. I don't need to be tucked in." He said the last comment to no one in particular. Part of his complaint undoubtedly had a kernel of pain at its center. Dementia slowly and mercilessly stripped you of freedom and privileges. Pop lost his driver's license four years back, and not long after I had to hire a team to keep him from accidentally hurting himself or others. The dementia constantly chipped away at his dignity, left both of us covered with invisible scars.

Pop grumbled some more as he puttered about the room, straightening up his small desk, putting out clothes for the next day, checking his alarm clock. Finally, he turned to me, nodded at the door.

"Valeria seems nice. You said she was a bitch."

I shushed him. "She's not. I mean, she isn't that bad. And thanks for not embarrassing me."

I'd meant it as a joke, a callback to my teenage years when I'd bring friends home. Pop gave me a hug.

"I'm not completely out of my mind yet."

I tried to say, "That's not what I meant," but the words dug their heels into my throat. I held back the tears, squeezed him while I fought the urge to give in to a good cry. I wanted to grab him by the shoulders, scream at him to hang on, that I was doing everything I could to bring Mom back, that he just needed to hold on *a little longer*.

When I thought I had it under control, I pulled away.

"So, what's the maybe-not-a-bitch doing here?" Pop asked.

I hit him lightly on the arm. "Whoa, you kiss Mom with that mouth?"

The words were out, hanging between us, before I realized it. I cringed, unsure where the phrase had come from. It was nothing I said on a regular basis. Why was I suddenly unable to open my mouth without shoving my foot into it? I searched Pop's face, waiting for the pain to surface, but instead he smiled at me. Pulled me closer, into another hug.

"I used to, Petal, every chance I got. And I was glad for the time we had together. Mostly, I'm glad for you. You were the best gift she ever gave me."

I did not need this. Not now, not with Martinez in the other room, not with Yuri dead. My vision blurred as tears slid down my cheeks. I wiped my cheeks, sniffled my nose, and tried to smile my way out of the sudden sadness.

"It's okay, Petal. Don't fight it all the time. Nothing wrong with crying."

"Says you."

Pop had a father's intuition like nobody's business. Trying to keep up a cheerful facade for him only made things worse, but wasn't that often a woman's lot in life? Pretending to be happy for the sake of someone else's happiness?

"So, Martinez," I said. "She's here because Mei assigned her to me. For this case. Martinez is shadowing me twenty-four-seven."

"A round-the-clock partner? Her? Did something happen at work?" His face grew serious. "What did you do?"

"Thanks for the vote of confidence."

"Well, am I wrong?"

I frowned, trying to decide if I wanted to give him the satisfaction of being right or lie and let him think I was yet again a blameless victim of office politics. Looking into his eyes, I couldn't lie.

"No. I've been bending the rules lately-"

"More like snapping them over your knee if I know you." Pop searched my face. "This is serious, isn't it?"

I wasn't about to go into Gerrald's bogus claim and the IA investigation. Already said more than I wanted.

"Enough. Maybe. I don't know."

Dad pursed his lips, offered one of his canned lines of encouragement. "I'm sure you'll sort it out, sweetheart."

I wish I had your confidence.

This time I opted for a half-truth instead of an outright lie. Summoning up levity I didn't feel, I gave him the stink eye and said, "You bet your ass I will."

Dad threw his hands in the air. "That's it, I'm going for the soap."

"Good luck with that, Pop. See you in the morning."

"Love you, Petal."

"Love you, too."

I closed his door and stepped into the family room, found Martinez tapping away at her phone. She looked up.

"Your caregiver, I think her name's Sumiye, she's in the kitchen."

"Thanks. Sumiye usually watches TV in here or hangs out in the kitchen at night. Just in case you're up."

"Sure, that's fine. Um," she looked around, "do you have anything to drink?"

"Yeah, water, orange juice, maybe a soda. Or did you have something else in mind?"

"I was thinking something a bit stronger."

It was past midnight, and she wanted a drink? Another point in her favor.

The day's demands had weighed on even my Yōkai-boosted stamina. Emotionally, I was drained, and all I wanted to do was sleep things off. Beni, Gerrald, Yuri…last night seemed like an eternity ago. I needed rest.

Still.

Fuck it. One drink, and screw all the studies saying alcohol didn't help you sleep.

"You read my mind."

TWENTY-THREE

TURNED out Martinez loved red wine. I dug up a bottle from the kitchen pantry and poured her a glass. As for me, I made a dirty gin martini and dropped a skewer of three plump olives into the glass. And when I say dirty, I mean filthy.

I told Sumiye about Martinez and passed along Chika's report from the day. I invited Sumiye to hang out with us, but she excused herself, went to the kitchen. Smiled as she left, said, "I'll let you two have some time together."

She probably thought I was being social by bringing home a co-worker, and while she was way off base, her gesture sparked a feeling of gratitude in me. My aunties always had my back.

Martinez and I settled into the chairs in the family room. I kicked off my boots, raised my glass in the air.

"To short cases."

"To short cases."

The gin was heavenly, and I slowly swirled the olives around, enjoyed the cocktail's salty tang and gin's aroma.

"Listen, I just want to reiterate that I truly have zero interest in Mei's office. We may have our differences, but you don't need to worry about me stabbing you in the back."

Martinez sighed, frowned. "Thanks." She looked at me over

her glass. "You know, what I really want is a post in Kyoto. But it's-"

"Super competitive. Hey, if it makes you feel any better, you've got the best chance at cracking Kyoto as far as our office is concerned."

I hadn't known just how lofty her goals were. Kyoto was the main headquarters for the Bureau, and it was a dream assignment. Some agents worked their entire careers hoping to call that place home, apparently Martinez among them.

"Too bad you can't write me a recommendation." Delivered with a grin that quickly disappeared. "But I'm realistic enough to know it's a pipe dream. I've settled on something outside of Japan, a position much closer to home."

"Be a lot easier working for another agency. What about Vigilance or Cazador de Espíritus?"

A snort from Martinez. "I'd never work for Vigilance, and my family — my life — is here in the states. Cazador de Espíritus? I've been to Japan eight times, but I've only crossed the Mexican border twice. Can you believe that? And yes, I thought about a Bureau post in Europe or maybe Australia. But I love it here. My life is here."

She hated Vigilance and loved L.A.? I added a few more points to her "Like" column.

I racked my brain for any trivia I had on Martinez's personal life, came up empty except for the fact that she wasn't wearing an engagement or wedding ring. I didn't interact much with the co-workers I liked, and I avoided those I didn't, even though that made me even more of an outsider. Bureau agents couldn't share their problems with people at Vigilance or other LEO groups. Our work was special. We were special. Different.

After-work fraternization wasn't uncommon at the Bureau, but with Pop's condition, I felt trapped. I was reluctant to bring anyone home for fear he might have an episode. The last thing I'd want is for him to do something he'd be embarrassed about later. And even though I had round-the-clock angels looking after him, it was increasingly harder for me to feel comfortable going out for drinks, dinner, or a movie.

I had nightmares about coming home one day and finding he couldn't remember who I was. Each day felt precious, and I had decided the best thing to do was limit my social life for now. Lately, the only thing I'd leave him for was work, my research in Archives, and the increasingly infrequent night out with Renee and my friends.

But then there was Beni. His drawing was still in my jacket, and I'd entered his number into my phone.

What was that all about? Was I seriously considering tearing down my walls? Could I let him inside?

Inari knows I'm toying with the idea.

Time to change the subject.

"So, you have any family in town?"

A shake of Martinez's head. "Used to. They're all back east now. Folks are in Connecticut, my brother's up near Annapolis, sister's down in Augusta."

"Boyfriend?"

"Not as of a month ago."

I made a face. "Ah."

"The Bureau isn't great for relationships, and what we do doesn't endear us to a lot of people."

Some people had a romanticized notion about our work, but the reality was a mix of boring paperwork and stuff that makes for shitty chit chat. After a while, it was a depressing topic you felt better avoiding. Work became this separate part of your life, something you weren't comfortable talking about.

I understood exactly what Martinez meant.

"So you throw yourself into work hoping to get recognized, maybe climb the ladder a little faster? Take on extra cases, pick up any extra tasks the Chief throws your way?"

"Pretty much," she said.

"Welp, that explains it."

"What?"

"Why you're always in the office so early, why you're there on the weekends, why you always follow the textbook no matter what. I just thought…" I stopped talking, not wanting to finish my sentence. But Martinez knew where I was going.

"I was a suck-up, uptight bitch?"

"Um. Yeah. Something like that."

"I suppose some of that's true."

I almost dropped my glass. Did Martinez just admit to being a bitch? Or a suck-up? Or maybe uptight? She wasn't clear what she was admitting, but whatever she meant, it was the first truly humbling thing I'd heard come out of her mouth.

"Wow," I said. Martinez looked up at me, confused. "I mean, I just…I never thought you'd say something like that."

She frowned. "Things you do to get noticed. To get promoted, you know?"

"I can honestly say I don't."

"What's your goal, then, Miller?"

The one that came to mind was the one that kept me in Archives so much: to reunite my parents before my father's dementia completely robbed him of his memories. A few others surfaced. Taking care of Pop. Helping unstamped Yōkai when I could, even if it broke Bureau policies and U.S. law.

Huh.

I realized none of my goals were about me specifically. They were about helping other people.

Across from me, Martinez had only one goal, and it was all about her. She wanted the Chief's desk. The why wasn't important. Fame, wealth, power, recognition — none of it mattered. Point was, she wanted something for herself. I couldn't remember the last time I had gone after something that was so self-centered. I struggled for some kind of answer.

"I don't know. Keep L.A. safe. Do my job. Take care of my dad. Not much time or energy for anything beyond that."

"How far along in the dementia is he? If you don't mind me asking."

"No, it's fine. It depends. Some days are good, some not so much. I never quite know what I'm waking up to or coming home to. He normally recognizes me but not always. One night I woke up when he climbed into bed with me, thought I was my mother."

"Jesus."

"He didn't try anything, just said good night and rolled over. And trust me, that's not the worst of it. Seeing him stare at me, him knowing he's supposed to recognize me but not being able to? That's ten times worse. Then there's his tendency to take a flyer, decide he's back in his thirties and try to go to work at his old brokerage firm downtown. Or he's knocking on a neighbor's door and thinking it's his old apartment in Kyoto. After that episode, I called in the extra help. I knew I couldn't trust him to stay home, and I freaked out at the idea of him wandering the streets in his pajamas."

"I had no idea."

"How could you? Not like we're BFFs." My martini was already half gone, and Martinez was nearing the bottom of her glass. She yawned. I drained my glass. "I'm toast. Your room is down that hall. Should be all ready to go, but let me know if you need anything."

"Thanks."

Two minutes later, I closed my bedroom door, fell on my bed without bothering to get undressed. I rolled over, stroked Madara's side and scratched under her chin. Felt like I'd run a marathon, and I closed my eyes for a minute. Just a brief rest before I changed and got into bed. I felt Madara settle into a curled position on my chest.

Hours later, I woke with a racing heart and clothes damp from sweat. No memory of what brought it on. I put on a t-shirt and flannel pants, slipped under the covers, realized I'd done zero research for Mom in two days.

Took me a while to fall back asleep.

TWENTY-FOUR

I WOKE to the screams of a woman. Scrambled out of bed while I rubbed sleep from my eyes, stumbled down the hall towards the source, noted Pop's bedroom door was open. Madara flicked about, trying to figure out what had me so out of sorts.

Quick sweep of Pop's room showed an empty bed, covers thrown back. I ran into the family room, met Martinez. The front door was open, and I heard voices from outside.

In the hall, I found Sumiye, Pop, and one of our neighbors, Elena Caralt, standing at the elevator. Elena was shouting. I stepped in between Pop and Elena. A couple of heads were peering from doorways, and a few neighbors were standing a discreet distance from the elevator.

Oh, fuckity fuck, fuck, fuck.

Pop had knocked on Caralt's door years ago, convinced it was the apartment he and Mom shared back in Kyoto when they first met. My nightmare had surfaced again in a whole new incarnation.

"Come on, Narumi. Don't be so dramatic." Pop looked at me. "Your mother can be a little extreme at times."

"Yep, I know, Pop. Let Mom run her errands. Come on, let's go

137

back home and have some breakfast, okay? Sumiye will make your favorite."

"Sure, sure." He waved to Elena. "See you tonight, sweetie."

I gently pushed Pop into Sumiye's arms, and she guided him back to the apartment. Martinez poked her head out of the door. I gave her an all-clear wave. She nodded, disappeared. I turned around to face Elena, who glared at me like I'd just slapped her.

"That man is a menace to everyone in this building!"

The Bureau thankfully trained all agents how to remain calm and focused during high-stress situations: a shooting, dealing with uncooperative and abusive suspects, having someone physically intimidate you. I have drawn on this training every single time I've had to deal with Elena.

"That man is my father, and he's suffering from dementia. He has no idea what he's doing, Ms. Caralt." I spoke calmly, softly.

"That doesn't change the fact that he made me afraid for my safety." She dropped her voice, took on a threatening tone. "I've done my research. I've spoken with an attorney. I know my rights, and they include the right to quiet enjoyment of my condo." She nearly spit the last part out at me, daring me to say she was wrong.

Like a lot of people who thought they knew the law after five minutes of online research, she was wrong, of course. I'd *studied* the law after Pop starting having his episodes, precisely for this reason. She was referring to a statute that didn't apply to this situation, and I was willing to bet she hadn't spoken to any attorney.

But my training guided me away from correcting her and towards calming her, not least because Pop's behavior was gathering ground for a different and far more legitimate legal action.

"Ms. Caralt, I'm so very, very sorry about this. I'm sure this was a harrowing experience for you, and I understand how being around someone with dementia can be scary. That's why I've hired round-the-clock help to keep an eye on him, but clearly, we need to review the steps we take to keep him and everyone else in the building comfortable. I can't change what happened, but is there anything else I can do going forward that would make you feel safer?"

Her chin came up as she soaked in my words. I think she was hoping for a fight, something that would give her the ammunition to argue for my eviction, too. With nothing to push against, she floundered for a response that wasn't personal.

"You think I'm just some angry lady who hates you because," here she gestured helplessly, "whatever. And you probably think that little badge on your belt gives you some special status. I've got news for you. I don't care who you work for or what magic powers you have, I'm not scared of you. And I don't care about the color of your skin, if you're Chinese-"

"Japanese."

She frowned, sighed. "Japanese. Fine. Look, we're both minorities, we both have challenges. None of that changes the fact you and your father don't belong here. He needs more medical help than you can provide him here. If it was me, I'd hope my daughter would realize that and move me to a place that could meet my needs."

Caralt's words left me spinning. This was only the second time she'd had a run-in with Pop like this, but I understood her reaction. Scared. Upset. Angry.

Still, her casual misidentification of my ethnicity echoed and amplified her comment about me and Pop not belonging here. *Here*, like this building? Or *here*, like this country? Was I being overly sensitive?

"Ms. Caralt, I appreciate your candor. I obviously want what's best for my father, as I'm sure you would for yours. I'd like-"

"Then move him into an assisted care facility where they have everything he needs."

Everything except me.

I got a text on my phone from Martinez: <*Anything I can do to help?*>

"Ms. Caralt, this is work. I'm afraid I have to go, and I'm sure you want to be heading to work as well. May we continue this conversation at a later time?" She nodded with a smirk, apparently happy with how things had gone. "Thank you. And again, I'm incredibly sorry for what happened."

Elena didn't look placated, and just because the conversation hadn't ended in a screaming match this time certainly didn't signal any kind of truce. She absolutely wanted Pop out of the building. A fight was coming, though probably not today.

Which was good, because I'd had more than enough conflict for one day, and I was still in my pajamas.

———

"I DIDN'T REALIZE how bad it was." Martinez picked at the breakfast Sumiye had made us before leaving. Salmon, miso soup, sliced banana, pickled daikon, and white rice.

"What? Want me to make you a rolled omelet?"

"No, no. The food's fine. I mean, it's great. No, I meant your father."

I picked up a mouthful of salmon with my hashi. "Comes and goes. The worst part is the bad episodes start coming more frequently and last longer. It's a shitty way to live out your remaining years."

Pop was in the family room, watching a history documentary. Niko Pressman, one of the few mortal caregivers in the group, pushed through the swinging door to the kitchen.

"He's had breakfast and is watching TV," she said with a smile.

"Great, thank you."

"I'll keep an extra eye on him today, don't you worry."

I'd given Niko a rundown of what happened, and she and Sumiye had discussed ways to help keep Pop from wandering off again. Sumiye was still feeling awful when she left, even though I'd told her several times it wasn't her fault. We'd work out a better system tonight.

Niko nodded, went back to the family room.

Martinez poked at her rice. "I'm sorry. I didn't realize what you were putting up with here."

I sliced the air between us with my hashi. "No pity from you."

"Fair enough. How about some fashion advice, then? Like, what's with the t-shirt and flannel pants?"

I looked down at my standard sleepwear. What could she possibly have against flannel?

"These pants are hella comfortable." I pointed at the picture on the front of my shirt. "And this is one of the smartest shows on TV. You've never seen it?"

A gut-busting laugh from Martinez at that.

"Um, no. I have better things to do with my time than watch cartoons."

"Like shopping for an over-priced blouse at some snooty boutique store?"

"Have you even stepped inside a boutique store before, Miller-san?"

I could feel my annoyance simmering. Wouldn't take much to push it to a full boil. Elena had bled my day's reserve of patience, and my training faltered, failed me. I parroted Martinez.

"Um, no. I have better things to do with my time."

And my money.

Martinez held up her hands in frustration. "Fine, fine. Just trying to help, that's all."

"I don't need your help, Martinez-san, if that's what you call good fashion."

I regretted the words as soon as they left my mouth.

Inari guide me.

Martinez looked down at her silky pajama set and equally silky — and matching — robe. She'd even brought a pair of slippers from her house. Her expression showed she found my comment utterly incomprehensible. She pinched the collar of her striped robe.

"This is Asceno. The finest Italian sand-washed silk."

"And probably cost more than my car payment."

"I don't care to discuss money. It's vulgar."

"Like your presumption I need fashion advice," I tossed back at her.

Martinez narrowed her eyes. So much for dealing calmly with stressful situations. I could stare down a dozen oni, but heaven help me if I tried having a conversation with Martinez. I took a deep breath, miraculously found a droplet of patience. "Sorry. That was uncalled for."

"That is certainly one word for it."

One word certainly leapt to my mind, one I wanted to use on Martinez, but I reined in my tongue, tried again to defuse the situation.

"Tell you what. I'm going to get dressed so you won't have to look at my t-shirt and flannel pants any longer, and we'll have a do-over for today's truce. Deal?"

Martinez's face softened. She nodded. "Deal."

I cleaned the dishes, showered, dressed. I pulled my katashiro from the safe in my closet, made some adjustments to the wardings — bit more resistance to physical damage, bit less from magic, add in a ward against thrall. If I ran into Goth Guy again, my biggest danger was being torn to shreds or falling under the sway of his thrall. Nikusui had no offensive magic to worry about.

When I finished, I found Pop on his laptop in the family room.

"Okay, I'm off to work. Be back around dinner-time."

He gave me a hug. "Be safe, Petal. Love you."

"Love you, too, Pop."

On the way out, I stopped in the dining room, silently offered prayers to Inari and my ancestors to watch over Pop while I was gone. The shrine to Inari was something I fretted over. After the Parting, a lot of mortals began worshipping kami, so having a kamidana for the kitsune deity wasn't immediately a confession to my Yōkai side. But it was still a gamble having it in my house.

Martinez had given no indication about her spiritual leanings, and she'd said nothing about the shrines. No openly worn religious symbols, no kami keychain, no verbal pleas to deities I was aware of. She might be an atheist for all I knew. I was just glad she'd kept mum about my prayers, didn't poke around for details about my beliefs.

We stepped into the hall, and I surreptitiously checked the wards along the doorframe while I locked the door. They seemed fine.

I punched the elevator down button.

While we waited, I texted Dinks to make sure he was okay. Then I typed out a second text, hit the send button before I changed my mind. Hoped I wouldn't regret it.

TWENTY-FIVE

MORTALIZATION CASES WERE JUST part of my job. Other assignments ranged from hunting down suspects to prisoner transports and lot of stuff in between.

Now, why in the world would a Yōkai want to become mortal? Why not stay magical and keep their cool powers? Invisibility, shapeshifting, unique creative talents: why give that up?

Many Yōkai were originally mortals. They self-identified as "sunrise" spirits. Their involuntary Yōkai transformation resulted from of a tragic event, a horrific experience, or simply through any number of emotions that got out of hand: jealously of a neighbor, anger at a co-worker, grief from a loss, excessive pride. They never wanted to be a spirit, and for some of the mortals-turned-Yōkai, their life could be a living hell on earth. Literally.

That wasn't as true for the Yōkai who were created or born as Yōkai. These "sunset" spirits, loved their powers and used them to open doors around the world. They weren't living in a perpetual state of torment.

While sunrise spirits made up the majority of mortalization cases, both sunrise and sunset Yōkai faced the same pressure to mortalize. The kind of persistent and not-always-explicit pressure Yōkai felt to conform.

Now, technically, mortalization was a voluntary option. The Bureau didn't aggressively push the program. If you were applying for a stamp, it wasn't supposed to matter at all whether you were currently in the mortalization program or not.

My experience? For a lot of Yōkai, they believed they didn't have a choice if they wanted to find a modicum of safety on the physical plane. Mortalization was a no-choice choice.

Case in point: Shohei, one of the employees at the Grounds Floor cafe. The cafe was a regular stop on my way into work, and my go-to drink of choice was a mocha with a double shot of espresso.

They say when you're a LEO, you should never be predictable, and that's an excellent motto, believe me. However, I'm pretty sure the folks who came up with it never had a Grounds Floor dark chocolate and mint mocha made by a former abura akago Yōkai.

"Morning, Shohei-san."

"Agent Miller! Usual?"

"Please."

"What can I get you?" Shohei asked Martinez.

She glanced at the menu overhead. "Just a regular coffee, thanks."

"Coming up."

I scanned the place while Martinez and I waited near the counter. Madara wasn't detecting any Yōkai, and most of the patrons were like me, popping in for a hit of caffeine on their way to somewhere else. A few were having meetings, and the rest were tapping at their laptops.

My phone buzzed.

<Hey! Can't afford standard modeling rates, but I can spring for a coffee!>

Beni, returning my text.

Sweet guy. Artist. Muscles in all the right places. A warm smile. A talented artist. No dick pics, no comments about my boobs or me being Asian. Not even a weird or offensive joke text. Funny and self-effacing at the same time.

I didn't know what was weirder: the idea of giving Beni a shot, or the realization I wasn't weirded out about it.

Either way, I'd made the opening move, put this whole thing in motion. I typed out a reply, deleted it, tried again, deleted that one, too.

I'll get back to him later.

I subtly pooled some kitsune power into my palm, fed Madara. Pop had told me he and Mom risked everything to ensure my Yōkai side stayed a secret. They'd arranged for Madara to be imprinted on me when I was just a few weeks old.

As a child, I'd taught Madara a variety of commands. If I told her to hide, she'd disappear. Super helpful for when I needed to concentrate on a test or didn't want the temptation of playing with her when I was supposed to be doing something else, like homework.

Sometimes she'd disappear on her own, too. Pop said the first time that happened when I was old enough to be aware of it, I had a complete meltdown. I sobbed for ten minutes even after Madara popped back into view.

I could also have Madara maintain a certain position. If I pointed above my head and told her "stay," she'd dutifully hang out there instead of swimming around me. Eventually, I taught her to respond to hand gestures so I didn't have to speak to her.

As I got older, I developed the distinct impression I wasn't training her so much as I was finally catching on to just how intelligent she was. Also got the feeling I was the spirit being trained.

Shohei handed over our coffees. I held out my credit card.

"On the house."

"Thank you, Shohei-san." I dropped a couple of dollars in the tip jar.

Shohei was one of my very first mortalization cases, and he rarely let me pay. A few centuries ago, he was a mortal living in Osaka whose occupation was a lamp oil thief. For his sins, at the time of his death he transformed into an abura akago, a Yōkai cursed to forever search for oil in people's homes. When he did, he'd lick the oil from lamps and paper lanterns. Not exactly a pleasant existence, especially as he craved the stuff no matter how much he drank.

Between Nurarihyon's oppressive control and a lot fewer oil lamps and lanterns in Japan, it didn't take long for Shohei to read the kanji on the wall. He worked hard, kept his nose clean, and got lucky enough to get stamped. Headed straight to Los Angeles and applied for mortalization through the Bureau.

"Any word from Kondo?" Martinez asked as we walked the last block to the office.

"Nope. About to pay him a visit, ask him nicely to move the autopsy to the top of his list."

I wasn't expecting anything shocking from the autopsy, but sometimes you got lucky. I made the rounds with our coroner, Paul Kondo, and our forensics team. Asked them to put a rush on it, pretty please with mochi on top.

Yuri's killers had roughed her up, no doubt, and the marks on her throat pointed to strangulation. The cause of her physical death felt straight-forward. Not much to go on. But the why of her death was a much better question, and neither Kondo nor forensics were likely to turn up anything I didn't already know. Martinez and I had plenty of other leads to run down.

Or leads that seemed willing to come to us, as it turned out. I'd just made my second cup of green tea when I got a call.

"I understand you've been trying to reach me, Agent Miller. What do you want?"

"Mikasa-san. You got my message."

"You are not a subtle mortal. What do you want?"

"Just a talk. Clear the air."

"Bottomless Bowl. Noon."

"I'll be there."

TWENTY-SIX

MIKASA HAD a reputation for being a wild card. She didn't hew to tradition, and all indications were she was gunning to take over the entire gokudō network in Los Angeles any way she could. The old rules didn't apply, and she'd taken off her gloves years ago.

Which made her choice of The Bottomless Bowl a relief. Just off Vine in Hollywood, the exclusive, high-end ramen shop was a Switzerland-like neutral territory for gokudō. Run by Sammy "No Face" Takeno, the Bowl was sacred ground, always available for parlay between feuding gangs, and in the seventeen years Takeno had been slinging soba, not a single Yōkai or mortal had met their demise on the restaurant's property.

That didn't mean I was stupid about my meeting with Mikasa. We got to the noodle shop thirty minutes early.

Takeno was a nopperabō, obtained his stamp years ago. As for his nickname, it was utterly unoriginal. Nopperabō were faceless Yōkai vendors who sold noodles to the unsuspecting. Faceless in that where you'd expect to see eyes, a nose, a mouth — it was just a smooth stretch of skin instead. Historically, they would open their carts at night. Customers didn't know they were dealing with a nopperabō until they'd finished their meal and tried to pay. That's when they'd realize the vendor literally had no face.

Unsettling if you're hitting a street cart at two in the morning on a moonless, rainy night. Nowadays, nopperabō generally focused on perfecting their craft instead of spooking mortals. Given how old Yōkai lived, that meant a lot of practice. In my book, nopperabō were the most talented hot udon chefs. Takeno had been at it for nearly three centuries, and his udon was the best I'd ever tasted. He'd built a small but mighty chain of restaurants around the world in just a few short years after the Parting. I counted myself lucky he chose to man the pans at his Los Angeles location.

The hostess greeted me, bowed as I entered. I asked to speak with Takeno, waited at the hostess stand. Within a few minutes, the Yōkai emerged from the kitchen.

When Takeno left Japan, he'd presented as a stick-thin Japanese male. Bald, with brown eyes surrounded by wrinkles that gave him the appearance of always being in thought. That day, he was manifesting, and several heads turned, some less discreetly than others, as the chef crossed the room. I'm sure they were wondering who this mortal woman was who could have warranted such a show of honor.

Takeno gave me a respectful bow, which I returned.

"It's good to see you, Miller-san, welcome back." Perfect Japanese. I replied in kind.

"Good to see you, too, Takeno-san. How is your family?"

"Quite well, thank you for asking. And yours?"

"My father is still trying to figure out how to retire."

Takeno smiled. Well, the skin on his face moved in a way I'd learned was the equivalent of a smile. "I wish him luck. I have yet to solve that riddle."

"Takeno-san, may I present Agent Valeria Martinez?"

The Yōkai gave Martinez a shorter and shallower bow, but it was far from insulting.

"It's a pleasure," Martinez said, returning the bow. "Agent Miller thinks very highly of you."

"I hope to continue to earn her praise," Takeno replied. "How may I help you today?"

"We're having lunch," I said. "And meeting someone."

"Oh?"

"House rules still in effect?"

Sammy nodded slightly. "Of course. As long as I'm behind the counter."

"Wonderful. And I'd very much like to use the private room if it's available."

"For you, I'll make it so, Miller-san."

"Thank you very much."

"Would you like your usual?"

"Please."

Takeno nodded at a server. "I'll check in with you shortly. Please do not hesitate to ask for anything."

A kimono-clad server showed us to the private room, an eight-mat tatami floor. The Bottomless Bowl was making no concessions for non-Japanese customers, and, frankly, it didn't need to. The place had a two-month waiting list for reservations.

I knelt down seiza-style, the bottoms of my socked feet resting against my butt. Martinez gave seiza her best effort, made it twenty minutes before she started fidgeting.

The server arranged a large bottle of Nirasa, two empty glasses, a pot of tea, and two teacups on the table. She filled the eight-ounce glasses with beer, bowed, and left.

"I never got the hang of this," Martinez said, switching to a cross-legged position. "You must have no nerve endings left."

"You get used to it after a while."

"You mean like after thirty years?"

I laughed. "Something like that. It's okay, you don't have to stay in seiza."

"I know. I just wish I could master it."

Another interesting insight into Martinez. I had the impression she didn't reject Japanese culture so much as embraced a few bits here and there under the slightest duress. Never occurred to me she might have tried, failed, and just given up in frustration.

The door slid open, and Takeno stepped through.

"Your meal is almost ready. Is there anything I can personally do to ensure your experience is superb?"

I sipped my tea, placed the cup on the table.

"This is more than superb already, Takeno-san, thank you." He gave me another smile and a brief bow. "I would never ask you to break the rules here, but I could use anything you have on Mikasa."

If he'd been presenting, Takeno's eyebrows would have arched. "Are you asking as an agent or as a customer?"

"I'm afraid it's as an agent."

"Then I'm sorry. I have little to share."

"No apology necessary. As I said, I don't want you to break house rules."

He held up a hand, waved it for a second. "I said I have little, but I have something. Mikasa's scared. The other bosses are discussing the need to put their differences aside in order to eliminate her."

Whaaaat?

"You really believe that, Takeno-san?"

A shrug of his shoulders. "Gokudō are unpredictable. If you figure them out, please call me."

I chuckled. "Don't hold your breath. If you can't figure them out, how am I supposed to?"

"You're a Bureau of Souls agent. I'm just a no-face noodle man."

"The most talented in town," I replied.

Takeno shook his head a few times, embarrassed at the compliment. "Far from it. So, your guest is Mikasa?"

"Yes."

"I would be distressed if anything unpleasant transpired at your meeting, Miller-san."

"Come on. You know me better than that. This is just a talk."

"You are a very intelligent mortal. Perhaps not so intelligent if you're intentionally tangling with Mikasa. Would you like some extra company?"

I considered the offer. Takeno was supposed to be strictly neutral in situations like this, but he'd boost his own security team if he thought a meet had the possibility of getting out of hand.

"I don't think so, but thank you."

"As you wish. I'll let you enjoy the rest of your meal, then."

A text came through from Dinks: <*Fine, thanks. But let me know if you hear anything I should be worried about.*>

I gave it a thumbs-up.

Fifteen minutes later, the server returned with a tray of dishes. Using both hands, he placed a steaming bowl of tanuki udon in front of me, spun it an inch, bowed low. He repeated the process for Martinez. The thick, pearl-colored noodles rested in a light brown broth and were topped with scallions, wakame seaweed, tempura flakes, and kamaboko.

I put my hands together, leaned forward, said, "Itadakimasu." I snagged one of the kamaboko slices with my hashi, popped it in my mouth.

Absolutely delicious. When I first learned it was ground up white fish mixed with flavorings, pressed into a mold, cooked, and then sliced, I almost swore off it completely. But then I tried it at the Bowl, and I was hooked.

I pinched a noodle, lifted the bowl to my mouth, loudly sucked the string of pasta into my mouth.

"It's amazing," I said to the server.

The server waiting just long enough to ensure we were happy. He smiled, bowed again, left.

"You must be pretty high up in the Yōkai crowd to swing a private room at the Bowl without a reservation." Martinez poured me a cup of tea, and I did the same for her.

"Not high enough to snag the chef's private table."

She frowned at me. "Pretty sure we'd be sitting there right now if you asked."

"What can I say? I have a sparkling personality."

"You've got something, that's for sure." But the smile on her face neutralized the sting of the comment. She was toeing around the question but not in an accusatory way. I didn't feel like explaining myself. "So, you planning on putting this on your expense account or mine?"

"Mikasa's, actually."

Martinez almost choked on her udon. "You're serious?"

A private room was never cheap in a high-end restaurant. It was astronomically expensive at the Bottomless Bowl because it was well and truly private. Takeno had it warded to prevent anyone, including himself, from being able to eavesdrop. There were rumors several gokudō deals had been cut in the room, though I'd never had the ill grace to ask Takeno about it directly.

"Hey. Sparkling personality, right?"

"I can't wait to see her face when you drop the bill on her."

At that moment, the private room door opened. Across the restaurant, I saw Mikasa roll in with two Nate in tow. They were all presenting, but Madara pinged all three of them.

Mikasa's outfit was a deliberate clash of styles. An expensive-looking low-cut untucked silk blouse draped over distressed jeans whose rolled cuffs capped a high-heeled sling back pair of shoes that made my feet hurt just looking at them. Long, wavy blond hair. Lots of jewelry: rings, necklaces, and bracelets.

I could hear her from across the room. She presented as a middle-aged Japanese woman. The two Crazy Nate were lean and wiry, near opposites of the two guys I'd seen on Evie's security feed. Takeno appeared, walked towards Mikasa.

I slurped another mouthful of udon, watched the Nate peel off Mikasa and make a point of sweeping the place. It was an insult to Takeno, a suggestion the Bowl was not perhaps totally safe, that he no longer held the same amount of power he used to command. Takeno's posture stiffened, but he said nothing.

If Mikasa was willing to piss off Takeno, she was desperate, scared, or extremely confident. Takeno was practically royalty compared to Mikasa's more peasant-level status when it came to age. Easily her senior by two centuries. The fact that he was stamped and still held enough clout in the gokudō world to run the Bowl should have given Mikasa pause.

Kids. What are you going to do?

The itachi ditched her shoes, entered the private room. The two Nate took up station outside. Mikasa knelt at the other end of the table.

"Agent Miller and..." Mikasa raised her eyebrows at Martinez. She either already knew what I looked like or had gotten a description from the Roku Roku crowd. I went with the former.

"Agent Valeria Martinez."

The Yōkai's mouth twitched. Her eyes slid back to me. "How's the udon?"

"Oishī desu." I noisily sucked up a large noodle, rested my hashi on the small porcelain holder. "But I didn't ask you here so we could discuss Takeno's cooking skills. I need information on a hakushi who was killed two nights ago." I slid a copy of Yuri's photo across the table. "She was in DTLA that night. Her body turned up in Griffith Park yesterday morning."

Mikasa looked at the photo without touching it. "And this involves me how?"

"Every lead I uncover miraculously points to you. Unless you can give me a reason to think otherwise, you're number one on the suspect list."

Mikasa smiled. "Does that mean you'll be frequenting my favorite haunts from now on?"

"Let's just say my schedule's very open right now."

Mikasa rippled, manifested as an itachi weasel. She leapt quietly up on the table, padded slowly towards me. Sniffed my udon, slurped up some broth.

"You're chasing the wrong rabbit, Agent Miller."

Wow. She was supremely confident.

"Give me a target, then, Mikasa-san."

"Why don't you go ruffle the feathers of those Shiny Kites pigeons and see what they say?"

I expected her to do exactly this. Point me at a rival gokudō gang, get me to do her work for her. By the time I figured out she was lying, if I ever did, she'd have a few less Shiny Kites to worry about. But her attitude, her assured cockiness, had me thinking otherwise. I couldn't sniff out truth versus lies from a Yōkai like I could with mortals, but Mikasa had me buying what she was selling.

"You're saying Tollerson and his crew killed Yuri?"

"I'm saying she took something from Tollerson that he wants back."

Martinez leaned in. "Which is why all the gokudō gangs have been at each other's throat for the past two weeks?"

"I never said the two were connected," Mikasa squeaked.

"Are they?" Martinez asked.

Mikasa took a bite of the pork, wiped at her whiskers. "You're a couple of smart agents. You figure it out. Now if you'll excuse me…" The weasel hopped off the table, transformed back into her mortal form. "I've got somewhere I need to be."

"Good seeing you, Mikasa-san," I said. "Oh, do be a dear and pay for the room on your way out, will you?"

That garnered a sneer, but I knew she'd foot the bill.

"Think she's lying?" Martinez asked.

"About the Shiny Kites and Yuri? No. But she's totally hiding something."

Gokudō are unpredictable, indeed.

TWENTY-SEVEN

"OKAY, how do the Kites and Tollerson fit into this?" I asked. "Given what we know, is there any way we can rule them out right off the bat?" Martinez was writing notes on a whiteboard at the office, visually laying out the key facts and potential suspects. I still hadn't shared with her my encounter with Yuri at Hana or what Yuri had told me about her time in the states. A part of me held out hope I could solve the murder without the connection coming up.

Even adding what I knew to the whiteboard's meager information, we still didn't have much to work with. Yuri's autopsy had come back. Kondo listed the official cause of death as asphyxiation. That was not exactly a surprise.

The eyebrow-raising revelation in the report was the possibility someone had extracted her soul before she died. If true, if her soul was stuck in a tamashi box somewhere, then she was effectively in limbo, unable to cross the Veil. That meant she couldn't begin the process of forming her Yōkai body again, much less return to the physical plane. Short of a firing, Yuri's fate was as close as a Yōkai could get to being dead. Now I wasn't just trying to find her killers, I was possibly searching for her soul, too.

The rest of the picture was fuzzy at best. But I was beginning to see the edges at least.

Martinez put up pictures of the suspects and their known contacts. We'd agreed to include Mikasa for now.

Chemistry had said all the gangs were after the object Yuri took, an artifact of some kind. Maybe. Gumdrop said he'd heard some Shiny Kites had paid a visit to Evie's motel. I'd dismissed that at the time, but now I wondered if that might be true.

Then we had a nikusui running around town asking about Yuri and a tamashi, most likely Goth Guy from last night. Felt like Goth Guy was the same nikusui from the Omagatoki Motel, though that was just a hunch. And Dinks had mentioned some of the gokudō were asking about a tamashi with someone's soul in it, not an artifact. Takeno said the other bosses were considering a coordinated move against Mikasa.

Finally, there was the uptick in gokudō activity, which corresponded with Yuri escaping from the soul shop. And the two guys who took Yuri from the motel.

Altogether, it seemed someone's soul was up for grabs, and all the gangs were upending L.A. in an attempt to find it. Mikasa might have been right about the Shiny Kites killing Yuri, but that didn't explain why Yuri had taken a tamashi or why all the gangs were fighting over it. If they were after a tamashi, it didn't contain the soul of some random mortal with a gambling debt to the gokudō. No, it had to be someone the gokudō would give a shit about.

"Hang on, who are those two?" I pointed at the pictures Martinez was taping to the whiteboard. Heavy-set guys listed as bodyguards for Isaac Tollerson. Presented as Japanese males. Suits. Hair pulled back into ponytails.

Martinez read off her CMS tablet. "Jiro and Juro. Oni Yōkai. Stamped. Been Tollerson's personal detail since they landed here a year ago."

Tollerson was the exception to the gokudō boss rule. Even in an area where Yōkai would be expected to completely dominate, a mortal had pried their way in. Tollerson was one of the few confirmed mortal bosses in the gokudō gang universe.

Wouldn't have been the first time a Japanese community had welcomed a White Westerner only to watch the newcomer assume control and start gate-keeping the members. Intel suggested Tollerson's closest mortal allies were attempting similar ploys in other cities, trying to recruit gokudō under their non-Yōkai banner.

I wasn't certain, but Jiro and Juro could have easily been the two guys who'd grabbed Yuri at the motel. No way they were the nikusui and the other Yōkai who'd visited Evie earlier. And maybe the nikusui wasn't working for the Shiny Kites after all, which meant he could be working for any of the gokudō gangs.

He'd clearly still been on the hunt for Yuri after she'd been killed. That strongly implied he hadn't killed her, even if he'd paid Evie a visit. I didn't remember seeing the bodyguards at Hana, though they could have been staking out the bar from the street. Or they could have caught Yuri when she went to the motel.

"Son of a bitch."

"What?"

"I think Mikasa was telling the truth."

———

"MILLER-SAN, THIS IS NOT A GOOD IDEA." Martinez and I were in the elevator, on our way to Containment.

"So don't do it."

"I want to solve the case as badly as you do, but this is going to blow up in your face. You can't see Gerrald because of the charges he's brought against you."

"That's why I'm asking you to talk to him. He used to run with the Shiny Kites, always hoping they'd let him join. They treated him like a dog, strung him along. Finally, he realized they just wanted to make fun of him and use him for entertainment. That's when he left. At least, that's his story. I want you to find out if he's still in touch with them."

Martinez didn't seem sold on the idea of questioning Gerrald herself.

"Why would he talk to me? I've never even met him."

"Lay out the deal, just like I told you. He'll bite."

Yua Noguchi was working Containment. She signed us both through after reiterating I was forbidden to have contact with Gerrald. One of the Jewels brought him to a debrief room, Martinez in tow. I sat with Noguchi and observed the meeting over a video feed.

As Martinez predicted, Gerrald had little to say to her, even when she dangled the possibility of takeout food in front of him. He was rocking back and forth, muttering to himself. Crimson Candy come down. Martinez started going through the script I'd given her, but she was fucking it up, failing to connect with him. Gerrald stopped making eye contact, turned away from her.

"Gerrald-san, I'm not here about the Crimson Candy or your voyeurism. That's between you and Agent Miller. I'm here about this Yōkai who was murdered the night Agent Miller arrested you." Martinez showed Gerrald a picture of Yuri. He had no poker face at all. He seemed surprised to learn Yuri was dead.

"I don't know what you're talking about."

"Gerrald-san, we know you're just a pawn in all this. Help us out, be the good guy you are deep down, and tell us what you know so we can bring the killer to justice."

"How am I supposed to help? I can't tell you what I don't know."

"Well, let's start with what you do know. It's possible you have some information that's important, even if you don't realize it."

"Look, like I already said, I was minding my own business that night when I spotted a taka onna peeping into a window. I performed a civic duty and tried to stop them. That's when that crooked agent tried to shake me down for protection money. Said she'd arrest me if I didn't pay her. I told her that's bullshit, and she planted the drugs on me. I don't know anything about a dead hakushi."

The Yōkai crossed his arms, stared down Martinez. I couldn't tell if she'd caught Gerrald's misstep, but I could see he'd shut down. Martinez wouldn't get anything more out of him. I started walking towards the debrief room.

"Miller-san, where are you going?" Noguchi asked.

"To sort this shit out."

I ignored Noguchi as she warned me not to set foot in the debrief room. I stepped inside, closed the door behind me. Martinez stood up.

"Miller-san, you shouldn't-"

"Just sit tight, partner. This won't take long."

A day in a Bureau holding cell hadn't taken the piss or vinegar out of Gerrald. If anything, he was jacked up more than usual, thanks to Martinez.

"You're a dead agent walking. As soon as my boss finds out about this, he's-"

"And who would that be, exactly? Tollerson?" That garnered me a defiant stare, but I caught the shift in his body posture. I'd guessed right. "Skip it. I've got good news. You're a free Yōkai." Both of them were now looking at me like I'd lost my mind. "I'm serious. You can walk right out the door. I'll take the cuffs off myself."

Gerrald frowned. "Bullshit."

"Not at all. I know Tollerson had the Jane Doe Yōkai killed, and I'm going to put him away. He won't be able to hurt you."

"Don't know what you're talking about."

"Yeah, Gerrald-san, you do. And I'm trying to help you, even if you can't see it. I understand why you were too afraid to talk to me the other day. I don't blame you. In fact, I'm sorry I busted you."

The swagger settled back on Gerrald's shoulders, and he lifted his head.

"Damn right you're sorry. Wait till I sue the Bureau for false arrest, imprisonment, and...and mental anguish." He seemed particularly pleased he'd come up with the last one.

"Your call. But I'm dropping the charges either way."

He didn't see that coming. Took several seconds for him to process what I was suggesting.

"You're lying. Why would you do that?"

"I'm just trying to find out who killed the Yōkai, Gerrald-san, and I think you can help me."

Roll of his eyes. "This again? I told you, I don't know anything about that Yōkai with the backpack. Never seen her before in my life."

I pointed at Yuri's photo. "There's no backpack in that picture. And we never said she was hakushi."

He realized the dead-end path he'd chosen. He got to his feet, paced the room in tiny loops.

"I want my lawyer now."

I flipped through his case jacket. "Says here you already spoke with a defense attorney."

"Well, I want to speak to them again."

"If you want. Doubt they're going to come over just to see you get released from jail."

He paused, looked sideways at me. "You're serious."

"I don't know how many times I have to say it. You're free to go."

"No catch?"

"No catch. I'd appreciate your help bringing some killers to justice, but it's your call."

Gerrald reluctantly sat down, sighed, stared at the floor. "What do you want?"

"I want to know why you were following me."

The agony played out on his face. He could taste freedom, but there was something else, too. Pain. Hurt. A soul-wrenching loss I knew something about.

He was close to tumbling, but he'd need a final nudge. I took a guess at what was eating him up.

"I bet you think I'm disappointed in you. I think you're unhappy because life in the U.S. isn't what you thought it'd be. You keep trying to make it all work, but it never holds together for long, right? Sooner or later, you're hooked on Crimson Candy again or trying to claw your way back into the Shiny Kites. But you know deep down neither of those are what you need."

Gerrald's head dipped, and his body shook once, twice, three times. Tears fell onto his pants.

"It's so fucking hard. So fucking hard."

"I know. That's why I sent you to Yōkoso. Why I keep trying to help you."

"I never thought...I figured things would be fine once I got here. But it's, it's not what I thought. I keep trying to fit in, but...I miss Japan. I should never have come here." The tears fell faster. He swiped angrily at his face. "I don't want to help Nurarihyon, but I'm not wanted here. There's no place for someone like me here."

"I think there is," I said. "And I'm going to help you find it."

TWENTY-EIGHT

I HAD to get Mei's sign-off to release Gerrald. Vigilance would pitch a fit, and Mei would be the one to have to deal with it, so I looped her in. She was totally on board with dropping the charges when I laid it out for her.

Gerrald didn't have all the answers I wanted, but he gave me enough to roll with the information I was hiding from Martinez, allow it to surface so she could use it, too.

Gerrald was, indeed, still trying to work his way into the Shiny Kites, mostly by feeding them whatever scraps of information he could get off the streets. When he heard they were looking for Yuri and willing to pay a lot of money to anyone who'd help them, Gerrald started scouring the area. He lucked out when he spotted her in DTLA. Gerrald had called Tollerson, who instructed the Yōkai to continue tailing Yuri but not to get too close. Tollerson wanted Jiro and Juro to make the actual grab.

Gerrald followed Yuri on foot, losing her a few times but always managing to find her again. The bodyguards had met up with Gerrald after Yuri entered Hana. They paid Gerrald in Crimson Candy and told him to fuck off, they'd handle it from there. He took a hit and was about to leave when he saw me exit the bar with Beni.

Gerrald didn't mention seeing me with Yuri, but he was smart enough to question whether my presence at Hana was pure coincidence. He called Tollerson again, thinking he could parlay my appearance into some more good favor with the gokudō boss. Tollerson told him to follow me, just in case.

"Honest, Agent Miller, I don't know what happened to the Yōkai after I left. All I knew was they were looking for her. And I never heard from Tollerson again. I didn't think they would kill her."

Easy words to say after the dominos had fallen, but I thought he was being honest.

"How about where Tollerson was keeping the Yōkai?" More muttering as he turned his gaze to the ceiling. "Hey, Gerrald-san, look at me, man. You're doing great. Just one more question, okay? Where did the tamashi come from?"

"Some place in Hawthorne. It's a pawn shop on top, but they do the soul swapping underground, in a basement."

More pieces slid into place. Gerrald's expression turned remorseful. "Agent Miller, Tollerson…he's coming after you."

I shrugged, played down the severity of the warning. "His choice, but he'll regret it if he does. I'm going to start working on your release. While I'm doing that, will you do me a favor, please?"

"What?"

"Would you tell Agent Martinez here what really happened at the apartment the night I busted you?"

He did, and Noguchi got it all recorded. There was still going to be paperwork and interviews with IA, but I felt like I was out of the woods as far as Gerrald was concerned. A slight relief, a tiny victory lap, but a success nonetheless. And it meant I could focus more of my energy on putting the final pieces of Yuri's murder into place.

Martinez and I updated Yuri's case timeline based on Gerrald's information. We felt confident we were getting close to figuring out whose soul was in the tamashi, and finding that soul shop might get us all the way there. We pulled a search for all registered pawn shop business licenses in Hawthorne. Six hits came back. We dug into them, looking for anything that might tell us which one had connections with the gokudō. Two hours later, we still had nothing concrete.

"Let's drive out there, eyeball them directly," Martinez said.

"Only if you drive." I wasn't ready to let Martinez give up her chauffeuring duties just yet.

———

WE SHOULD HAVE TAKEN A CROWN. Martinez's BMW didn't exactly blend in. On the other hand, it didn't scream "police." We cruised all six locations, ruled out one because it had an underground parking deck and ruled out another because it was on the third floor of an outdoor strip mall. We'd need to narrow down the remaining four to a likely candidate if we wanted to pull a search warrant. Neither one of us wanted to drive all the way back to DTLA without marking at least a couple more off the list.

"That stand-alone green building on Carson, what's it called? Second Lives? Didn't it say it was open twenty-four hours?"

"Yeah," I said. "Why?"

"Every other place closes no later than six. And if you were swapping souls, when would be the best time to do it?"

Not bad, partner.

"Okay, you want to call in for a warrant?"

Martinez thought about it. "Let's take a peek inside, since we're already here. Nothing illegal about window shopping. If it smells funny, we'll come back with a warrant."

"Sounds good to me."

Martinez parked across the street and a block up so we had a view of the shop's entrance. The first thing I noticed about the Second Lives pawn shop was its a-bit-on-the-nose name. Might have been intentional, a deliberate middle finger to the LEO community. The second thing was how little stuff there was inside for sale. On our first drive-by, we'd noticed the mostly bare walls.

"Feel like taking a look?" Martinez asked. "I've always been in the market for a black light Elvis velvet painting."

If I hadn't just seen her home, I'd have thought she was having a stroke.

Did she just crack a joke?

"Young or old?"

"Young Elvis, of course."

Of course.

Martinez went in first, I followed a few minutes later. No hint of Crimson Candy or anything else illicit in the air, but I caught something. Dirty laundry, maybe, or the smell of someone who hadn't showered in a few days. Very faint.

There were three customers inside and a woman behind the counter. Madara pinged the woman as a Yōkai, the rest as mortals. Of the customers, a female looked through a small collection of LPs, a male admired a *Wizard of Oz* poster, and a redheaded male stood at the counter opposite the Yōkai.

Copper Top had both hands on the glass counter and was leaning over, literally trying to get in the Yōkai's face.

"I told you I'd be back today, cash in hand. What did you do with my card?"

"Sir, as I already said, we sold it. Our policy clearly states," here the Yōkai lifted an open hand to indicate the large sign on the wall behind her, "all items become immediately available for sale once they have been placed on the floor. We do not hold or set aside items, period, end of sentence. If you have something to buy or sell, I'm happy to help you."

She'd quoted the sign verbatim. Not for the first time, either, I was sure.

The guy pounded the counter hard enough to make the coffee cup dance. "That was a 1953 Topps #82 Mickey Mantle. It's worth at least two grand. It took me years to get my hands on it!"

"It's worth considerably more, actually. I believe we sold it for closer to three thousand."

The fury smoked off the guy so hard, I didn't need to see his face to know where this was going.

"Motherfuckers! You only gave me a grand when I sold it to you! Where's the manager? I want to speak to the manager. Now!"

The woman looked up from her magazine. "Sir, I am the manager."

"Then I want to speak with the owner!"

"I'm also the owner. And the bookkeeper, too. In fact, as far as this conversation goes, I'm the only person you can speak with."

"God damn it all, do you know how many followers I have online? I'm going to burn this place with reviews. I'm going to put you assholes out of business!"

"I look forward to retiring early, sir. Until then, unless you have any business to conduct, please leave the shop."

The guy folded his arms, smirked. "If I don't leave here with my card-"

"It's already been sold, sir, I can't give back something I don't have."

"-I'm going to post on Yelp, too. And then I'm going to call the FCC and file a complaint."

"I think you mean the BBB, sir. The letters make it confusing, don't they?"

The Yōkai's voice didn't even hint at being anything but bored, perhaps a little amused. The customer, however, launched into another profanity-laced tirade. The Yōkai picked up the phone behind her, dialed a number.

"Oh, you better call your boss, lady, better call them right now before I come across this counter."

The Yōkai stared blankly at the man, spoke into the phone. "Yes, I'd like to report a disturbance at Second Lives Pawn Shop located at 40231 Carson Street-"

I couldn't make out the rest, as the customer started saying how much he'd love for the police to come, how he couldn't wait to see the look on their faces. When he paused to catch his breath, the Yōkai covered the phone with her hand.

"I'm not calling the police, sir," she said.

The guy froze in silence, looked around the store. The female customer had left, but the Oz lover was watching. I stayed put, comfortably far from Copper Top and not blocking his way out of the shop. Martinez was somewhere behind me.

"Look, I didn't mean-"

The woman cut him off. "No need to apologize, you can explain it all when they get here."

"Okay, look, I flew off the handle, I'm sorry about that. Why don't you just give me back my money, and we'll call it square? You're still in the black."

The Yōkai began describing the customer, what he was wearing, even gave his name. The man got more anxious, said he'd take five hundred. The Yōkai ignored him. He dropped it to two-fifty before nearly sprinting out of the store.

I watched him go. The Yōkai stopped talking mid-sentence as soon as the customer had gone, hung up the phone.

Interesting.

I stepped up to the counter. That smell from earlier cranked up a notch or two, but I doubted Martinez or any mortal would have noticed it. "Excuse me, I'm looking to purchase something. Something unique."

"What you see is what we got." She went back to flipping pages.

"I think what I'm looking for is in the back."

Flip.

"You looking for some cardboard boxes? Past due invoices? Maybe a pot of cold coffee?"

I looked up, found not one but two cameras covering the counter. Made a point of staring into each for a few seconds. "Sorry for not being clearer. What I'm looking for is in your basement."

Slight hesitation before she turned the next page. "We don't have a basement."

"I'm thinking you do."

The woman's eyes tracked up to meet mine. "That so?"

I took a chance. "Yeah. I'm thinking you've got a particular something downstairs that belongs to an acquaintance of mine. I'm here to discuss a negotiation."

"Who's your acquaintance?"

So much for denying there was a basement.

"Someone who wouldn't want me kept waiting by a flunkie like yourself." I tilted my head at her. "In fact, I'm done talking to you. Why don't you scamper into the back and tell the grown-ups I need to speak with them."

The Yōkai said nothing, turned and went through the door behind the counter. I did a casual turn, noticed Martinez by the front door. We didn't acknowledge one another, but her expression made it clear she didn't approve of me interacting with the woman.

A minute later, a guy walked in from the back. Well, Madara pinged him as Yōkai, but he was presenting. Frayed hair under a baseball cap, scraggly beard, greasy jeans, and a t-shirt. The woman followed, closed the door, leaned against it. Beardie Boy stepped to the counter.

"What do you want?"

My hunch had paid off so far, and I was pretty sure Gerrald was right about souls being bartered, pawned, and sold here. Figured I'd roll the dice one more time. "My acquaintance needs more time."

"And who would that be?"

I glanced at the cameras. "Someone who doesn't want their name being said aloud. Someone who likes their privacy."

Beardie Boy rolled his eyes. "This again? Look, you tell that self-righteous piece of shit he better have the money by Friday, or he can forget about the whole thing."

"He only needs until Sunday. He'll pay you an extra ten percent."

Beardie Boy laughed. "Midnight Friday. No extensions. No negotiations. We have a deal, and he better stick to his end of it. Anything else?"

"You're getting a ten percent boost for an extra forty-eight hours. Not sure why you're thumbing your nose at the offer. Unless you already sold it."

"I haven't." He lowered his voice. "It's still in the cage."

Bingo.

Well, mostly. Beardie Boy hadn't said the words *soul* or *tamashi*, but I knew these guys were swapping souls.

"Prove it. Show me the tamashi."

Beardie Boy's eyes narrowed. "Can't do that."

Good enough.

This is where I should have grumbled, made a show of being shut down, and ultimately left the shop. Where I should have checked in with the office, gotten a search warrant, organized a proper breach and sweep of the place. Where I should have done what Martinez would have done.

I didn't.

Instead, I pulled my sidearm and showed my badge.

"Bureau of Souls. I'm arresting you under suspicion of the illegal possession of souls, which is a violation of Chapter 137 of the U.S. Code and California Health and Safety Code 12802. Please put your hands up and do not move until I instruct you to." I heard Martinez behind me, and based on the looks of the two behind the counter, her weapon was out as well.

Beardie Boy frowned. "Pawn shops aren't illegal. Don't you ever watch TV? They got an entire show devoted to that pawn shop in Vegas. Besides, I don't deal in souls. No clue what you're talking about."

"In that case, you won't mind if I take a look." I pointed my gun at the door.

"You're going to need a warrant, agent, if you want to step behind that counter."

Why do criminals always think they know the law better than LEOs?

"And you're going to want to stop relying on police shows for your legal training. Probable cause. You just became my warrant. Move away from the door, take five steps to your right, and put your hands on the counter." The female walked to the end of the counter, Beardie Boy in tow.

When they were both safely away from the door, I came around the counter, stepped to the side, and tried the handle. The door opened, revealing a security code punch-panel on the inside lock.

Those were usually on the outside to keep customers from accessing employee-only areas. Only reason to put one on the inside was to prevent someone from getting out of the back of the store.

I took a step into the hall just as a young male rounded a corner thirty feet from me, shotgun in his grip. He must have been nervous, because the weapon went off as he was still raising it towards me. I felt the sting of buckshot on my right shin.

Thank you, Hachiman was all I had time for before I returned fire. I fought my training to go for the chest, aimed instead at the guy's right arm, sent three rounds down the hall. Two hit, one in his upper arm, the other near his shoulder. He dropped the shotgun, clutched his chest, dropped to the floor. The boom of the shots left my ears ringing. I thought I heard noises farther back in the store, couldn't clearly make them out. From the front, Martinez's voice floated in, muffled and muted.

"Miller-san!"

"I'm good! Stay there!"

The kid reached for the shotgun with his left arm, but I closed the distance and yelled at him to freeze. He looked up at me, eyes tracking my Sig, and he stopped. Couldn't have been older than eighteen or nineteen.

Come on, Inari, help me out here.

I used my foot to move the shotgun out of his reach, ordered him to stay on the ground. He did, and I placed my left hand over the chest wound, delivered a healthy dose of han healing. Did the same to his arm.

His eyes blinked and stared at the ceiling, but he was breathing, and the han magic had stemmed the blood loss. He'd live. I patted him down for another weapon, came up empty, cuffed him.

"Martinez-san, call for an ambulance. He's cuffed and stable, but he took two rounds in his arm and chest."

"On it."

I emptied the shotgun, tossed it well out of reach of the kid. "And stay in the lobby with those two. I'm going down the hall."

"Roger."

I walked to the first door, tried the handle. Locked. "Martinez, see if Beardie Boy has any keys to these doors."

I heard the ding of a bell, followed by a lot of footsteps and shouted orders to freeze. How in the world could local PD be here so fast?

"Hey, Miller-san," Martinez called out, "you better holster your weapon and slowly step back into the lobby."

"What is it?"

"Vigilance."

TWENTY-NINE

THE VIGS WERE BESIDE THEMSELVES, and it didn't take long to figure out why. Vigilance was crying foul over me and Martinez stepping on a multi-month undercover operation they claimed they had been running on the shop. Said they'd been surveilling it for some time and were now accusing me of royally fucking up their entire investigation.

Calls went out to Mei and her counterpart at Vigilance to determine who was in charge of said fuck up. The Vigs taped off the area and put up a perimeter, waited for orders on who was going to inspect the crime scene. LPD showed up but stayed on the sidelines to see who won the turf war.

While we waited, I stayed by the kid, whose name was Peter. Han spells had a declining effectiveness, and I'd hit him with a high-dose healing spell in the hall. I waited until the paramedics had wheeled his stretcher into an ambulance, made sure there wasn't anything more I could do.

The Procs, short for the Jewels Procedures team who evaluated any discharge of a Bureau firearm, would demand half a day of my time at some point, going over the incident ad nauseam. Had I followed proper procedures? Was the shooting justified? Had I endangered any civilians?

It was necessary, a good check and balance, but it would be time consuming. And then there was the lengthy report I'd have to write and file. I pushed all that to the back burner for now.

Martinez used a han of seeing to discern who was Yōkai and who was mortal. I already knew Peter was mortal, and Beardie Boy and the woman were Yōkai. I couldn't tip my hat, of course, though I kept an eye on them. Not knowing what type of Yōkai they were meant I didn't know what kind of powers they had. While I waited, I healed my leg. Minor scratches, thankfully, but my pants were a lost cause.

The Vigs had snagged four of the six suspects who had bolted out the back door after my shootout with Peter. While Martinez was casting, one of the Vigs strolled over to me. Darnell Durante, who, it happened, was the Vig assigned to Yuri's Jane Doe case.

"Miller."

"Hey, Durante."

He smiled, hands in his pockets. Sported a boyish face that almost hid the telltale signs of the forty-some-odd years he'd actually logged.

"FUBAR situation, huh?" The statement was clearly ambiguous about where the blame belonged.

"One way to put it. You guys stake out a suspected gokudō business without getting us involved, this is what happens."

"Hey, this one's above my pay grade, but I agree. Listen, I owe you a call about the Jane Doe."

"No worries."

"That why you're here? You working a lead on that case?"

"Not really. Just running down a tip from one of my sources. Might be connected, but I was here for something else."

Durante nodded, grinned wide. "Damn good lead, I'd say."

"Lost a couple of suspects." I kept the statement neutral.

"Happens. We've put out an APB and requested an airship. Might find them."

"And I might inherit the Queen's jewels. We've got a better chance that one of the other suspects rats them out."

He didn't argue. "I'll make sure we give it the full court press."

"You think this is going to stay a Vig op?"

"Nah. But the mortals are coming with us. Pretty sure we can get at least one of them to turn."

"Maybe. Call me if you do?"

"Yep."

Martinez finished her last cast, confirmed two of the back door runners were mortals, the other two Yōkai. The Vigs had the mortals cuffed and huddled together. We had the Yōkai looped with shimenawa cuffs. A sweeps team was still inbound and would process and transport them regardless of who got control of this scene.

I didn't think Vigilance would find the entrance to the basement. The gokudō would have it magically hidden and probably warded. Even if the Vigs had discovered it, they'd kill themselves trying to open it. At the least, they'd stomp around the shop and probably fuck up the evidence. But if I could find the basement, Vigilance would have no choice but to turn the scene over to us.

I slipped under the strip of yellow Vigilance tape, walked towards the shop. Two Vigs casually moved into place, blocking me from entering.

"This is a Vigilance investigation, agent. Can't let you inside."

"Gentlemen, there's a high probability-" I looked over their shoulders, into the shop. My hand slowly went for my Sig as I whispered, "There's an oni moving around inside. Don't turn around."

Of course, one of them did. A half-second blur of burgundy motion disappeared into the doorway behind the counter, an unmistakable horned head atop a massive body. I finished my draw, and their weapons cleared their holsters.

"Jesus. How'd we miss that?" one of the Vigs muttered.

"I think you'd better warn whoever's guarding the back door." I called Martinez over. "There's an oni inside. I'm going in. How about you circle around to the back?"

The Vig officer who'd been silent up to now looked over at his superior. "I think we should pull back and secure the area first."

A howl echoed from inside the shop.

"Yeah, well," I said, "I think the oni might have something else in mind. You two fall back. I'll check it out." I looked at the Vigs. "Unless either of you want to join me?"

They shook their heads, stepped aside. I gave Martinez a nod, and she jogged off to the back of the building. I entered the shop, moved through the room to the door behind the counter. There were no more howls, no sign of the oni. Of course, there hadn't been an oni to begin with.

Being half kitsune had its perks.

I passed a couple of rooms and offices I would have loved to search, but I wasn't sure how long the Vigs would wait before coming inside. I settled for focusing on finding the basement entrance.

A han of seeing revealed the basement entrance, hidden behind an illusion of a full-length mirror. With the illusion dispelled, I could see a recessed door handle and wards outlining the door frame. Curiously, they appeared inactive. The door had a bar-style handle, and I used my elbow to prevent my prints from getting on it.

The door swung in, revealing stairs descending to a finished hallway. My nose picked up a mix of scents but mostly a stronger version of body odor. Madara went nuts.

At the bottom of the stairs was a wide hallway that stretched for fifteen yards. Finished drywall, carpeting, and overhead lighting. Two cameras mounted on the ceiling at each end of the hall. Three open doors on either side of the hallway, evenly spaced, plus a closed door at the end of the hall.

I eased up to the first door on the right, gave it a quick peek before ducking back. First impression was a messy but empty office. Crossed to the opposite door and did the same.

Not an office. Also, the source of the odor I'd picked up.

The room was about twenty by twenty, and it held seven

large metal cages, each around five feet on a side. Three were occupied, all Yōkai according to Madara, though they were presenting. Two males and a female, grungy clothes, tangled hair.

My heart rate jumped at the unspeakable horror of what I was looking at. Yōkai, caged like animals and forced to do Inari knows what until they died or were killed. The icing on the cake? This wasn't the work of some mortal fringe group demanding the spirits be purged from the physical plane. This tragedy had been inflicted on Yōkai *by* Yōkai.

Over the last four years, I've brought home images from work I'll never fully get out of my head, stuff that would haunt me the rest of my life. This basement became the latest entry.

What if I hadn't made it out of Japan? What if Pop had been forced to smuggle me into the states like Yuri had been? It wasn't a huge leap to think I was standing on the outside of these cages by sheer luck.

I held my finger up to my mouth, showed my badge. The Yōkai wordlessly shrunk back in their cages, probably figuring they were about to be in a different kind of trouble. The three occupied cages were locked. I didn't know if the basement was safe yet, much less where the keys were, so I reluctantly moved back into the hall.

I quietly checked out the rest of the basement. There were two more rooms with cages, much like the first, though the cages were empty. I also found two rooms with operating-style tables and all the necessary gear for conducting the soul transfer rituals. Little doubt now that Gerrald had been right. Even less doubt about whether some seriously illegal crap was going on.

The room at the end of the hall was clearly the storage area for souls. Shelves of large ceramic and wood containers. Some vase-like, others box-shaped. They ranged from extremely ornate to utterly plain.

Boxing a soul was no easy feat, and keeping it contained wasn't any easier. You needed industrial-grade wards and runes, applied properly and in the correct order. The slightest error with a single stroke could cause a failure and destroy the soul.

Of the three dozen or so vessels, only four were sealed and appeared to have a soul. They had name cards placed on or in front of them. But my eyes snagged on a card in front of an empty space on the shelf.

It read "Mikasa."

So many pieces of this puzzle fell into place.

Having finished a sweep of the basement, I returned to the cages, explained I was there to help the Yōkai, that they were safe. The female told me to check the room across the hall for keys, and I found a small ring of them in a desk drawer. I wasn't worried about fingerprints anymore.

I had no way to confirm if the Yōkai had stamps or not. None of them had any kind of documentation on them, though they swore they had received stamps. It was the safe thing to say, especially as it would take some time for the Bureau to sort out the truth. If I'd been in their position, I wouldn't admit to a Bureau agent I'd committed the crime of sneaking across a border. At least, not until I was out of my cage.

I desperately wanted to help them escape, but I couldn't see it happening with Vigs surrounding the place. My illusion abilities were limited. And even if I could pull off a distraction, I couldn't count on the Yōkai surviving on the street as safely as Yuri had done. Vigilance of the Bureau might easily scoop them up. Or, worse, the gokudō might find them and decide not to renew their "employment."

Don't want that on my conscience, too...

No, better they took their chances with the Bureau than just stumble into the night. They might get temporary asylum, maybe even avoid a deport.

I unlocked the cages, told them to stay behind me as I led them up to the first floor. I went for the back door, knowing I'd sent Martinez there. Less chance of a trigger-happy Vig letting their nerves get the better of them if an agent was standing nearby.

I paused at the back door, picked up a familiar-looking backpack, turned it around. My heart sank when I spotted the oval omamori charm on it. Stamped into the gold-colored metal was an image of the o-kami Jizo, a deity known as a protector of children, women, and travelers.

Looks like I wasn't the only one who'd let Yuri down.

THIRTY

I SEARCHED THE BACKPACK, found nothing. No cash and no Whisper cell phone. Yuri's cell was either in a landfill or being used by one of the gokudō in the shop. Nothing pointed defini-tively to me having met with her, and I left it in the shop.

"Clear! We're clear!" I shouted as I nudged open the back door with my foot. "Officer coming out with three victims!"

"Where's the oni?" Martinez asked as she and the Vigs next to her lowered their weapons.

I shrugged. "Got me. Might have been a shapeshifter. I checked the entire building. I suppose it might still be in there."

Based on the looks on the Vig officers, my comment had the desired effect. They wouldn't be going into the building at this point.

As I expected, with the new wrinkle of living Yōkai and extracted souls being found on site, the Vigs were forced to turn the scene over to us.

I stood with the three Yōkai near the back of the store, didn't want them anywhere near Beardie Boy and his crew. I tried to assure them they were safe, but the words felt hollow even in my own ears. Were they safer than they were in the basement? For now, yes. But truly safe? No.

The Yōkai said nothing while I waited for the Bureau sweeps team. Not a word while the Jewels draped blankets around them and helped into the transport van. Just blank stares and numb compliance with our requests to watch their step.

The Jewels would interview and question the Yōkai back at the office. If we were lucky, they might agree to testify against the mortals and gokudō who ran the shop. That kind of cooperation might even help them avoid a deport.

The sweeps found nothing significant on site beyond what I'd already found, though it would take weeks to go through all the evidence. There were dozens of file cabinets and several computers in the building.

There would be a metric crap ton of paperwork to file tomorrow, but all I could think about at the moment was Yuri. And not just Yuri. All the other Yuris in Los Angeles she represented. The unlucky ones who were invisible and ignored, and the even more unfortunate souls who were oppressed and abused.

I loved Los Angeles, but sometimes the people here broke my heart into a million pieces.

————

MY ALARM WENT OFF FAR, far too early the next morning. I'd gotten home last night to find a note from one of my neighbors. He wanted me to stop by his apartment at eight before he left for work. The smell of green tea and a freshly cooked breakfast helped get me out of bed and into my clothes.

I ran two fingers down the sides of Madara, fed her some of my Yōkai essence.

"Okay, girl, time for me to eat."

Niko had arrived early and, with help from me and Sumiye, rolled out a traditional Japanese morning meal. Steamed rice topped with leftover natto from Sumiye, grilled salmon, a small dish of kale, soy-vinegar pickles, and miso soup. Sumiye had chopped green onions as a topper for the natto, and I finished it off with a bit of karashi, a spicy mustard.

Martinez earned some points for displaying a talent with her hashi, picking up a single natto. She lost most of those points when she sniffed the bean and wrinkled her nose. Then she scored double for tasting it anyway.

"Wow. Never knew they could taste this good."

"You never had Sumiye's natto before," I replied. "Try it with the mustard."

She did, and then some. Nearly finished off the jar of karashi.

Well done, partner.

Martinez went to change after breakfast, and I talked to Pop about Elena.

"About yesterday morning. I think we need to have some new rules."

"Yesterday morning?" He didn't seem to know what I was talking about at first, then his expression changed. "What happened?"

I summarized his encounter with Elena. He sighed. "I'm sorry, Petal, it's-"

"Not your fault, Pop. It's not your fault. Just wanted to make sure you were part of the discussion about how we can protect you and everyone else."

"Of course. Whatever you think's best."

"I think we need to install a chime on the front door, maybe on your bedroom door, too. And the ladies will be keeping a closer eye on you."

Pop nodded silently.

"It's because we love you, Miller-san." Sumiye came around, gave Pop a hug. He patted her hand.

"I know. I know. I think I'll-" he paused. "I think I'll watch some TV. Maybe later Sumiye-san and I can take a walk around the block."

"Any time," she said.

Pop left the kitchen, and Sumiye gave me a hug, too. I let myself have a quiet cry.

———

FRANK DELAMONT AND HIS WIFE, Annie, lived two doors down from us. I knocked on the Delamont's door, heard Frank's shuffling footsteps, a metallic scrape as the safety chain came off its hook. Frank was in a short-sleeved, button-down shirt and slacks, clearly ready for work.

"Morning, Frank." I held up his note. "This a good time?"

"Morning, sunshine." He waved me in.

Modern jet plastic models filled his condo.

"How are the models coming along? Working on a new one?"

"Yup. Annie just got me a big one. Gonna take me a couple of weeks at least. With these hands, anyway."

"Let me know when it's done. Pop and I would love to see it."

Nod of Frank's head. "Will do, will do." His expression turned concerned. "About David. I heard from Elena again. She's gone door to door to petition to have David evicted. And rumor is if that fails, she's gonna to take him to court."

"For what? Losing his memory? Having a brain slowly wither away?"

"Course not. She's talking assault, sexual harassment, mental anguish." I must not have done a great job of hiding my shock. The wrinkles around Frank's eyes eased, and he put a hand on my arm. "I'm so sorry to be the one to tell you this."

"He never touched Elena. Sumiye saw the whole thing."

"Having a witness will help. Might not be enough, though. And I hope I didn't step out of turn, but I asked a friend of mine about the situation. She said Elena has enough of a case to make it drag out forever. Can't get David kicked to the street, but she might get a restraining order."

"Which is the same thing."

Frank sighed. "I'm so sorry, sunshine."

"Thanks." I dug up a smile, pasted it on my face. "No, it's okay. We'll be okay. And thank you for asking your friend. I owe you."

"Nonsense. But if you want to make some extra soba noodles next time you find yourself in the kitchen, maybe set some aside, maybe they wind up here in 12C, hey, I'm not gonna complain."

A chuckle. "No, you won't, but I'll never hear the end of it from Annie."

Frank drew himself up, stuck out his chin. "I'm not scared of her. I'm a grown man. She can't tell me what I can and can't eat."

"Frank, we both know you're petrified of her."

He pretended to be giving the matter some serious thought. "On second thought, I suppose you're right. Guess I better come over to your place and eat those noodles where she can't see." He gave me a wink.

"I'll whip some up this weekend, promise."

"You just made an old man very happy."

"I live to serve, Frank, I live to serve."

———

My morning was pretty rotten, and it didn't improve once I got to work. Mei waved me and Martinez in as soon as she saw us.

"I understand you met with Kevin Gerrald yesterday, Miller-san. Were you aware that was in violation of the policies regarding IA investigations?"

"Yes."

"But you did it, anyway."

"Yes."

"Lucky for you, your stunt paid off. Gerrald's confession and the withdrawal of his accusations allow IA to put a nice little pin in this one. You dodged another bullet."

"I dodged a blank, Chief. He was lying from the get-go. IA would have cleared me."

"It was still a risky idea, and you're fortunate it didn't backfire on you." She turned to Martinez. "And where were you when this happened?"

"In the debrief room with Miller and the suspect."

Mei pursed her lips, took a deep breath. "I just spent the last twenty minutes listening to the Bureau's U.S. Section Chief explain to me how he just spent the last half hour getting dressed down from the Director of Vigilance. The Section Chief is not happy. I am beyond furious. Vigilance is apoplectic. All of which means someone is going to have to explain to me why you felt the need to be in the Second Lives shop, and why you felt it wasn't necessary to obtain a warrant."

Martinez opened her mouth to respond, but I waved her down.

"None of this was Martinez's fault, Chief. I got the lead, I told her we were going to check it out, and I'm the one who pulled first. If anyone's head is going to roll, it should be mine."

"You're both to blame. I assigned Martinez to you to avoid exactly these kinds of problems."

Martinez cleared her throat. "Chief, I think this Jane Doe case is linked to the soul shop somehow, which is definitely run by gokudō. Three of the Yōkai we busted had priors, and all have been connected to the Shiny Kites at one point or another. That puts us on very safe ground for making the arrests. Gokudō are strictly outside of Vigilance's jurisdiction."

"That may be," Mei countered, "but they *do* have authority to interact with Yōkai if there's reason to believe non-interaction will place lives or property at risk."

She was right. That one little clause in the federal criminal codes allowed Vigilance to put their sticky little fingers in the Bureau's business, and they abused it all the time. The Bureau of Souls had lost some gokudō collars because Vigilance over-reached, bungled the case, then pled the non-interaction clause as their defense.

"That's for situations when they have to make a snap decision," I said. "No time for proper clearance. You said it yourself, Chief.

They were working this case for months. Plenty of time to inform us of the operation as well as bring us in to help."

"They claimed they filed it," Mei continued, "but there's no record of it in the Cross-Clearance System. They're calling it a data entry error." The look on Mei's face told me she didn't buy that any more than I did. "And they're saying your actions were the trigger for the non-interaction clause."

"That's bullshit!" I couldn't stop myself. "Sorry, Chief, but that's a crock and a half."

"The Section Chief has ordered me to discipline you both. He left the specifics up to my discretion."

Here it comes: a month of desk-duty and paperwork; suspension without pay, pending further investigation; a disciplinary entry in our records. The list of possibilities was long and unpleasant.

"Effective immediately, you are both to file a detailed report about the incident. You're not allowed out of this office until I've read your reports. That's all."

I'm not sure who was more stunned, Martinez or I. We got to our feet.

"And?" I asked.

"And you better get your reports done so you can get back to working the case."

Okay, then.

THIRTY-ONE

WE'D JUST FINISHED our reports when I got a call from an outside line. Durante from Vigilance. One of the suspects from Second Lives was insisting on speaking with me. Told the Vigs to use her one and only call to contact me.

"Who is this?" Martinez asked as we walked to the DTLA Vigilance office.

"One of the female mortals from last night. Said she's got something important to tell me."

"Do you know her?"

"Never met her before in my life."

"I'm curious what she has to say."

"Makes two of us."

———

DTLA HAD CHANGED CONSIDERABLY over the past three decades. Developers leveled lots of older buildings, replaced them with condo and apartment buildings, mixed-use projects, high-end restaurants and bars, retail locations, and grocery stores. When I was a kid, much of DTLA was a ghost town after five o'clock. Now there were plenty of reasons for sticking around or driving over in the evening. And thanks to massive redevelopment efforts, there were tons of great places to live, if you could afford them.

What struck me the most was the number of high-rise buildings sprouting up all around the area. Growing up, I remember seeing DTLA's "skyline." Lots of recognizable buildings fingered their way upwards, thumbed their noses at the dangers posed by earthquakes. The Bonaventure Hotel was my favorite. A massive cylinder of glass and metal at the center, with four similar but smaller cylinders attached to it. But the kicker was the placement of the windowed elevators, which were mounted on the *outside* of the building.

I'd pictured myself riding all the way to the top, hands and forehead pressed up against the glass, watching the ground fall away as I came eye-to-eye with the other skyscrapers, the horizon receding in the distance.

Sad side note: I never got around to it.

But after the enormous influx of investment dollars, the Bonaventure wasn't just dwarfed by the super high-rise buildings, it was nearly hidden from view. And new ones were popping up along the 110 Freeway all the time. My prediction? In less than a decade, the view of DTLA's skyline from the 110 would become lost behind a wall of buildings squatting right next to the freeway.

Another prediction? The L.A. Vigilance headquarters would always be located in the tallest building in DTLA.

At the moment, that honor went to the Wilshire Grand Center, which topped out at over a thousand feet. And the tenant claiming the top five floors? None other than Vigilance. Meanwhile, the Bureau enjoyed the amenities of a three-floor building dating back to the Stone Age.

Martinez and I checked in at the lobby, filed through a security line dedicated for Vigilance visitors. Worse than flying in terms of identification checks, bag inspections, and a brutish attitude from the Vig security team. Once we were cleared, a guard escorted us up a dedicated elevator before handing us off to another guard working the second checkpoint, which was right outside the Vigilance office.

I saw a lot of visitor badges, many worn by the equivalent of Vigilance in other countries. A few Cazador de Espíritus folks. A handful of red-jacketed Royal Canadian Mounted Supernatural Ministry Police officers. Fun fact: they had the longest name in the Canadian government. Also, very few of them rode horses.

Eventually we were ushered through the outer doors and into the Vigilance office proper. A Vig took us to their detainment center, where we once again underwent a security check and clearance before being dumped in an interrogation room.

The room was standard LEO decor. Acoustical-tiled walls, a one-way glass mirror, and two security cameras quietly observing from their perches in the ceiling corners. Apparently, this was the only place Vigilance felt comfortable leaving us alone. A table and four chairs comprised the room's entire inventory.

I didn't have to prep Martinez to limit our conversations. Vigilance had a reputation for being the Hoover of intel — they sucked up as much as they could from everyone else but gave almost nothing back.

The door opened. In the opening, two Vigilance officers flanked a young woman in full restraints: handcuffs attached to a martin chain around her waist, which in turn connected to a pair of leg irons. Mid-twenties, light brown eyes, shamrock green mohawk.

Her eyes darted about the room as she entered.

One of the Vigilance officers stepped to the table, pointed at a large metal loop welded to the tabletop.

"The suspect will present her handcuffs over the restraining loop."

The woman complied, and the officer locked her cuffs to the loop.

"Can I at least sit?" she asked.

The other Vigilance officer placed a chair behind her, and she sat down. I'd seen Vigilance in action up close before, and their demeanor always seemed not just over the top but intentionally asshole-ish.

"Is it necessary to keep her cuffed to the table?" I asked.

"Until such time as the suspect is given a reduced risk assignment."

I gave up. Their house, their rules, especially since the suspect wasn't a Yōkai. I took a seat across the table from her.

"Which one of you is Miller?" the woman asked.

"Me," I answered. At least I wasn't wrong about not having met her.

Mohawk girl lifted her chin at Martinez. "Who's she?"

"My partner, Agent Martinez. And you are?"

"Vicki. Vicki with an 'i'." She glared at the Vigs. "Any chance these dickheads will give us some privacy?"

I nodded at the mirrored window. "Not seeing that happening. But maybe the officers would be willing to kindly wait out in the hall?"

They both stood still long enough that I wondered if they caught my question. Then one of them said, "We'll be outside." When the door closed, Vicki collapsed back in the chair.

"Thank God. They give me the creeps."

"They may be gone, but someone's still watching and listening."

The woman shrugged. "What I got to say, it doesn't matter. These guys couldn't find their own asses with four hands and a map." She glared at the large window, flipped off whoever was behind it.

"Given we've never met before," I said, "I'm curious why you wanted to see me."

"S'okay, here's what you need to know. That Yōkai who was killed a few days ago? She took something from the Kites. Something that's got the gokudō community all riled up."

Yeah, I know. Mikasa's soul.

But I played dumb. "What might that be?"

"Something they all have an interest in, but one gang is far more interested than any other."

"And I'm supposed to care because…?"

"Because these gangs will continue ripping the town apart until they find it. I'm talking collateral damage of the highest caliber. Unless, of course, you find it first."

"I don't even know what you're talking about, much less what I'm supposed to be looking for. How about you at least point me in the general direction?"

"I don't work pro bono, but trust me when I say the object is still out there. If the Kites or some other gang had gotten it, the streets would either be quiet or there'd be a pile-on for the person who'd found it."

I couldn't argue with her logic. Like a lot of criminal networks, the gokudō may have been united against outside forces, but they were viciously territorial when it came to their own power bases.

"How do you know all of this?"

For the first time since she entered the room, the young woman shifted uncomfortably, her eyes skittered away from me, focused on nothing.

"I cared about her."

"Who?"

"Yuri."

"Did you help her escape?"

Vicki snorted. "And what? Have my own soul caged before they tortured me to death? No Yōkai's worth that."

I gritted my teeth, ignored the implication Vicki might have sacrificed herself for a mortal but not a Yōkai.

"But you looked after her?"

A shrug. "Did what I could. Gave her extra time out of the cage. Talked her up to the gokudō, said how good she was doing. When she got out, I was relieved."

"Okay. Where is this all-important something?"

Vicki leaned forward. "Uh-uh. Not until I have guarantees. I have info, valuable info, on the gokudō. Stuff that isn't even on your radar. All yours if you get me transferred to the Bureau and promise to drop all the charges."

Man,, if I had a nickel...

"You're a mortal, Vicki. The Bureau has zero jurisdiction over you." Technically not true. I could request a transfer on the grounds Vicki had information only the Bureau could act on, that the Bureau should have purview over her. Mei invoked that right about as much as Vigilance complied with it, which was to say rarely.

And the last thing I needed to do was get into yet another pissing contest with Vigilance, which would no doubt splash all over Mei, only to find out Vicki was saying anything she could to get out of Vigilance's grip.

Vicki banged her fists on the table, the chain rattling on the metallic top.

"But I have dirt on some of the biggest gokudō activity in town! I could literally give you the head of one of the biggest bosses in L.A., served up on a silver platter. You'd be a hero. I'm talking key to the city, promotion, the whole nine yards. That's got to be worth something."

I sketched a dubious look. "Why would you want to flip on your gokudō partners?"

"You think I wanted to work there? They blackmailed me. I was as much a prisoner as the hakushi."

Having seen the soul shop's basement, I bristled at the comparison. Yuri and Vicki might have both been trapped, but one of them got to leave every night and sleep in her own home. One of them at least had the option of seeking help.

As for who Vicki was talking about, several names came to mind. The first was Kazuko "Two Tails" Eto, boss of a nekomata gokudō clan called the Deadballs. Nekomata looked like very large cats with two tails. As they got older and more powerful, they could walk around on their hind legs, cast fire spells at will, and control corpses. The Bureau had confirmed the first two capabilities and was still looking into the third.

Another possibility was Natsuko "Stiletto" Ono, who ran the all-female Kisu, a Jorōgumo gang out of San Fernando Valley. Legend said Jorōgumo were regular spiders who transformed into mortal-looking Yōkai after four hundred years and started hunting young men instead of insects. Most Jorōgumo had left that legend in the history books.

Then there was Tollerson and, of course, Mikasa. Based on what I'd seen at Second Lives, I knew Vicki meant Mikasa.

"Tell you what. You give me something right now, something I can verify, something big enough, and I'll request a transfer and a waive of charges."

I imagined the chuckling behind the mirror: *Those Bureau agents must be out of their minds if they think we'll give up this chick.*

Vicki began talking, but it wasn't English. Instead, she made a string of vowel-heavy sounds, ones mortals struggled to enunciate. A kind of private patois used by lots of the gokudō. Not exactly a secret code, per se, more of a thieves' cant.

She was also making signs in the air with her hands, an ancient form of Yōkai communication. More widespread back in Japan, the cant and sign language were rarely seen here in the states. I'd taken the optional training when I signed up, but almost never had the need or opportunity to use either.

Took me a second to understand what she was doing, because what she was saying didn't really make sense. I stopped her, made her repeat it more slowly. Then I realized why I was being thrown off. Vicki was alternating her words between the cant and the signs, one word in cant, the next in signs, the next in cant, and so on. I watched her hands while I listened to the growling, stitched it all together: *Yuri stole a gokudō soul, and she hid it somewhere in Grand Central Market.*

THIRTY-TWO

BASED ON HER EXPRESSION, Martinez had no clue what Vicki had just said. Guess she skipped that part of her Bureau training.

"How do you know this?" I asked.

In cant, Vicki replied that Yuri had texted her with the tamashi's location.

I nodded at Martinez. "Let's step outside."

"Hey," Vicki said, "what about me? We have a deal?"

"I'm going to submit the transfer request," I said.

"Don't fuck me over on this. What I told you will cost me my life on the street."

"I'll do everything I can. That's a promise. Besides, if what you told me is true, it shouldn't be a problem."

I rapped on the door. The Vigs on the other side opened it.

"We're done," I said as we stepped around them and headed for the elevator.

From behind, Vicki shouted, "Guess I'll just be here until then!"

Martinez and I made idle chitchat until we were well away from the Wilshire Grand Center building. I pulled her into a hole-in-the-wall sandwich shop.

"I need you to do me a favor, Martinez-san. A big favor."

"Okaaaaaay."

"I need you to submit a transfer request for Vicki."

"Sure, no problem." Puzzled look on her face.

"While I run an errand."

A wary look replaced Martinez's confusion. "You have got to be joking. Tell me you're joking."

"Sorry. One hundred percent serious."

"What did she say?"

I bit my lower lip. "It's hard to describe."

"Try me."

"I think Vicki just gave us a lead on the Jane Doe case, but if we don't move quickly, like right the fuck now, we may lose it. I need you to get to the office and convince the Chief we need the transfer request submitted ASAP."

"Meanwhile, you're doing what, exactly?"

"Hopefully finding something that tells me who killed the vic."

Martinez sighed, long and slow. "You're asking me to disobey a direct order."

"I'm putting my trust in my partner, who I hope now trusts that I'm telling the truth here. We have an opportunity to break the next lead on the Jane Doe case, as well as snag a valuable informant from Vigilance. If Vicki told me the truth, she could help us put a big dent in the gokudō network. But we need to get her transferred ASAP."

I didn't enjoy playing the guilt card, but I was surprised to discover I didn't feel bad about it. I really did believe everything I said, including me trusting Martinez not to turn me in.

"All right. What am I supposed to tell the Chief? She's going to wonder where you are."

"Hey, you're one of the Bureau's finest. I'm sure you'll come up with something. Just get the hell out of there as soon as you get the request submitted. Text me when you do, I'll tell you where to pick me up."

She was still wrestling with the idea. "Miller-san, this goes sideways, we're both in deep shit. Forget IA, we're going to be on the street, and that's if we're lucky."

"I wouldn't ask if I didn't think it was important."

Martinez stared at me for a few more seconds, then waved me off. "Go."

I ran.

———

I ZIGZAGGED from Wilshire and Fig on my way to Grand Central Market, picking up a cheap backpack on the way. The open-air market was a collection of eateries, mini food stores, and takeout restaurants, spanning the entire first floor of an office building that sat between 3rd and 4th streets. You could enter the Market from the north, on Hill, or come in from the south, off Broadway. Both entrances were completely open — no doors and as wide as the building. You could literally see right through the ground floor.

It started off over a hundred years ago with the staples: a butchery, fruits, egg, vegetables, seafood. Over time, it reflected DTLA's appetites, and vendors rotated in and out of the Market. A few decades ago, the owners overhauled the space into a hipster goulash of international tastes. Asian. Mexican. Americana. Italian. Greek. You name it, Grand Central Market probably had it.

Super popular for anyone working in DTLA, as it had every imaginable kind of cuisine. Predictably packed at lunch, you could easily get in and out in minutes for breakfast or dinner. Amai Ramen was my go-to place in the Market, with a close second being Beggs, which served the best breakfast bagel sandwich in town: two scrambled eggs, Swiss cheese, and block bacon with extra butter. They tossed it into a Panini press right before serving it to you. I've tried recreating it at home, could never quite match it.

Point was, I knew the Market inside and out, the entire layout and every food stall in the place. Which meant I also knew I was looking for a needle in about a hundred haystacks.

Gerrald said he'd lost sight of Yuri three or four times. She'd have had more than enough chances to stash the tamashi somewhere in the Market. Maybe she explained her situation to a sympathetic employee, convinced them to hide the cage. She also had plenty of time to ditch the tamashi when she'd temporarily given Gerrald the slip.

Vicki wasn't lying about the tamashi, according to my kitsune nose. To be more accurate, she believed it was somewhere in the Market. Through her coded cant, she'd told me Yuri thought she was being followed, and she'd hidden the cage in the Market as insurance. Afterwards, she'd called Vicki, told her that if anything happened, Vicki might be able to use the location of the tamashi as her own ticket out of the gokudō operation.

Either way, knowing the tamashi was in the Market sounded great on paper, but standing at the north entrance, I felt my hope evaporate, smoke in the wind. The place was still crowded. Plus, the soul could literally be anywhere in the thirty-thousand square foot space. And that didn't include the underground level seating.

A han of seeing would work, but there were two problems with that. I'd be drawing a lot of attention to myself and tapped out of magic long before I could have swept the entire Market. The next best idea was to use Madara as my divining rod. I'd get lots of false positive hits from every Yōkai in the place, but it was the best I could do.

I methodically worked the aisles, pretending to shop but keeping my eyes on Madara. Tamashi has insanely powerful signatures, and I'd expect Madara to flip out if we got near one. Problem was, she'd also flip out over a couple of powerful Yōkai.

I took the far-left aisle and began working that side, heading south towards the Broadway entrance. When I reached the end, I doubled back and worked the other side of the same aisle.

If Madara found something, I'd stop and wait, try to determine if she was pinging a Yōkai or something else. The process was frustratingly slow, and each minute that ticked by meant Vigilance might be that much closer to figuring out Vicki's coded message. They weren't as well-versed in Yōkai culture as the Bureau, but they weren't complete morons, either.

Or maybe Yuri confessed the location before she died. Maybe it's already long gone.

Almost thirty agonizing minutes later, I'd finished a full pass of the ground level of the Market, circled back to the half dozen stalls where I wasn't entirely sure if Madara's ping was a red herring. Another ten minutes went by, and I was beginning to fear the tamashi was, indeed, gone.

The downstairs area was less crowded, the air thicker and warmer. Doubtful Yuri would try hiding the tamashi in the pharmacy, and I already knew there weren't a ton of hiding places in the underground seating area. Mostly open space, tables, and chairs. My eyes stopped at the entrance to the ladies' restroom.

So, maybe not a ton of hiding places down here but definitely at least one.

I hadn't even touched the door, and Madara was front and center, looking for all the world like she was struggling to swim against a strong current. Inside, a couple of women were checking themselves in the mirror, another was in one of the stalls. I moved down the row, stopping at the last stall. Madara pointed up at the drop ceiling tiles. I stood on the toilet rim, poked at the tiles. One didn't move at all. Something heavy was holding it down. I awkwardly pushed aside an adjacent tile, spotted a vase-shaped object.

"Bureau of Souls," I said to the ladies who were now eyeing me in the mirror. "Nothing to worry about." They shrugged, apparently satisfied with my answer, left. I brought the vase out of the ceiling, inspected it.

A heavy, beige ceramic container wrapped with a couple of loops of thick shimenawa rope and a metric crap ton of wards inscribed on it. I didn't need to use a han of seeing to know I'd found what I was looking for.

The tamashi fit snugly in the backpack, just a matter of getting this back to the office and into Oshiro's hands to confirm whose soul was inside. I was nearly at the south exit of the Market when Madara began darting side to side. I heard a voice to my left.

"You must be part bloodhound. Well done."

Another voice to my right. "Indeed."

And for the first time since my Bureau training, I felt the full-body arc of muscle spasms in response to a Taser's electrical discharge.

Jiro and Juro each grabbed an arm, eased me to the ground as Jiro removed the backpack.

"She's having a seizure!" Juro said. "Is anyone a doctor?"

I couldn't do much more than watch and listen as Jiro parted the circle of people forming around me, walked away with the backpack in his grip.

"I'm a nurse." A male voice that soon matched up to a guy's face looking down at me. "What happened?"

"She pushed her way between me and my brother, then collapsed to the ground. I think it's a seizure or something." Juro moved out of view, disappeared into the crowd. Madara raced up and down my body, just like she had when I was first tased in training. The Bureau wanted its agents to know what it felt like to be on the receiving end of the devices. It wasn't pleasant then, and it was even less pleasant now.

Like before, Madara sped up my recovery. I had no idea how she did it, but my muscles were already loosening up, responding to my brain's commands to *Get the fuck up*.

The nurse checked my pupils. "Doesn't look like a seizure to me."

I grunted, forced myself into a sitting position, pushed the nurse's hands out of the way. My tongue was jelly, and I hurt like hell.

"Bureau. Of Souls." All I could manage through gritted teeth as I struggled to get to my feet. The nurse tried to keep me on the ground.

"Easy, easy. Let me have a look at you."

"Fine. I'm fine." I brushed his arms away, got upright, searched for the two bodyguards. "Which...way? Which way...did they go?"

Someone pointed, said, "There."

Once I was out of the Market, I spotted the pair of oni walking east along Broadway. I fell in behind them, matched their pace for two blocks. My movements were still jerky, though numbness was giving way to pins and needles. The oni walked into an underground parking lot. I eased up to the entrance, slipped around the corner, picked up my pace. The oni were walking down to the lower level, and I started jogging. My instinct said they'd make me any second. I drew my Sig.

"Bureau of Souls! Freeze!" The pair stopped, turned. My backpack dangled from Jiro's hand. "Drop it."

They didn't move. I closed the distance until we were twenty feet apart. I repeated my command, this time with my Sig pointed at Jiro's head.

"Last warning." I knew they spoke English, had heard them in the Market. But I switched to Japanese. "Drop the backpack now."

The oni lowered the pack, set it on the ground. I heard a car coming up the ramp ahead of me, hoped whoever was behind the wheel wouldn't go civilian vigilante on me. I pulled my badge from my belt, held it up, a sign to the driver that this wasn't what it looked like.

"Now back up," I said to the oni, and they did, their hands still at their sides. Their expressions were anything but intimidated. I slipped the pack over my left shoulder. "On the ground, face down."

Neither moved. The oncoming car came into view, a dark blue sedan, maybe a German luxury model. It accelerated up the ramp, and I thought it was going to run over the oni. Turns out I was the intended roadkill.

The car swerved around Jiro and Juro before turning its grill towards me. I jumped in between two parked cars, heard the crunch and grind of metal as the sedan sideswiped the row of vehicles, screeched to a halt. I was not going to let them have Mikasa's soul, but I didn't have any intention of dying in the parking deck, either.

Tapping my kitsune speed for the tiniest bump, I jumped onto the hood of the car next to me. The two oni were manifesting now and closing in. The sedan backed up, trying to get clear of the other cars. In those seconds, I vaulted across the row of vehicles until I was near the top corner of the lower level. Another small tap of speed propelled me up the ramp towards the entrance, but I knew the oni were right behind me. No need to look for the sedan, I could hear the howl of its engine.

If this spilled into the street, civilians could easily get caught up in the crossfire. Which left me with only one option: keep things in the parking deck.

I spun, went down on one knee, raised my Sig. As the car cleared the corner, I fired at the front right tire. It blew. The sedan dogged off its trajectory. The echoes boomed in the concrete deck, and I could be sure of one thing: any civilians near the entrance were going to be scrambling out of the way now.

The sedan swerved, plowed head-on into a parked minivan. I kept my Sig on the tinted passenger door, waited to see if anyone got out. Instead, the driver shifted gears, floored it. The sedan raced down the ramp in reverse. I got nothing off the temporary license plate beyond the first three characters — BX6 — before it was too far away to read. I went after it, noting the oni were now also backing down the ramp.

"Freeze!" I shouted as I moved into a sprint. The momentum of the encounter had shifted, and I leaned into it. The sedan cornered at the bottom of the ramp, sparks flying from the rim of the blown tire. Jiro and Juro ran as fast as they could for the stairwell. The sedan moved farther down into the parking deck, disappeared.

I slipped my right arm through the backpack strap, settled it squarely on my back, and tapped some kitsune speed. Faced with having to choose between the oni and the car, I chose the oni. I hit the stairwell just as I heard a door bang open above me. A dozen more steps, and I was outside, on a small street. The oni were nowhere in sight.

I called in the shooting, relayed my location and that I was on foot and in pursuit of two oni suspects. I provided descriptions of Jiro and Juro, plus the sedan. The Bureau would loop in LPD, who would add eyes and establish a perimeter around the garage. Maybe they'd pick up the sedan if I was lucky.

"Search," I whispered to Madara, and she did. I followed her back to Broadway, turned right. Pedestrians moved along the sidewalk. I didn't see the oni, but Madara kept moving, still on their trail. The honking of a horn half a block up caught my attention. Jiro and Juro were presenting again as they crossed the four-lane road. I stepped into the street, holding up my badge to the oncoming traffic. Took me a lot longer to get across than I liked, and by the time I did, the two oni were out of sight again.

I ran to where the oni had crossed, hoped the tamashi on my back was still intact. Madara picked up their trail again. We got as far as another block before Madara slowed, began darting back and forth as we approached a restaurant with a long line stretching down the sidewalk. A dozen Yōkai, some manifesting, some not. Madara didn't seem able to pick out the oni's Yōkai signature from those in the line, and she spun about, a compass surrounded by magnets.

Shit.

I'd lost the oni and, most likely, the sedan. Upside: I still had the tamashi. Downside: there was no way to prevent Mei from finding out Martinez and I had separated. I texted Martinez, told her to tell the Chief I'd intentionally given her the slip after our visit to Vigilance. At the very least, I owed her the opportunity to dodge a disciplinary writeup. I sincerely hoped she took it.

I pressed on, looking in store windows and moving up Broadway for another ten minutes before heading back to the parking deck. LPD had beaten me there, and we started coordinating logistics, everything from how much of the garage to tape off to how to methodically search it in case any suspects were still around. Under normal circumstances, I'd have been looking at a few hours at the scene plus a lot more back at the office. That was on top of yet another visit with the Procs.

A single text summons from Mei put all of that on hold.

THIRTY-THREE

"I'M SORRY, WHAT?" I couldn't cover my surprise. The Chief had called me into her office, where I braced myself to take the weight of the insubordination, but my partner had beaten me to it.

The Chief nodded at Martinez. "As incredibly dubious as her claim is, Martinez assures me you reluctantly went after the tamashi at her explicit request. She's taken full responsibility for this fiasco."

"Chief-"

"Miller-san, you are to stay within the confines of this office until I give you permission to leave. Is that understood?"

I started to object, read her face, reconsidered. "Yes." I gave Martinez an *I'm sorry* look as I left. I had tons of paperwork to complete, plus the Procs debriefing on the shooting. Hadn't even started the process for the first one. Instead of my desk, I headed for Archives SL1.

SL1 was basically one long hallway. At one end was the elevator and stairwell. At the other was our warded safe room. In between were a handful of examination rooms and a dozen small offices.

The safe room was a heavily warded space where it was theoretically okay to perform spells or examine dangerous evidence without worrying about reducing the entire building to a rubble of bricks. Or, say, release a bunch of demons onto the physical plane.

The Bureau designed the door to be hermetically sealed when necessary, and the Mirrors had reinforced the room physically and magically. When the long overdue big earthquake finally hit Los Angeles, the entire building could collapse, but the safe room should still be intact. That's what the Mirrors told me, anyway.

I found Oshiro and another Mirror, Emi Saito, in the safe room. With less than a year's experience at the Bureau under her belt, most agents considered her a rookie. They underestimated Saito at their peril. She was smart, not afraid to work hard, and got along with just about everyone, Martinez and Balingford included. She was beyond excited about the soul cage.

"This is an incredible find, Keiko. One of the oldest tamashi I've ever seen. My guess is it's been used two, maybe three dozen times. And the wards are some of the most intricate and secure I've come across. Whoever's inside, they must be important. Or powerful. Any ideas?"

"A hunch. But I'd prefer you crack it cold."

Like me, Saito was a Nikkei transplant from Japan. Unlike me, she'd leaned hard into the SoCal surfer girl lifestyle. Eternally upbeat, laid back, and not overly taken with the LEO office protocol of using last names. Saito steadfastly ignored it with everyone except Mei, and she politely requested we did the same when addressing her. Despite the more strait-laced and conformist attitude in the Bureau, Saito's good-natured personality endeared her to most of her co-workers.

"Challenge accepted." Saito alternately typed away at her laptop and scribbled in her notebook. Next to her was a large leather roll, like archaeologists used. The roll was open, revealing the top half of a variety of objects I recognized from my research on soul cages.

The tamashi rested on a lazy Susan in the center of the warded table. Several of the tabletop's kanji symbols slowly blinked, blue beacons indicating they were active. Compared to the amount of han power stored in the table, what I could cast on my own wouldn't even move the needle. The table would have buried it.

Next to the tamashi was a lunchbox-sized octopus kind of device with cords and cables, one of which was plugged into Saito's laptop. Oshiro worked at a desktop computer with a monitor attached to a moveable arm, currently pivoted to allow him and Saito to view it.

I noted several ceremonial items carefully laid out in preparation for the Bureau priest: a wooden wand tipped with thin paper streamers, a mirror, a small bowl of salt, a wide but shallow bowl of water, and a small dipper.

The L.A. Bureau's Shinto priest, Shuji Ishī, entered the safe room and began the purification process, both on the tamashi and us. Ishī was fifty-five and sported a thick wave of dark brown hair with natural highlights most women would pay three figures to have. His amiable smile, light brown eyes, and runner's body still turned a couple of heads, not all of them female.

Ishī purified his hands with the dipper and water, allowing the water to fall back into the bowl. He purified our hands, one at a time. Setting the bowl and dipper aside, he clapped his hands three times, bowed before the tamashi. The priest used the paper wand as part of an incantation to expel from the area any spirits who meant harm and to invite any o-kami who would be willing to protect us and oversee the ritual. When he finished, he collected his items and, with a deep bow, exited the room.

"If you don't want to stick around for the entire decryption process, now's the time to leave," Oshiro said to me.

"I'm good."

Oshiro sealed the door, and the Mirrors got to work. Oshiro reviewed a scrolling river of text and numbers on the monitor. Saito positioned another of the octopus cables near the tamashi, used a tool from her leather roll to calibrate the large stethoscope at the end of the cable. Saito clipped the sensor to a stand, pointed it at the vase. She flicked a switch on the box, and I heard the whisper of something electronic spin up.

I'd witnessed a tamashi box being opened once before, and I'd watched videos of the decryption process the Bureau had on file. The process was scientific in a few ways, namely that for optimum results you should be consistent and methodical in your approach. Rush things, overlook a step in the ritual, do something out of order — screwed up any little thing — and you'd either have to repeat the ritual from scratch or risk permanently damaging or destroying the soul inside.

If I was right, Mikasa's soul was inside the vase, trapped as much as any prisoner in a physical jail. I didn't know how her soul came to be in the tamashi, but I knew all too well the ramifications.

If Mikasa's physical body died right now, her soul would be stuck in the cage, unable to cross the veil to Furusato so she could begin reconstructing herself. Provided the tamashi remained intact, Mikasa could be a prisoner for all eternity.

Opinions varied — that was an understatement — but I didn't embrace the idea that a Yōkai convicted of a crime, regardless of how heinous it was, should have their soul removed and permanently stored in a Bureau vault somewhere. It was a position more than a few hardliners in the Bureau advocated, calling it the "humane" alternative to firings. If the soul continued to exist, and the potential for a Yōkai to reconstruct itself hadn't been permanently eliminated, could you still call it murder? They claimed yes.

I claimed bullshit.

It was a moral equivalency that put us on a dangerous, slippery slope. What if the world gravitated towards a "better safe than sorry" policy and started harvesting Yōkai souls "as a deterrent" and "a preventative measure?" Thanks to Madara, I wouldn't be identified if the U.S. or any other country decided Yōkai no longer had an automatic right to exist in the physical plane, regardless of whether they had committed a crime. Other Yōkai?

They could easily wake up one morning to find themselves guilty of the crime of simply existing.

So, yeah, I stuck around to watch Oshiro and Saito do their thing. They were extremely knowledgeable and talented, but they weren't infallible. I didn't want Mikasa's soul damaged or destroyed because a couple of Bureau agents accidentally fucked up. I'd brought her soul in, and I felt responsible for it.

"Here we go." Oshiro tapped at the desktop, and the river of text shifted to several panes of graphs and meters. He kept his attention on them, occasionally opening a pane for a more detailed view. Saito watched her laptop, which displayed a similar but different set of data. The process was boring and fairly technical from here on out. No incense or candles. Just the quiet hum of the computers and a warbled kind of thrumming from the table.

The Bureau had scripted the decryption process down to a bunch of sub-routines in a program, much like an autopilot on an airliner. The program caused the wards in the table to fire in the proper sequence at the right time and with the correct amount of power. Theoretically an automated process, but regs required a Mirror to monitor the progress and shut the program down if anything went sideways. We were always finding nuances with the tamashi, new twists on the storage and encryption process that required tweaks in the program.

Which was why the two Mirrors were so focused. Oshiro worked the decryption program, and Saito monitored the tamashi. If Saito noticed anything strange, she'd let Oshiro know, and they'd decide whether to halt the process.

Things moved along fine for the first hour. I switched my attention between Saito's laptop to Oshiro's monitor. The program surgically peeled away the layers of magical encryption, bit by bit. Once the soul's signature had been recorded, the Mirrors would reapply the encryption wards in a reverse procedure. The warded table supplied the necessary protection while we temporarily unwound the tamashi wards.

A flare of yellow on Saito's screen caught my attention.

"The attenuation frequency's out of bounds," I said.

"I know." Saito typed furiously, a frown on her face. I watched one of the visualizations of the program's effect on the tamashi, a single sine wave. The frequency increased, as did its amplitude. "Koji…"

"Reducing power factor by twenty-five percent," he replied.

I watched another reading on Saito's screen flash to yellow, then a third. I leaned forward for a better look.

"Wards are still getting hammered," Saito said. "I think the algorithm's parameters are off."

"Oshiro-san, what algorithm is the decrypt using?" I asked.

"Nemoto-Fujita."

"Was it tuned for micro-quantum modulations or macro?"

"Micro. The scans indicated an interweaving of the outer wards."

Parts of Saito's screen turned crimson. I looked at the data on Oshiro's monitor. Despite reducing the program's power, something was still seriously messing with the outer wards on the tamashi, a persistent pounding that would eventually cause the wards to collapse. Normally, the table's wards would shield the soul. Since the source of the problem was the decryption program itself, however, the wards wouldn't stop Mikasa's soul from being disintegrated.

"Pull up the scans," I said, trying to keep my voice calm as Saito's screen went nearly all red. Oshiro's monitor flickered, resolved into a multi-dimensional scan of the wards surrounding the tamashi. I could see the interweaving patterns he mentioned. An unusual and rarely seen technique. Interweaving the wards produced powerful but also volatile results. I didn't remember finding a lot of info on them in the Archives.

At first glance, Oshiro's algorithm choice looked good. Nemoto-Fujita would have been my call, too. So, why wasn't it working?

"There's the problem." I pointed to the numeric output of the scan. Saito had guessed correctly. It was the proper algorithm, but Oshiro hadn't properly tuned it for the encryption we'd asked it to crack. "The wards are interwoven, but they're also *inverted*. You need to-" Loud beeping from both computers. The wards on the table flared a bright blue.

We're out of time.

I bumped Oshiro aside, tapped at the screen as fast as humanly possible. Maybe a little faster. Even if we killed the decrypt, the program would take several seconds to fully wind down. The outer wards wouldn't sustain the barrage for that long. I pulled up the algorithm's parameters, tweaked the frequency of the modulation and offered a heartfelt plea to Inari.

I held my breath, watched one panel on Saito's screen turned yellow, then two more. The panels slowly blinked from red to yellow to green. When the beeping stopped, I stepped back from the monitor.

"My apologies, Oshiro-san. I should not have taken over without asking first."

Oshiro tapped at the monitor, checked various diagnostics. He nodded his head once. "You were correct. I'm grateful for your intervention. I overlooked the inversion."

"It was easy to do," I started, "the only reason-"

"You're more knowledgeable about tamashi than I am. That's the reason." He didn't look angry or upset. If anything, he looked impressed. I opened my mouth to object, but he stopped me. "It's a fact, not an opinion. If you were not here, her soul would be gone."

"I was just trying to help."

"And you did. Shall we continue?"

Watching a soul being released from a tamashi was one of the most beautiful sights I've ever experienced. Impossible to put into words, it's far more of an emotional experience than a sensory one. You felt reborn afterwards, filled with awe.

We weren't releasing Mikasa's soul, though. Just lifting the wards long enough to snapshot the soul's signature. It took another two hours for the decrypt program to work its magic. Oshiro and Saito adjusted the algorithm's parameters when the decrypt started to run astray, nudged the process back on track. We watched the final subroutine finish its work. Three soft tones from Oshiro's computers confirmed the process was successful.

Oshiro saved the data from the decrypt, pulled up the snapshot program. "Now for the signature. Emi, would you, please?"

Saito nodded, moved a couple more of the sensor cables into place around the tamashi. She pulled tools from her leather roll, calibrated the sensors. Thirty minutes later, we looked at the soul's signature on the monitor, a two-dimensional representation of a living being's multidimensional soul. The slowly spinning spirograph was the equivalent of a soul's heartbeat, unique as a snowflake or a fingerprint. A few minutes later, our database found a confirmed match.

Mikasa.

THIRTY-FOUR

I ASKED Oshiro and Saito to keep Mikasa's soul under wraps for now, leave it listed as unknown. I also asked if they could help me with a little project. Oshiro was dubious, Saito not as much.

"Give us a day or two, I think we can have something ready to test."

"You'll have hours, not days," I replied. "This is the very definition of a rush job."

"What are you planning, Miller-san?" Oshiro asked me.

"Less you know, the better, but here's a hint: two gokudō, one soul."

I went upstairs to find Martinez. She was quiet. Not angry, just super subdued. Made it clear she wanted to finish her report of our trip to Vigilance and our subsequent insubordination. Write now, talk later. Maybe.

I felt like shit, even though we'd recovered Mikasa's soul. I should have been elated. This could be the leverage we needed to crack the case. It certainly explained why the gokudō had been so hot to find Yuri. Also explained what Mikasa had been hiding at the Bowl.

For now, all I could think about was the hit to Martinez's

record, the speed bump on her way to Mei's office. Said speed bump being me.

I finished my report, and when the Procs worked their way through the Pen towards my desk, I didn't bother trying to put them off. Nearly three hours later, the Procs called it quits and cut me loose.

Even with the partial license plate, LPD came up empty on its search for the blue sedan that tried to turn me into roadkill. The APB on Jiro and Juro was also proving to be equally unproductive.

I found Martinez at her desk. When she didn't look up, I cleared my throat.

"Hey, partner."

"Hey." She continued typing.

"I was going to get something to eat. You hungry?"

"Not really."

"I've been thinking about a way to bring all of this to a resolution. Might be able to sideline two gokudō bosses and confirm the Jane Doe's killer, all in one go."

"Great." Still typing.

"Come on, Martinez-san, I told you to hang this on me."

She looked up. "No, what you asked me to do was lie to the Chief. Lie about me intentionally disobeying a direct order."

Fair enough.

"I thought I was saving you from any fallout. But I see your point. I'm sorry. I really didn't mean to put you in the crosshairs."

Martinez sighed. "Yeah, I know. It just sort of happens when you're around." No edge to the statement. I took the hit without complaint.

"I'll make this right," I said. "I promise."

"There's nothing to make right. I agreed on letting you go. I'm a grown adult. I can handle the consequences of my actions, okay?"

I felt even more miserable. She wasn't playing the martyr, and she was decent enough not to say *I told you so*. Stoically accepting her fate without deflecting blame, not asking for or expecting any help. And I ruffled her feathers by implying she needed my help. That hurt the most.

"Okay. Well, I'm still hungry, and I'm pretty sure you need to eat, too. What do you feel like? My treat."

We settled on takeout from Katsu Prime, a tonkatsu place in Little Yōkai, and hunkered down in a briefing room. I laid out my idea as we ate.

"Mei will never sign off on that, Miller-san. No way she's going to give a gokudō boss her soul back."

"Even if it means losing the chance to catch Yuri's killers and take down the Crazy Nate? Not to mention cooling down the scavenger hunt that's tearing up Los Angeles? What's not to like about this?"

"With Mikasa's soul under our care, she's not likely to step out of line any time soon. And if we can knock together a solid case, she'll be deported, maybe banished. Her soul is leverage we can use. That's a sure thing. You taking her soul out of Archives is just asking for trouble. What if you lose the soul? What if we don't catch the bigger fish? The optics on either scenario will make it look like the gokudō have our office on their payroll."

Too true, that. The prejudice against Yōkai wasn't limited to the spirits themselves. Plenty of conspiracy theorists adamantly believed the Bureau was a cover, a way of secretly smuggling unstamped Yōkai into countries across the world. Apparently, the end goal was total subjugation of the humans. Or a complete purge of all mortals. Or something like that.

I'd tried teasing some coherence out of the blogs and social media posts. None of it really made much sense if you spent more than five minutes thinking about it, but that didn't stop the tinfoil hat crowd from spinning up their crocks of spiritist shit.

"It doesn't have to be made public. I think it's a risk worth taking."

"Sorry, I'm just not sold on this," Martinez said. "We can punt

Mikasa across the veil when we have a case. In the meantime, we keep going after Tollerson. I think we can nail them both without taking the chance that Mikasa gets her soul back."

"All right, how about this, then?" I laid out my second idea.

"Oshiro said he could do it?"

"Well, Saito said she could."

"You'll still need the Chief's sign-off."

"No sweat." I sounded far more confident than I felt.

My idea intrigued Mei, and she gave me the green light.

"Miller-san, I want the terms of the release of Mikasa's soul to be crystal clear. She needs to be a key component to bringing solid charges against Tollerson. If she doesn't deliver actionable evidence, there will be no deal."

"I understand. Chief, there's one more thing."

"Does it have anything to do with Martinez?" I nodded. "You wish to tell me she was lying to protect you. That you were the one who proposed splitting up. That I should look the other way when an agent disobeys a direct order, then lies about whose idea it was."

"When you put it like that,..look, Chief, I don't want any blowback on her record for my insubordination. Put me on leave, take me off the case, whatever you want. Just don't punish Martinez."

"Hmmm. A few days ago, I never would have thought I'd see you provide cover for Martinez."

That makes two of us, Chief.

"What can I say? I'm as surprised as you. But I'm serious. Please don't ding her record on account of me. It's not fair."

"I'll consider your request."

Which was about as close to *you got it* as I'd hoped to get. Now I just needed to convince Mikasa to go along with my plan.

———

IT HAD TAKEN QUITE a bit of tree shaking to reach the gokudō boss earlier. This time around, I got her on the phone within an hour. I ran the deal past Mikasa: she sets up a meet with me and Toller-son, at which we get him to talk enough about Yuri's murder for me to charge him, and in exchange, Mikasa gets her soul back, no strings attached.

"Come on, Mikasa, where's the downside here? The Bureau gives you back your soul in exchange for helping us nail Tollerson on the Jane Doe murder. You won't have to wear a mic, because I'll be right beside you. Just get him to talk. We get a solid case, you get your soul, and L.A. has one less gokudō boss to worry about. Everyone wins."

"Forgive my reticence to take you at your word, mortal."

"Your soul is on its way to Kyoto this time tomorrow if you can't get me to Tollerson. I can't hold things up for much longer. Help me, and I'll do everything in my power to keep your soul here in the states."

"I'll need proof." I texted her pictures of the tamashi and the screen caps of her signature. "Give me an hour."

Thirty minutes later she texted me an intersection in DTLA and a time to meet.

————

"THIS IS WAY TOO LOOSE, MILLER," Martinez said in a low voice. "Not nearly enough prep time. Plenty of ways this operation can go sideways, and you'll be alone, no support."

I was touched Martinez seemed more concerned about me than about the outcome of the op. And I was increasingly inclined to believe her. Walking in to Tollerson's den with zero Bureau support? With Mikasa at my side? My initial enthusiasm for the idea was rapidly waning.

"Well, you do your job, and I won't be."

She grimaced, turned back to the board on the wall. Mei had tapped the L.A. office's most senior agent, Daniel Yoshida, to organize the op. That gave me no small amount of confidence, as

Yoshida had been in the L.A. office for almost thirty years. He knew the Bureau, and he knew this town.

Like me, he was also a hafu, though his father was Japanese, his mother White. His mentoring and guidance since I joined the Bureau had been a bright spot in my career.

Knowing Martinez was in the mix made me feel better, too. Our past friction aside, she was an outstanding agent.

Yoshida aimed a laser pointer at a map on the wall.

"Mikasa will pick up Agent Miller at Figueroa and 4th at 7pm. Miller will have the tamashi with her. No wire or tracker. We can use GPS to track her phone, but we can't count on that. We have no confirmation on where the meet with Tollerson is or even if there's a meet. Mikasa might skip the get-together and make a play for the tamashi."

Said play ending with me punching the veil.

"But," I said, "we've got an angle to mitigate that threat." Thankfully, no one asked for details. It was a pretty weak angle.

Yoshida used the laser to point out five X's marked on the map. "Tollerson has three known residences, and his companies own at least two buildings in the area. He might go for neutral territory, though that's unlikely. Bottom line: we could wind up anywhere. Ground transportation to the meet is most likely. Might be a lone vehicle or a caravan and anything from coupes to SUVs. After that, air and water transport are a possibility. Tollerson has a private jet at LAX and a large yacht moored at Marina del Rey. We can pull in an airship from LPD or Vigilance if necessary. For now, we're planning on two teams, each driving unmarked cars and trading off pursuit of Miller's transport vehicle. Once Miller's at the meet, teams will form up, assess the environment, and proactively work the situation."

The other agents nodded, picking up on the underlying message: *you're going to have to improvise*. Improvisation was a deadly ingredient for ops like this. The team asked a series of logistical questions, most of which we didn't have concrete answers for. After thirty minutes, the questions stopped, and Yoshida dismissed the group.

"You sure about this?" Martinez asked me.

"About as sure as I'm likely to show up tomorrow in a pair of Jimmy Choo's."

"You pull this off, I'll buy you a pair myself."

THIRTY-FIVE

I DIDN'T WAIT LONG for Mikasa to pick me up. A large white SUV rolled up to the corner. The back-passenger door swung open. I saw Mikasa on the far side of the middle row, climbed in next to her. Two Yōkai, in mortal form, were in the front, plus two more in the back row. Mikasa patted me down. I'd left my Sig at the office, knowing it wouldn't stay with me for long.

The SUV headed west, towards the 110 freeway.

"I want to see the tamashi." Mikasa eyed the backpack at my feet.

"Knock yourself out."

I put the tamashi on the seat between us. Mikasa placed a hand on top of it, closed her eyes, started casting a han. Minutes later, she opened her eyes, pupils massively dilated behind half-closed lids. Reminded me of how some Yōkai reacted to Crimson Candy.

She tapped the driver's seat. "To the restaurant." Her words came out like slushed ice.

We passed under the freeway, moved along Wilshire.

"Mikasa-san, let's go over how things will unfold at the meet. I need you to-"

Mikasa placed a finger across her lips. "Shhhhhh."

The itachi in the front passenger seat turned around, aimed a large handgun in my face. The barrel was less than a foot from my nose, and the barrel looked insanely large.

"Agent Miller, please tell me why I shouldn't dump your body on the side of the road."

So much for trust, then.

I had a pitch ready to go if I thought Mikasa was going to cut and run. A mix of fact and fiction. Hopefully, she'd swallow it all.

"Well, the rampage you and your fellow gokudō have been on for the last couple of weeks pushed the mortals and Yōkai over the edge. Know what a scorched earth policy is? The Bureau got clearance from Vigilance, the Governor, and the Mayor to fill the Valley with Crazy Nate bodies if I come back with so much as a hangnail. The gloves are off. No more due process, no more adjudication. Agents can execute sentence in the field and at their personal discretion."

"You're lying. The mortals would never go that far."

"You underestimated just how many of them hate you. Not just the gokudō, Yōkai, too. A lot of mortals are tired of the bullshit the gokudō brings to the shores, and they'd be happy to have the lot of you gone, regardless of how it's done." Here I was again, talking like I wasn't a Yōkai myself, lying about my dual identities. In some ways, I had more in common with Mikasa than the agents at the Bureau.

Now, the bit about the scorched earth policy approval was grade-A bullshit. The bit about some mortals hating all Yōkai, sadly, wasn't.

My life hung in the balance of the next few seconds, wholly dependent on whether Mikasa would buy my outrageous claim. And it was outrageous, a total fabrication, but one she wouldn't have time to verify until it was too late.

"All right, agent. My soul for Tollerson." The Yōkai in front faced forward, and the others relaxed a bit. I returned the tamashi to the backpack. Mikasa didn't look away until I'd zipped up the backpack.

"Good. Let's talk about what I need you to do when we're in front of Tollerson." I ran down a series of protocols and contingencies, what Mikasa should and shouldn't do, what she could and couldn't say. What to do if things went south during the meet. How we'd handle her soul if things went well.

I also told her about my plan to use the tamashi with Tollerson, warned her not to give things away. "No matter what I say, just go with it. Don't react, okay?"

She spent most of the time staring out the window, offered the occasional acknowledgment only if I pressed her for it. She wasn't distracted so much as disinterested. I chalked it up to her knowing how close she was to getting back her soul.

The SUV pulled up in front of a Cuban restaurant, stopped at the valet stand. A high-end establishment, one I'd heard about but never visited. I resisted the urge to look for Martinez's or Yoshida's unmarked cars as I got out. I slipped the backpack over a shoulder and followed the Yōkai into the restaurant, two of the Crazy Nate trailing me.

Mikasa walked past the hostess stand, across the dining floor, and into the kitchen. Kept going until we hit the emergency exit in the back. An employee used a key to turn off the fire alarm, and Mikasa pushed open the door. Two large black Mercedes sedans idled in the alley behind the restaurant. The back door of the lead car opened. Mikasa gestured at the vehicle.

"After you," she said. I had little choice. She got in after me, and the Mercedes pulled away. Mikasa was smart, no question about it. I shouldn't have been surprised at this kind of elaborate deception, but she had a few more tricks up her sleeve.

"Don't bother," she said when I pulled out my cell phone. "Only authorized devices will work in here."

Sure enough, I had zero signal on my cell. Martinez would have been tracking it but not accurately enough to register what happened until it was too late. I'd be miles away and trapped in a mobile Faraday Cage by then. Martinez had been right about me winding up on my own.

I put my phone away, kept a casual attitude.

"So, how did Tollerson manage to get your soul?"

Mikasa scowled. "Turned one of my Nate against me."

"I'm guessing they lost their club membership privileges."

The sneer on Mikasa's face was predatory. "Permanently. As did a few others whose sole job was to protect me from this kind of treachery."

She frowned, looked away. I think she'd said more than she meant to. No doubt about the animosity between her and Tollerson, and it went far beyond the typical rivalry between two gokudō gang bosses. The irony of Mikasa being shocked by Tollerson's actions was amusing, if only because I was absolutely certain she had tried the same thing herself. She was mad he'd succeeded first.

Less amusing was her admission to killing a fellow Yōkai. On reflection, I'd missed the importance of that confession.

"Mikasa-san, you may want to consider your words a bit more carefully."

She smiled, and my kitsune nose twitched. I didn't like how she was acting, any more than I liked being cut off from my support team. I stowed the anxiety, focused on the aspects of the situation I still had control over.

"Do you consider yourself to be lucky, Agent Miller?" Mikasa asked.

"Don't really think about it all that much."

"So much of our lives turn on chance, so many of our high points and low points are the result of random encounters."

"I suppose. You planning on having a random encounter tonight?"

"I think one of us is going to be very lucky tonight."

THIRTY-SIX

AFTER PULLING out of the alley, the two Mercedes got on the 110S and then the 405S. Yoshida's map showed Tollerson's homes, one of which was in Venice. We were headed in that direction, though the knowledge did me little good. No way for me to notify the support teams, and whatever was going to happen tonight would be over long before another agent got to the house.

We stopped in front of the driveway, and I offered a prayer to Inari. As an afterthought, I offered one to Hachiman, too. Figured it couldn't hurt.

Electric gates parted, allowed the two cars to pull straight into the open garage. Mikasa waited until the garage door had closed before turning to me. She held out a small grey bag.

"Your phone. Tollerson doesn't allow them anywhere near him. You can have it back when we're done." I handed it to her. She turned it off, dropped it in the bag, left the bag on the seat. "Let's go."

I stepped out, the backpack in my hand. A couple of manifesting Kites stood by an elevator. Mikasa had brought three of her Nate with her, and they formed up in front and behind her. They remained in their mortal forms. My guess was they didn't want to lose the height advantage.

The kotengu Kites inspected my backpack, patted me down. They did the same to the Nate.

"This way," one of the Kites said, and directed us to an elevator. They let us ride up alone. When the elevator doors opened on the first floor, two more Kites were waiting for us. The house was super modern, fairly new construction or a recent remodel from the studs on up. The floor we were on was elevated ten feet off the ground outside. Composed of nearly all glass, the two-story west wall offered a gorgeous view of the sunset, purples and pinks giving way to the perpetually muddy grey that was as close to night as Los Angeles ever got.

Tollerson sat behind a desk composed of a steel frame and a thick, solid glass top. Music — Bossa Nova? — floated in from somewhere. Jiro and Juro flanked Tollerson, and I counted off four more Kites in the room. Jiro and Juro were presenting as mortal, but the other Kites were in their true kotengu form. Madara had pinged everyone except Tollerson as Yōkai.

Going just by the numbers, Tollerson tipped the power scale by five and that wasn't counting the two Kites in the garage. Good bet he had more kotengu around and out of sight, but I had a hunch Mikasa wasn't nearly as outnumbered as she appeared.

Tollerson beamed as we walked in. He stood, his arms stretched out. If he'd been closer, I'd have thought he was asking for a hug.

"Mikasa-san, I can't tell you what a pleasant surprise it was to receive your call. Please, come in." He moved to one of two large chairs near the window, sat down. Mikasa took the other chair. I walked closer but remained standing. Madara painted a small yellow box on the bookcase behind Tollerson's desk.

Yuri's soul?

Our intel indicated Tollerson's strings were being pulled by a gokudō back in Japan, a kotengu named Hatobou, who reported to yet another gokudō. But the fact that Tollerson had been able to command the respect of the Shiny Kites said a lot about his powers of persuasion.

Tollerson's swath of wavy black hair over coal-colored eyes and an easy smile were disarming. A friendly face, one you wanted to trust. One that put you at ease. He looked even more at home in the beach house with his ivory linen shirt and jeans.

"Who's your guest, Mikasa-san? I don't believe she's part of your regular retinue."

"You know my name, Tollerson," I said. "And I'm the one who asked Mikasa to set up this meet."

Slight raise of Tollerson's eyebrows, his mouthed formed a silent "oh." Nearly nonplussed, and his two oni bodyguards didn't flinch a bit.

"Yes. Miller. Rings a bell somewhere. I believe you're the first Bureau agent I've hosted here. May I offer you something to drink? I have an extraordinarily talented tea master on site." He addressed Mikasa directly. "I also have a fresh batch of honeysickle if that's appealing."

Honeysickle was a super-sweet, brewed beverage, supposedly hard to make, as it required ingredients from both sides of the veil. Kama itachi loved the stuff. Common wisdom held their affinity for the drink inspired its name, which included a reference to the blade-like appendages the itachi could sprout when manifesting.

The Yōkai shook her head. "No. Just want to get this over with."

"It's so rare that we sit down like this, Mikasa-san. I welcome the chance to clear the air, as it were. We needn't constantly be at each other's throats." Mikasa looked ready to claw Tollerson's eyeballs out. Barely restrained rage. I hoped she wouldn't blow this. Tollerson turned to me. "Though I believe our guest from the Bureau might welcome our continued self-inflicted fighting."

I shrugged. "The last couple of weeks haven't been all that bad. Except when the collateral damage started taking a toll on the innocent mortals and Yōkai."

Tollerson adopted a sympathetic expression. "A regrettable outcome, truly. And if I may, such eruptions of violence would be far less likely if my peers chose to pursue more agreeable under-standings amongst themselves." Said to me, meant for Mikasa. "So, Agent Miller. Mikasa mentioned you had some questions for me."

"In a manner of speaking." I pulled the tamashi out of the backpack.

Show time.

"I have here the soul of a Yōkai killed earlier this week. Foren-sics has traced it back to a soul shop we busted last night. A shop we can connect to you." I watched Mikasa out of the corner of my eye, hoped she'd listened to me in the SUV.

A bemused grin spread across Tollerson's face. "What a fasci-nating bit of fiction."

It wasn't all fiction, but I was so far out on a limb, I was nearly touching the ground. "Fact is, we've got nearly a dozen counts against you. You confess to half of them, we'll drop the others."

"I never went to law school, but I believe you have to charge me with something before we can begin any kind of plea bargain-ing. Aren't you jumping the gun on this?"

Something was wrong. Tollerson was far too comfortable, too relaxed, and Mikasa was on her feet, pacing slowly around the room, eyes on the tamashi.

"I'll run down the list if you like. Might even let you choose which ones to toss. Call it professional courtesy," I said.

"Very generous of you. However, I'm afraid I won't be confessing to anything tonight, least of all to killing some piece of trash hakushi."

Bingo.

"Maybe you didn't pull the trigger, but you ordered it, Tollerson."

"Saying something doesn't make it so, Agent Miller. You've got no proof. Worse, you've overplayed your hand."

Mikasa stopped in front of me, put her hands on the tamashi. "I'll take that now."

My hands and arms went numb, my legs refused to function, and I collapsed to the ground.

THIRTY-SEVEN

I KICKED myself for not seeing this coming. No wonder the Kites had barely reacted to the tamashi. And Mikasa must have placed a han on the tamashi box when she was checking it in the car. She just needed me to be stupid enough to hold it when she fired off the spell.

"Were you followed?" Tollerson asked Mikasa.

"No. And her phone's been bagged."

"Well, I suppose this is where I thank you for your help, Mikasa. I'm going to enjoy dispatching this agent."

A hesitation. Mikasa held up a hand. "Won't that just cause more problems? She said the mortals have taken the Bureau off their leash. If she's hurt-"

"Lies, Mikasa-san, lies. Just like her ability to connect me with that hakushi or the soul shop. They've got nothing on me. I'm safe."

The room came into focus from my floor-level view. Tollerson and Mikasa stood over me. Madara was doing the same thing she'd done when I was tased, flicking up and down my arms. My fingers started tingling. I'd still be outmatched, even if I was armed and standing. But if I could surprise them...

Patience.

Mikasa cradled the tamashi, moved out of my sight.

"Now," I heard her say.

Behind me, sounds of shuffling and a wary, "What the fuck?" In front of me, a look of surprise on Tollerson's face. He pulled a gun from inside his jacket.

"Mikasa-san, you're about to step off an extremely high ledge. Last I checked, itachi can't fly."

I couldn't turn my head just yet, but Madara had started working on my legs, which were feeling like an acupuncturist's pin cushion. Mikasa's voice floated in from across the room.

"I don't need to fly to put you in your place, mortal."

Tollerson looked between Mikasa and me before breaking into a laugh. "That's not your soul. I've still got it locked up."

"Now you're the one full of lies, Tollerson. I tested it. It's my signature. It's my soul."

Tollerson cleared his throat. "I don't know what she told you or what you think is in that tamashi, but I assure you, I've still got your soul. We found the hakushi who stole it. Jiro and Juro grabbed her from a downtown motel." He turned to me. "And for what's it's worth, yes, I had the little bitch killed. Sucked her soul, too, for stealing from me. Mikasa-san, if you want your soul back, you need to choose your next actions very, very carefully."

I gave Tollerson props for his Oscar-worthy performance. If I hadn't known Mikasa's soul was in Archives, I'd have believed him.

"Mikasa-san," I said, "I found your soul at the Grand Central Market. The Yōkai hid it there after she took it from Tollerson's shop. If Tollerson really had lost your soul, you think he'd admit that?"

"She's lying!" Tollerson screamed. "Your soul isn't in that tamashi. I'm telling you, I still have it."

"I'm willing to chalk up your betrayal as a momentary loss of logic, Mikasa-san," I said. "We have a deal on the table, and I'm not backing out of my side. You give me Tollerson, the Bureau gives you back your soul, and the Crazy Nate don't have to go searching for a new boss tomorrow."

Tollerson's expression morphed to something decidedly unfriendly as he learned of Mikasa's betrayal. I took a moment to savor his surprise before he turned his charm back on.

"There is zero chance she'd let that happen. Please, Mikasa-san, just leave. I'll dispose of her body, and we'll go back to our original arrangement."

Despite a laudable performance, Tollerson's face didn't have the same comfortable confidence from a few minutes ago. The room went silent.

Now.

I leaned on my kitsune ability for a slight boost in speed. Disarming Tollerson wasn't hard, but by the time I wrestled the gun from him and taken in the room, I found myself standing between Tollerson and the other Yōkai. Mikasa had retreated to a corner of the room near the beachfront window, her three Nate standing guard.

Jiro and Juro had manifested. The two oni were closing in on the Nate, one on each side of the sofa. Two Kites, the ones who had been closest to Mikasa, were down but moving. The remaining two Kites were coming at Mikasa, boxing her entire crew in to the corner, and I saw the pair of Kites from the garage tumble into the room to my right.

Mikasa was in mortal form, but her crew had gone full itachi. Weasels with sickle blades for hands and feet, many of them tinged in red.

I held out my hands, as much to protect Tollerson as to defuse the situation.

"Wait! No one has to die here tonight! Mikasa-san, I'm giving you one last chance. Let me take Tollerson in, book him through the Bureau, and you can head back to the valley."

The itachi leader shook her head. "Tollerson has incurred debts that must be paid. I will claim my payment before sunrise." She patted the tamashi, her eyes tracking back towards me. "I will have my revenge."

The three itachi slid their blades across each other, knives being sharpened before the butchering began again. Behind me, Tollerson tapped my shoulder.

"Agent, I'm turning myself in. I'm confessing to the murder of the hakushi Yōkai. I seek the protection of the Bureau and-"

"Tollerson, shut your fucking mouth and stay behind me." He did. I looked at Mikasa. "So, I'm supposed to hand him over to you? Just step aside and let you give him a slow and painful death? That about it?"

Mikasa smiled. "That or we'll simply leave one more corpse behind. I'm fine either way."

Would it be so bad to let Mikasa take out Tollerson and the oni? What if I did just walk out? Or simply wait until Mikasa had killed the Kites and then arrested her?

Yuri's face floated in front of me, her last hours on the physical plane certainly spent in fear and pain.

Gokudō like Mikasa and mortals like Tollerson were the source of so much pain and suffering in Los Angeles. Wouldn't this city be better off if they never saw the light of day again? Wouldn't that serve the Bureau's purpose? Hell, much as I hated to admit it, wouldn't Vigilance approve?

Really, who'd have blamed me for letting the gokudō take themselves out?

THIRTY-EIGHT

TURNED out that was a long list. For starters, Pop, Mei, Martinez.

And me.

"Sorry, Mikasa-san, can't do that."

"As you wish."

The tension in the room snapped, releasing the stored energy and putting everyone in motion. Jiro engaged the Nate between him and Mikasa. Juro took on another Nate, while the third itachi closed on the two Kites from the elevator. The two Kites from the garage took one look at the room and came for Tollerson, who I heard move to his desk, which was behind me and to my left.

I thought my sitrep training would have ensured I'd clocked every threat.

I was wrong.

Thankfully, Madara darted around, pointing furiously to my left. That's when I caught the flash of blue streaking towards the window.

I jumped back and right, closed the distance between me and Tollerson, heard the shattering of thick glass, smelled the salty tang in the cool evening air off the ocean. In the microseconds afterwards, I saw who the party crasher was.

Inari's nine tails. Goth Guy.

I got to Tollerson as he was reaching into his desk drawer, grabbed his collar, jerked him back behind me. My gun swung towards the approaching kotengu Kites. I'd already seen it wasn't a han-forged weapon. Not much use against a Yōkai but not entirely useless, either.

"Freeze!" I ordered as the first kotengu got within ten feet. They didn't, and I fired three rounds into their chest. The kotengu doubled over, stumbled back, tangled up the kotengu behind them. The pair were out of the fight for a few seconds, no more.

I scanned the room. Jiro was still standing, fighting off the nimble attacks of his itachi opponent through sheer mass. Juro seemed to be faring similarly, but one of the Kites next to him had gone down. The remaining kotengu Kite squared off against a wounded and bleeding itachi.

The explosion of the shot behind me was normal, but I caught the telltale blue glow of a han-forged weapon. Tollerson must have had it in his desk drawer. A couple of thoughts raced through my head.

How the fuck did Tollerson get his hands on a han-forged weapon? No one outside the Bureau is allowed to have one.

Also, *Do not end up on the wrong side of that barrel, Miller.*

The bleeding itachi bent over like they were looking for a dropped contact lens. Tollerson's gun sounded three more times, and the itachi went down. Their kotengu opponent moved in, delivered a brutal assault on the prone figure.

I swung my weapon towards Tollerson, closed the distance. He tried aiming at me. Bad idea. Threatening a Bureau agent with lethal force opened up a whole new list of options in terms of how I could legally respond. But I had the two kotengu from the garage coming up behind me, I sensed it. Not enough time to disarm Tollerson before his Kites got to me. I knocked his arm aside, spun him around, turned him into a shield between me and the kotengu. I put my pistol to his temple.

"Drop the gun, Tollerson!" He did, tossing it away. It hit the floor, gave a single bowling ball bounce. I aimed my gun at the two kotengu. They slowed to a stop. "Tell them to back off."

"Move!" Tollerson ordered. The kotengu did. Stalemate for now.

I dragged Tollerson backwards, into the southeast corner of the room but didn't let go of his collar. Juro launched an itachi into the air. The itachi weasel cartwheeled into the vaulted ceiling before tumbling squarely on Tollerson's desk. The glass top shattered from the impact, distracting the two garage Kites standing next to it.

Across the room, Mikasa knelt in her corner, casting a spell on the tamashi.

Jiro and the remaining kotengu managed to pin their itachi opponent. The oni gripped them by a leg, repeatedly smashed them on the floor until he noticed Goth Guy.

They exchanged words, unintelligible to me with the melee still going on in the rest of the room. Jiro swung a haymaker at the nikusui. A huge mistake. The attack was so telegraphed, Goth Guy casually leaned to the side a few inches, let the momentum of the swing bring the oni in closer.

Goth Guy delivered a flurry of attacks on the oni's neck and head. Jiro swayed, went down to one knee. The itachi that had been Jiro's rag doll staggered to their feet and began methodically slicing up the oni. The kotengu edged away from the fight, circled around to the safety of the two Kites from the garage.

The nikusui turned to Juro, who was looking for his next opponent. The oni let out a rumble of a shout, launched himself at the nikusui. Goth Guy sidestepped Juro like a bullfighter. I swear he even gave a little flourish of his hand as he did. Juro stumbled forward, crashed into one of the sofas, went down. With Juro on the ground, it wasn't hard for Goth Guy to deliver the next attack.

But he moved smoothly and insanely fast, almost too fast for me to see the punches and claw attacks. Juro kicked out at the nikusui, kept missing. He swung an arm, which knocked Goth Guy off long enough for Juro to get to his feet. The last itachi standing in the room besides Mikasa attacked the oni from behind, sliced his neck. A burgundy spray misted the air as the massive Yōkai collapsed.

The tide of the fight had turned almost instantly. The trio of Kites moved in between Goth Guy and me. There was blood in the air — literally — and I thought nothing would stop the slaughter until only one side remained standing.

Still, I tried, shouted for everyone to freeze, begged for them to stop. No dice.

The three kotengu squared off against the nikusui and the itachi. A noble effort, if not futile. I knew the fight was over before it had even started. The itachi were quick, which kept them in the fight longer.

"You don't want to fight me," the nikusui said. "You want to leave, go someplace far away." He was using his thrall, charming the Kites into believing what he said. "Go. Now. Get in your car and drive until you run out of gas."

The three kotengu exchanged glances. The nikusui's thrall was working.

"Don't listen to him!" Tollerson screamed when he belatedly realized what was happening.

"Go on," the nikusui urged. "It's okay." He made a shooing gesture, and the kotengu walked out. Tollerson ordered them to stay put, cursed at them, threatened them. All to no avail. The pair were under the thrall of the nikusui until it wore off.

"Noooooo!" Mikasa howled from the corner. She held out the tamashi like it was a rabid animal, stared at me. "How is this possible?"

"I told you, Tollerson doesn't have your soul. I do. Back at the Bureau office."

"But this…this is my signature!"

"Trust me, it's an empty tamashi."

"How?"

"Bureau secret, but the only way I could have done it was if I already had your actual soul."

She dropped the tamashi, started crossing the room. "Give it to me. You promised."

"I said if you got Tollerson to confess to the murder, you'd get back your soul. Instead, you double-crossed me and then tried to kill Tollerson."

Her betrayal didn't necessarily mean the deal was off, though. In a weird way, she'd upheld her end. I had a confession from Tollerson. Plus, one or two of the Yōkai in the room might turn on Tollerson, affirm his confession.

"Come on, Mikasa-san, cut your losses. Let me heal these Yōkai."

The gokudō eyed the carnage, stepped over the fallen itachi, oni, and kotengu. She seemed defeated, unable to understand how things had turned out this way. She knelt down, stroked the pelt of the itachi Tollerson had shot. Their eyes rolled up lazily, met hers, went white.

Mikasa looked slowly around the room, her gaze snagging on the han-forged gun.

Oh, shit.

"Get that for me." The words were barely out of Mikasa's mouth, and Goth Guy was already in motion. Unless I released Tollerson, I had no chance of getting the weapon before the nikusui did. I cranked off a couple of warning rounds. Goth Guy scooped up the gun with a speed that rivaled my own kitsune powers, tossed it to Mikasa. She hefted it in her hand.

"Agent, I know what will happen to me, and I will not become a plaything for you and your kind. I'll be back, one way or another, but it will be on my terms."

The Sig came up, barrel under her chin. She gave me a half smile before pulling the trigger. Once. Twice. A third time, and she crumpled to the floor.

Seconds swelled, the ringing in my ears not quite blocking out the crash and the surf across the beach. I felt the punch to my gut, the guilt of Mikasa's death.

She'd be back, of course. The Bureau would eventually release

236

her soul across the veil, and when she'd finished reconstructing her body, Mikasa could return to the physical plane. But for now, with her soul back in Archives, she was worse than dead. She was in limbo, just like Yuri.

Meanwhile, I was staring down a nikusui and an itachi.

The itachi knelt over the Nate Juro had tossed onto the glass desk. A few groans from some of the downed gokudō reassured my feeling that, except for Mikasa and possibly the itachi Tollerson had shot, we'd all have a chance to see the sun rise again. Presuming the gokudō were willing to press pause, that is.

"I don't suppose you're going to punch the veil, too?" I asked.

The nikusui smiled. "Not until you have my soul."

"Any chance you two will give yourselves up?"

Goth Guy stared at Mikasa's body. "I think not, agent. And it appears my contract just got cancelled."

I still had my gun trained on him, but we both knew how little of a threat it held at this point.

If he decides to go for that han-forged handgun, I'm screwed.

I couldn't let him walk away, and I didn't want him going anywhere near the magic weapon.

Jiro lurched to his feet, launched himself at the nikusui. Goth Guy snatched up the han gun, fired at the oni. Jiro didn't flinch, kept coming. The nikusui fired again and again until the gun was empty.

I was already in motion, praying as hard as I could to Hachiman and tapping my kitsune power for some extra speed. Hopefully not enough to tip my Yōkai nature to Tollerson. As the han-forged gun clicked empty, the nikusui dropped it, prepared to grapple with the oni, who evaporated right before his eyes.

My right hand grabbed Goth Guy's wrist while my left tried to clip my cuffs on him. He was too fast, raked a set of claws across my arm. I kept up my momentum, closed the gap between our bodies, tried to topple him. It almost worked.

We hit the ground on our sides. He had my left hand tied up, I had his right pinned between us.

"Well, well," Goth Guy whispered. "What a lovely little illusion. Who knew you had such talents?"

Fuck.

"You mean how strong I am?" I asked, hoping to play it off.

Goth Guy smiled. "Among other things. I think we'll dance again soon enough." He leaned close, his voice louder. "Until then, it's time to say goodbye, agent. Time to let me go."

I felt the words echo inside my head, fought the urge to loosen my grip. I screamed, tried to drown out the nikusui's words. A futile effort. I was already relaxing my hold on him. I told my brain not to let go, but my muscles responded to his instructions. Not quite like someone else was in my head but close.

"That's it, agent. Let me go. You want to let me go."

Despite my efforts, he twisted out of my grip, got to his feet. Put his fingers to his mouth, blew me a kiss, and jumped out the window into the night.

THIRTY-NINE

I CAUGHT Tollerson in the garage before he could flee, retrieved my phone, called Yoshida. The three garage kotengu Goth Guy had thralled were in the wind, but they were low priority at the moment. I cuffed Tollerson to the wrought iron frame of his now topless desk. Most of the Yōkai were stirring now, their natural healing abilities speeding their recovery. I poured a ton of healing hans into all of them, anyway, especially the one Tollerson had tagged.

The group nursed their wounds and cast threatening looks at each other, but with a han-forged weapon and a regular handgun, I had the room under control for now. I didn't bother telling the Yōkai the han-forged gun was empty.

I picked up the yellow box from the bookcase, placed it on the floor in front of Tollerson.

"This is hers, isn't it?"

"I don't know what you're talking about."

"Yeah, you do. And you're going to tell me."

"That was a gift, agent. I have no knowledge of its contents."

I held up my phone. "I'm going to make a call, and you're going to choose which number I dial."

"If you're offering, I'd appreciate a call to my attorney."

"I was thinking more like the Crazy Nate." That wiped the smug grin off his face.

"You can't do that. You just stared down Mikasa to save my life. I've confessed. I'm asking for protection-"

"Stop talking, Tollerson, or I swear I'll toss you headfirst out that window. Tell me who's in the tamashi, but remember that your answer will determine who I call first."

He swallowed, and a sheen of perspiration blossomed on his forehead. "It's the hakushi's. It's hers."

He was nervous, but he was telling the truth.

Out in the darkness, the persistent crashing of the Pacific Ocean waves rolled out in every few seconds. In the post-fight adrenaline crash, my thoughts turned to the nikusui and his knowledge of my powers. Neither Tollerson nor the itachi seemed to have caught my illusion but Goth Guy sure had. Would he use it against me? Or perhaps call in an anonymous tip to the Bureau?

My stomach churned at the thought that now, after all these years — after getting so close to finding a ritual to bring Mom back — my secret was out. I heard the ticking of a second clock, this one counting down to the day my secret would be public knowledge.

Nothing I could do about it for now.

LPD arrived first. I coordinated with them to search the area for the three missing Kites.

Vigilance arrived next. Tollerson continued demanding to see his attorney. When the LEOs rolled up, he claimed he was coerced into his confession, spun a wildly fabricated story about a conspiracy between Mikasa and me. For once, I was happy to see a Vig beat us to a scene. I handed over Tollerson, glad not to have to listen to his bullshit any more. A few minutes later Mei, Yoshida, Martinez, and a sweeps team arrived.

The Jewels went to work while I gave Mei a quick debrief.

"Mikasa held up her side of the bargain, Chief."

A nod. "So it appears. I'll make sure the release request for her soul goes through." She eyed the tamashi box in my hands. "What's that?"

"The Jane Doe's soul," I said.

"Really? I'll submit a release request for that, too, get them both off to Kyoto tomorrow."

"Any reason we couldn't handle the release ourselves? Does it have to go back to Kyoto?"

"I suppose not. Kyoto will still have to authorize it."

"I know."

Mei tilted her head at me, prompting me to explain myself. I stayed silent. "I'll see what I can do."

"Thank you, Chief."

————

WITH GERRALD'S withdrawal of his accusations, IA dismissed the investigation case against me. All great and well, but I'd promised Gerrald to help him finally find a place in the world. He asked if I would go with him to Yōkoso to start the process.

I tempered my enthusiasm with the reminder that progress in these situations wasn't always a straight line. This wasn't his first time visiting the non-profit service provider, and it may not be his last. Didn't matter. I'd keep extending a helping hand.

Mei unwound my assignment to Martinez, which was surprisingly bittersweet.

Knowing Yuri's killers would soon receive their due brought me some relief, as did watching gokudō activity drop back to normal within a day. With her soul in Bureau custody, Mikasa would be in the penalty box for a while. Politics and paperwork would inject a delay in her soul's release, though I didn't think it would be for too long.

I checked in on Vicki. She'd delivered a lot more info on the Shiny Kites, ensuring Tollerson wouldn't be walking around as a free man for a very long time. Durante and I officially closed the case on Yuri.

I kept Beni's drawing in my pocket. Couldn't bring myself to throw it away. Didn't want to throw it out. I'd call him at some point. Probably.

For the first time in days, I felt relief, like I'd been holding my breath until now. Things were, in the end, turning out okay. My life felt like it was back on track, and I was somewhat at peace. I thought the world was coming into balance.

Silly, silly, Keiko.

FORTY

AFTER I'D GIVEN the Procs my statements and filed my reports, Mei gave me three days off. Okay, she ordered me to take three days off. Said I'd more than earned it.

I haven't earned anything other than a lifetime of guilt for letting Yuri down.

I nearly slept through the first day of my leave, spent the second knocking around Little Yōkai with Pop. We hit Temple St. Market, had lunch at Katsu Prime. On our way back home, he told me a story I'd never heard before. Well, a different version of a story I'd heard a thousand times before.

"There's something you should know. Just in case I forget." He meant to say in case his mind totally went, and I felt the sting of the words. "When your mother and I realized we wanted to be together, we knew staying in Japan wasn't an option. She applied for a stamp, but in the first few years after the Parting, it was hard to get approved. Then we had you. Your mother used her illusion powers to make you appear mortal. We almost made it out of Haneda Airport, but the Bureau had developed some new detection tech. Neither of us wanted you living a life under Nurarihyon's thumb or falling under his thrall."

243

"I know all this, Pop. You and Mom got Madara so I could hide my Yōkai side."

"Yes. I'm getting to the part you don't know about." He kept walking, composing his thoughts, wouldn't look at me. "Narumi and I, we thought it best to keep this a secret. Actually, the Bureau ordered us to keep it a secret. Part of the deal we worked out."

"When the Bureau arrested Mom for not registering herself."

A nod. "Yes, that's technically true, but her banishment wasn't because she failed to register. It was because she was such a powerful Yōkai. Back then...well, even today, a powerful Yōkai in Japan is considered by some to be a potential threat. If they fall under Nurarihyon's control, I mean. Your Mom, she's a six-tailed kitsune. Seriously powerful. She agreed to be banished if you and I were allowed to move to the U.S. You already had Madara, so the Bureau thought you were mortal."

"Why didn't you tell me this before?"

He sighed. "The Bureau only agreed to let you and I go if we kept quiet. But after all these years, I figured you were old enough to know. You had a right to know."

I turned that revelation over in my head, wondered what other secrets were lurking in our family closet.

"Mom let them banish her. To save me."

Pop sighed. "Basically. We didn't have a lot of options. Your mother struck a bargain with the Bureau. Agreed to be banished, not put up a fight. Agreed to...well, she traded her freedom for you. In exchange, the Bureau got a powerful Yōkai off the physical plane."

"Why didn't they just let her leave Japan if they were worried about her?"

"This was decades ago. Things were, I mean, we were still sorting things out, trying to understand what had happened. There was a lot of fear and uncertainty. Today, the Bureau would likely stamp her and tell her to never come back to Japan. Back then, some awful decisions were made that seemed necessary at the time."

I may not be able to remember those early years, but I didn't need Pop to explain them to me. I'd studied them in school. Researched them. Learned where my education had stopped short, or, in some cases, had skewed the facts. And the definition of "necessary" had been pulled, stretched, and distorted until it was an umbrella for a whole host of shitty policies and practices some of us were still trying to unwind.

That was at the macro level. The impacts at the micro-level — the personal level — were continuing to unfold before me. After years of thinking the Bureau had deported my mother simply for not registering as a Yōkai, I'd just learned she'd cut a deal with the Bureau to secretly ensure my freedom.

The revelation left me on shaky ground, unsure of my footing. I sat with the unknowing and the indecision, resisted the urge to sort things out now. There was time to deal with it all later. The secrets were decades old as it was. Another few days would make no difference. Besides, I had an important promise to keep.

───────

OSHIRO, Saito, and I spent hours preparing to release Yuri's soul. After what happened with Mikasa, the Mirrors were more than happy for my help. And with good reason. We weren't just trying to decrypt the wards of the tamashi. We were going to open it up.

Things went smoothly, despite our collective nervousness. When the last ward was carefully unwound, Oshiro opened the lid of the yellow box. Brilliant light flooded the safe room, but it didn't hurt my eyes.

It's hard to describe seeing a soul with your naked eye. When you tried to put concrete words to it, they dried up. Empty husks, pale shadows of the object they were meant to reflect.

The light faded until the box was empty, and the room was dark. None of us said anything for a while. Eventually Oshiro turned off the cameras. I'd asked him not to record the release, but he said Kyoto would require a video, both for educational and reference reasons.

Filming Yuri's release felt like it turned a solemn moment into something less important than it was. This should have been a private event. Instead, it would be watched, over and over, by Bureau agents for decades to come.

Those agents wouldn't know the first thing about Yuri. About what she'd suffered through. About her innocent desire for a better life. A desire that led her down a dark path and ended with her being tortured to death and her soul imprisoned. About how she was worth so much more than what the world gave her.

But I knew. And I'd never forget.

KEIKO'S next case in *Hunted* starts off innocently enough but quickly becomes deadly:

Curiosity almost killed this kitsune.

When ordinary objects transform into sentient beings, I'm dragged into a far more sinister threat.

Rifts appear in the veil, the barrier separating the physical plane from the Yōkai home world. Objects come to life. People are dying. Par for the course for a Bureau of Souls Agent like me.

But when my magical koi fish, Madara, starts acting weird, things get super dicey.

Option A is solving the case but revealing my kitsune side. Option B means a lot of people will die, but my secret remains safe.

I really need to find option C. Like, yesterday.

Read Keiko's Next Case!

https://scottiswriting.com/little-yokai-series-hunted

PREVIEW OF "HUNTED"

Lilia Flores pointed at the large cypress tree in her backyard, and I understood why she'd called the local police. I also totally understood why, after inspecting her yard, LPD had kicked the report over to the Bureau of Souls. Which was how I wound up in the hillside neighborhood of Eagle Rock on a sunny November morning, squinting at something that didn't add up.

"Well," she said. "What do you make of that?"

The cypress looked odd, no doubt about it. One side of the trunk had a dappled look. I stepped closer, placed my palm on the tree.

The shape and feel of the bark were typical, but the coloring was off. Like, way off. A spectrum of colors streaked horizontally across the trunk, as if someone had run a paintbrush across a wet canvas. The ground was equally odd, a mixed pool of colors. The grass was brown and black, parts of the soil were green. Structurally, everything looked and felt okay, but the swirl of colors made for a trippy effect.

Reminded me of the sumi-e style of painting with a dash of impressionism thrown in for good measure.

I looked at my hand: clean. The colors were fixed, though they obviously smeared together at some point. Flores seemed convinced the coloring had been caused by a group of midnight trespassers she'd caught in her backyard earlier in the week. Kids messing around with fireworks.

What I saw wasn't lining up with her theory.

Madara, my supernatural companion, popped into view. She looked like a regular aka bekko koi fish: crimson-colored body with black spots. But she "swam" through the air and never left my side. Oh, and she could identify Yōkai by giving them a blue aura. And I was the only person who could see her.

Like I said, just a regular koi fish.

Except regular koi fish didn't normally roll upside down and hang in place.

Okay, weird.

Also: *holy shit!*

The only thing keeping my heart rate in a semi-healthy range was the lazy back-and-forth motion of her tail.

One of Madara's abilities was to prevent my Yōkai signature from being detected. She "ate" my signature as fast as I produced it, which was how I waltzed through the detectors at the Bureau every day without tripping any alarms. Now, even if I didn't have her, I could still appear in my mortal form. But without her, my days at the Bureau were over.

No big deal, except the only reason I was working at the Bureau in the first place was to mine their Archives for a ritual to bring my mom out of her banishment early. Early as in before my father's dementia completely ate his head.

I tried not to freak the fuck out.

On a hunch and prayer, I backed away from the tree, looked uphill at the back part of Flores' lot. Like most of the homes in the neighborhood, her house faced downhill. Her backyard was large and climbed up to the bottom of the house above. Flores' lot wasn't the typical postage-stamp-sized Los Angeles property, and the backyard transitioned from a neatly manicured lawn to a wilder, more natural thicket of mature trees and bushes. Thick enough to provide privacy from the neighbor above her.

"Where, exactly, were the fireworks?" I asked.

"Isn't it obvious? Right there, next to the tree. Can't you see the chemicals?"

Flores wasn't happy LPD had taken several hours to respond to her 911 call. Was less happy when they shrugged and said they couldn't help her. Was positively pissed the Bureau had taken three more days to show up. To be fair, most of that delay was on LPD for not forwarding her report in a timely manner.

Still, I understood her frustration, and I planned on getting her some answers.

"I can see the discoloration. I'm not sure if the cause is fireworks or chemicals, though." No sign of scorches around or on the tree. No leftover fireworks on the ground. I recalled the details from her report. "So, you and your husband woke up a little after one in the morning and saw a group of people standing next to the tree."

"That's right. Diego — that's my husband — went out to talk to them. I told him to call the police, but he said he'd handle it himself. He yelled at them to leave. They didn't. The moron walked over, started talking to them. I watched from our back-door, but I couldn't hear what they said. They talked for a minute, and then Diego came back inside. Said they were almost done, he was going back to bed." She made a face. "Don't know what got into him. I called the police and waited inside. Of course, the hooligans were long gone by the time the cops showed up."

Madara slowly righted herself, twitched, circled around me. I put my hand behind my back, pooled some of my kitsune power into my palm. Madara picked at it with her mouth. A dozen tiny nibbles later, and my palm was empty. She was acting normally again, and I thanked the kitsune kami, Inari, for that.

"Can you describe the fireworks?"

"It was one of those large sparkler ones. Lots of big, green sparks. But not the kind you shoot in the air. The kind you leave on the ground, you know?"

I nodded. She continued.

"And when I say lots of green sparks, I mean a ton. Those kids were standing under a shower of sparks. But they were too high to notice."

"How do you know they were high?"

She gave me the stink eye. "No sober person goes into a stranger's yard, lights a massive firework, and doesn't care when they're getting burned for fifteen minutes."

I smiled, refrained from saying out loud what I was thinking. "How long were they here?"

"Maybe fifteen, twenty minutes after we woke up. They moved up the hill, must have hopped the back fence. At least they had the decency to take their garbage with them."

"I'm sorry, garbage?"

She held up her hands like she had a basketball between them. "A small trash can or something. They took it with them."

I cast a han of seeing.

Okay, definitely not fireworks.

"Do you have gardeners, Ms. Flores?"

She narrowed her eyes. "What difference does that make?"

"I'm just curious who else has been out here besides you and your husband."

"Oh. Yes. They came here yesterday." Catching my drift, she smirked. "Guess you should have showed up earlier."

I walked into the thicket, moving slowly up the incline and searching for anything out of the ordinary. Despite the shade, I was sweating by the time I reached the top of the property. A large chain-link fence separated the lots. A mat of vines covered the fence, thick enough that I couldn't see the other yard. The hill rose steeply, and it had to be at least ten vertical feet from the ground to the top of the fence. No indication the vines had been ripped down in an attempt to climb the fence. Doubtful any mortals had scaled that. But plenty of Yōkai could. I turned around, headed back to Flores.

As I approached the tree again, Madara went loopy. I cast a new han of seeing, this time a more detailed and powerful one. I got a flare of magic, plus the telltale sign of a rift in the veil. The rift itself was a thin, curving vertical line of emerald energy about a yard tall. Sealed, thankfully. Surrounding it were blinking black spots like you got after looking at a bright light. The spots were the telltale sign of a rift's aftershocks, invisible waves of residual energy.

Since the Parting, we'd discovered temporary holes in the veil. Well, not holes, exactly. A more accurate description would be places where the lines separating the Yōkai homeward of Furusato and the physical plane thinned. While the rifts didn't fully pierce the veil, they did affect the physical plane.

For all their visual splendor, rifts posed no threat to life on the physical plane. A wonder to behold but not something to fear.

The Bureau had been studying the phenomenon since the Parting, thanks mostly to the fact that rifts regularly occurred in the famous Hell Valleys in Japan. The Hell Valleys had been the initial site of the Yōkai emigration onto the physical plane, and the area still experienced the highest frequency of rifts in the world. That was relative, though, as we might only record two or three rifts each year in the Hell Valleys. The frequency was even less for the rest of the world.

Point was, the event in Flores' backyard was super unusual. More unusual was the group that hopped her fence. If the rift in Flores' backyard had been random, how had a bunch of strangers known to show up?

"You're going to arrest them now, right?"

"Who?" I asked.

"You did your magic spell thing. I saw you. You know who did this, right?"

"I'm sorry, I don't. I do know this wasn't caused by fireworks. I detected a temporary rift in the veil."

"And that means what to me?"

"Honestly, not much now. The rift's sealed. It's not dangerous. And neither are the aftershocks I detected."

"Aftershocks?"

"Yes," I admitted. "After a rift seals itself, there are magical aftershocks. I detected those just now. But they're harmless."

Flores made the sign of the cross. "Magic? You mean like those Yōkai demons?"

"I mean traces of residual magic. And no, not Yōkai demons."

Flores broke in a flurry of Spanish, ended in English. "Do I need to have my yard blessed?"

The Parting caused many people to question their faith. Some double-downed on their beliefs, others rejected their lifelong religious convictions. I'd learned to take a diplomatic and respectful approach when possible. The Bureau's official position was it had no official position when it came to which religion was the "real" one.

The reality was far less neutral. If any single religion got a significant boost from the Parting, it was Shinto, with a close second being Shingon Buddhism. Outside of Japan, a lot of people wound up associating Yōkai most heavily with Shinto, even though Yōkai featured prominently in Buddhism, too. Sales of kamidana home shrines exploded in the years after the Parting.

Inside Japan, things hadn't changed all that much. Japanese had concurrently practiced multiple religions for a very long time and still did. Not at all uncommon for a Japanese person to be blessed at birth by a Shinto priest, married in a Christian ceremony, and honored at death with a Buddhist funeral.

The Bureau's "no official position" aside, it quietly began recruiting Shinto priests as agents and assigning them to offices outside of Japan. The Bureau classified the priests as Mirrors. These agents split their time between office duties and community outreach.

Shuji Ishī had been the L.A. office's Shinto priest for nearly a decade. Personally, I was glad to have him. A lot of the U.S. offices still lacked one.

All of this rolled through my head as I considered how to respond to Flores.

"If you feel better having the yard blessed, please do so. You can also request a visit from the Bureau's local Shinto priest or one from a local shrine. As for the discoloration, that's temporary. Your yard should be fine in a couple of days."

Flores looked around the yard, back at me. "What if they come back?"

I handed her my card. "I doubt it. But if they do, call 911. Or call me directly." She took my card, seemed to appreciate the gesture. "And if you don't mind, Ms. Flores, may I have some agents come by and take a look at this? Collect some data?"

"Yes. Yes, I suppose so, as long as they don't mess up my yard."

"Thank you. They'll be in touch to schedule a convenient time to come by."

I'd have chalked this up as a natural rift, except for the people Diego encountered. Who were they, and why were they at the rift? Had someone been trying to open the veil? Perhaps allow a Yōkai back across? The location seemed random, though. If you were going to open the veil, why do it in a stranger's backyard instead of somewhere more private, more controlled?

The Jewels team would give the place a thorough inspection. If we were lucky, they'd find something to get me closer to solving this mystery.

If not, I still had Madara's odd behavior to worry about.

———

Read *Hunted*:
https://scottiswriting.com/little-yokai-series-hunted

255

GLOSSARY

Caged contains several Japanese words and phrases, including references to Yōkai spirits and gods. The definitions below provide explanations for these terms within the Little Yōkai series.

Japanese Words / Phrases

Amanatto: A Japanese sweet made from cooked azuki (red) beans which are dried and covered in sugar.

Anpan: A sweet roll most often filled with a sweet red bean paste made from azuki beans.

Azuki: A red bean commonly used to make a sweet red bean paste.

-Chan (honorific): A suffix appended to a name to denote a degree of intimacy or closeness (e.g., a family member, spouse, or very close friend).

Daikon: A white winter radish used in soups and stir-fries. It can also be pickled and served as a side dish.

Furusato: In the Little Yōkai series, this is the Yōkai home world.

Gokudō: In the Little Yōkai series, this is a global network of criminal organizations populated predominantly by Yōkai (similar to The Triad or the Yakuza).

Hafu ("half"): A term referring to someone who has a Japanese parent and a non-Japanese parent.

Hakushi ("blank"): In the Little Yōkai series, this is a Yōkai who has illegally entered a county without obtaining the proper stamp on their passport.

Han: a direct translation is "size," "seal," or "stamp," but in the Little Yōkai series, han is also the word for magic (both for the han spells Bureau of Souls agents are taught to cast, as well as the kind of magic Yōkai can cast). The Bureau also uses han magic to forge the handguns and rifles used by its agents.

Haori: A traditional Japanese hip- or thigh-length jacket. The panels do not overlap like a kimono and are tied together instead of buttoned together.

Hoshi-no-tama ("starball"): The source of a kitsune's power, these small glowing globes were often worn on jewelry or held under the spirit's tongue. As the starballs also contained a small part of the Yōkai's life force, kitsune diligently guard them.

Hyakki Yagyō ("Night Parade of One Hundred Demons"): A nightly parade of Yōkai through the streets of Japan, led by Nurarihyon, Lord of the Yōkai.

Itadakimasu: Often translated as "I humbly receive" but when said before a meal, the meaning shifts closer to "bon appétit." In that context, the word is customarily accompanied with a slight bow while holding your hands together (palm-to-palm).

Kami: An umbrella term that can refer to deities, spirits, and forces of nature.

Kamidana: A miniature household altar used to worship one or more Shinto kami.

Karashi: A spicy, hot mustard.

Katashiro: A piece of paper or thin wood shaped like a rudimentary doll and used to represent a person during a religious ritual (usually to remove that person's sins or to provide protection against evil). Bureau agents often maintain a katashiro with personalized combinations of protective wards.

Kawaii ("cute" or "adorable"): Term used to describe the

culture of cuteness in Japan (e.g., Hello Kitty).

Kimono: Multi-layered traditional Japanese garment.

Kusari ("tattoo"): In the Little Yōkai series, this is a ring of permanent, magical marks all Bureau of Souls agents have around their wrists and ankles. The marks allow agents to punch and kick hard enough to inflict damage on Yōkai (who are resistant to most mortal weapons).

Mizu manju: Translucent jelly cakes made from flour or rice powder and filled with a sweet paste.

Natto: Fermented soybeans.

Noren: Traditional Japanese fabric dividers with one or more vertical slits. Used between rooms in a home or at entrances to businesses. Often decorated with designs or symbols.

Ofuda: A talisman constructed of wood, paper, metal, or cloth and commonly found in Shinto shrines and Buddhist temples. The talismans, usually displayed as upright rectangles, are believed to be imbued with the power of a particular deity.

Oishī desu: "It's delicious."

Omamori: Small charms issued by Shinto shrines and Buddhist temples. Omamori provide protection or other benefits.

Ryū Kiri ("Dragon Mist"): In the Little Yōkai series, this is an all-powerful, mysterious group of Yōkai secretly pulling the strings of Los Angeles. At least, that's the urban myth…

-San (honorific): A suffix appended to the last / family name of the person you're addressing.

Seiza: A formal posture for sitting where you kneel on the floor with your buttocks resting on your heels.

Sento: A Japanese bathhouse.

Shimenawa: Rope used to demarcate a sacred or spiritual location or object. In the Little Yōkai series, the Bureau adapted it for use with Yōkai suspects (either as rope tethers or embedded into handcuffs). The Bureau version of shimenawa has the capability of forcing Yōkai into their mortal forms and prevent them from using their Yōkai powers.

Shōji: A wood frame panel covered with translucent paper

used as a door or a divider in a Japanese building. Shōji may be hung in place or mounted on a sliding track.

Sumi-e: A style of ink wash brush painting using a special kind of black ink. Its minimalistic style is often compared to the Western art movement of impressionism.

Tamashi: In the Little Yōkai series, this term refers to an object used to store the soul of a Yōkai or mortal. Also called a soul cage.

Torī: A traditional Japanese gate — usually made of wood and painted red — placed at the entrance to a Shinto shrine. The arched structure symbolizes the transition from the ordinary world to a sacred one.

Tsukesage: A less formal style of kimono.

Washi: Traditional Japanese paper handcrafted from the long fibers of bark from one of three plants. Washi can last hundreds of years, and its durability makes it a popular choice for a variety of uses (not just books or scrolls).

Yōkai: An umbrella term for a variety of entities, including gods, demons, ghosts, strange phenomenon, and supernatural beings. The legends and myths that originally gave rise to Yōkai are sometimes conflicting, and accounts of a particular Yōkai can vary across regions of Japan. Some appear as mortal, others appear as otherworldly beings. Some were always Yōkai, others were born mortal but transformed into Yōkai. There is no single, definitive, exhaustive list of Yōkai or their descriptions, and that elusiveness is one of the reasons I'm so fascinated by them!

Zabuton: a Japanese cushion, usually rectangular, used to make kneeling or sitting more comfortable.

Japanese Gods (kami)

Ebisu: One of the Seven Gods of Fortune, Ebisu is known as the god of luck and protector of fishermen.

Hachiman: God of war and protector of Japan.

Inari: Goddess of fertility, rice, agriculture, and foxes (among other provinces). Fox spirits called kitsune are believed to be messengers for Inari.

Yōkai Spirits

The descriptions below are common interpretations of legends and myths, though the spirits in the Little Yōkai series often do not precisely adhere to their historical origins.

Abura Akago: Appearing as fireballs or babies, abura akago are fond of licking the oil from lamps and lanterns.

Ame Onna: Hag-looking spirits appear on rainy days and nights and are said to snatch newborn girls.

Azuki Arai: Resembling Buddhist priests, these three-fingered spirits are friendly and fond of ceaselessly washing azuki beans in rivers and streams.

Chōpirako: Luminescent spirits who take the form of children and bring prosperity to the homes they inhabit.

Daitengu: These spirits make up a small percentage of tengu and generally keep to themselves. When they get involved with mortal affairs, they usually do so peacefully and with good intentions. They can often be identified by their long noses.

Haradashi: Friendly spirits who may take different forms and often appear before sad or lonely people to cheer them up.

Hinoenma: Said to appear as beautiful women, legends claim these spirits like to prey on men.

Hitotsume-kozo: One-eyed priest boys known for appearing suddenly at night and scaring people.

Itachi: Weasels who possess the ability to shapeshift, cast magic, and start fires.

Jurōgumo: Spiders who have become Yōkai and then prey on men. Their Yōkai form is a giant spider, but they can also appear as beautiful, enticing women.

Kejōrō: Legends claim these spirits appear as women who style their hair to hide their face and live as prostitutes, which makes it easier for them to prey on mortal men. Kejōrō can control and animate their hair, allowing them to grasp, hold, and manipulate objects.

Kitsune: These long-lived spirits have the form of foxes and enjoy a close connection to the kami Inari. As kitsune grow older and more powerful, they gain additional tails. Kitsune have several magical powers, but they are known to enjoy masquerading as mortals in order to trick or prank their targets.

Kotengu: Refers to the larger segment of tengu spirits who are boisterous and extroverted, always fond of pranks and parties. In the Little Yōkai series, the presence or guidance of a daitengu has a calming effect on kotengu.

Kowai: The ghost of a gluttonous mortal who, as a Yōkai, is cursed with forever being hungry no matter how much food they consume. These spirits look human but have fox-like features, bloodshot eyes, sharp teeth, and a long, drooling tongue. They typically appear at night outside of food stands and restaurants.

Mujina: Shy shape shifters who generally prefer to live a secluded life. Depending on which legend you refer to, mujina resemble either Japanese raccoon dogs or badgers.

Nekomata: A cat who has transformed into a Yōkai. Nekomata have two tails and consider mortals to be inferior creatures.

Nikusui: A vampiric Yōkai who typically hunts mountain roads at night, usually appearing as a beautiful young woman.

Nopperabō: Faceless spirits fond of scaring mortals. Nopperabō will appear as mortals until they decide to reveal their faceless head.

Nurarihyon: Lord of the Yōkai. He appears as a short, old man with a long, gourd-shaped head. In the Little Yōkai series, Nurari-hyon possesses the ability to put anyone under his thrall and obey his commands.

Oni: Ogre-type spirits who are born after a wicked mortal dies. Oni often wield iron clubs and enjoy torturing mortals.

Tengu: Powerful mountain goblins known for their magical prowess and recognizable by their long or enormous noses.

Taka Onna: Resembling mortal women, these spirits love to spy on the romantic activities at brothels. They can elongate their bodies to peek into windows high above ground, and they enjoy scaring mortals.

Tōfu Kozō: Small Yōkai appearing as little boys wearing

kimono and wide-brimmed hats. Fond of tofu, these spirits generally avoid mortal company and often act as servants for more powerful Yōkai.

Yosuzume: Night sparrows considered harbingers of bad luck. Yosuzume like to gather into swarms and startle travelers at night.

Zashiki Warashi: House spirits who appear as children and bring good fortune to the homes in which they reside. These Yōkai love pranks of all kinds but are harmless.

ACKNOWLEDGMENTS

The list of people during my life who nudged me to explore fiction writing is far too long to include them all here. However, there are several individuals who directly contributed to the creation of the Little Yōkai series:

————

The Wesley Street Writing Group: E.J., Jackie, Jane K., Jane P., Jess, Max, Ruomu, Sam, Wil, and especially Maureen. You're all madcap fans of fiction and patrons of prose, and I'm forever grateful for your early feedback on *Caged*. Your enthusiasm was a much-needed boost of confidence and a great prompt to consider Keiko and her world from a new (better) perspective.

————

Sachiko Burton: I still give thanks to the Google gods for sending you my way. Little Yōkai is insanely far outside of my lived experience, and you were the *perfect* sensitivity/developmental editor for this series. Your always-patient, ever-insightful, and non-judgmental feedback helped me understand the full potential of the Little Yōkai world. Your comments led me to discover the real Keiko I was fumbling to find and constantly reminded me why I started writing this series in the first place. Thank you for joining me on this journey, being my guide, and elevating Little Yōkai to heights I didn't know were possible.

[Sachiko reviewed an early draft of this manuscript, which has gone

through several subsequent edits. I made every effort to keep Sachiko's guidance in mind during my revisions. All errors and problematic passages in this published version are mine and mine alone.]

———

Matthew Mayer's Yōkai resources: I relied on many research books for this series but none more so than Mayer's beautifully illustrated series highlighting hundreds of Japanese spirits: *The Book of the Hakutaku*, *The Night Parade of One Hundred Demons*, and *The Hour of Meeting Evil Spirits*. I also frequently referred to his yokai.com website.

———

Carrie and my three amazing kids: To say this book would not exist without you is a massive understatement. I could thank you a thousand times and still fall far short of my gratitude for your love, support, and encouragement. You all believed in me even when I didn't.

ABOUT THE AUTHOR

Scott Walker adamantly believes pizza is a food group, Han shot first, and *Serenity* is still flying somewhere out in the 'verse. Over the years, he's designed, crafted, and shared storytelling experiences via collaborative worldbuilding, tabletop gaming, and live-action role-playing. While Scott's imagination takes him to lands of mystery and wonder, he always returns to his hometown of Los Angeles. At least, he's pretty sure it's Los Angeles.

https://scottiswriting.com

facebook.com/scottiswriting
instagram.com/scottiswriting
tiktok.com/@scottiswriting